DEGREES OF DECEIT

A BAD VIBES REMOVAL SERVICES NOVEL

N. M. CEDEÑO

Lucky Bat Books

A Lucky Bat Book

Degrees of Deceit: A Bad Vibes Removal Services Novel
Copyright ©2019 by Noreen M. Cedeño

ISBN-13: 978-1-943588-80-0

Cover Design: Brandon Swann
Published by Lucky Bat Books
10 9 8 7 6 5 4 3 2 1

Also available as an ebook

Discover other titles by the author at *nmcedeno.com*

For Thomas, Jonathan, and Catherine
And Norbert and Lynn

Author's Note

WHILE THIS BOOK IS SET AT the University of Texas at Austin, all of the characters, including undergraduates, graduate students, teaching assistants, professors, and other support staff, associated with the university are fictional. Any resemblance to any real persons, situations, or scenarios is entirely unintentional and purely coincidental. Although street names and certain buildings mentioned on campus may be real, the dorm around which this story centers is fictional. The dorm had to be placed somewhere on the campus map, so it is described in the story as being located on the site of a real dorm. No one from the real dorm is associated with this story. In Britain, collegiate mysteries comprise an entire subgenre of mystery fiction. As with those books set at Oxford and Cambridge, while the university exists, the people and the story are fictional.

CHAPTER 1

D R. JENNY TREMAYNE, A PROFESSOR OF European history who specialized in the ancient Celts, ushered Lea and Kamika into her office in Garrison Hall on the University of Texas campus. She turned to Lea with mild concern. "Lea, how does my office feel to you? I'm guessing you haven't seen any ghosts, or you would have mentioned it to me."

Lea grinned at her. As a graduate student in history studying ancient civilizations, she'd visited Dr. Tremayne's office regularly for months, ever since one of her thesis advisors had died and Dr. Tremayne stepped into his place. Dr. Tremayne was aware of Lea's unusual ability to see ghosts. "No. No ghosts in here. It is claustrophobic, though. That sensation is imprinted on the space, which compounds the fact that the room *is* small and cramped." Lea began to unpack her infusing equipment and glanced around the familiar office space.

Though small, the office was well organized, reflecting Dr. Tremayne's working habits. Books on a shallow bookshelf filled one wall. The rest of the space was taken

1

up by a wooden desk with two chairs placed in front of it for visitors and another chair behind it for Dr. Tremayne. The desk was free of clutter, holding only a picture frame, a laptop computer, and a mug on a coaster.

Dr. Tremayne smiled, her anxiety relieved. She leaned against her desk and tucked her pageboy-cut, dark hair behind one ear. "Can you infuse something happy into the walls for me?"

"Yes, ma'am," Kamika said in a cheerful voice. "All bad vibes shall be removed and the atmosphere improved as you request." She stood with her hands on her hips and studied the office. "I can make some interior decorating suggestions too, if you'd like. A brighter color on one wall would really cheer this space up."

"I wish I could paint, but I'm not allowed to," said Dr. Tremayne with a rueful smile. "However, I do like the feeling of history in this building. It dates back to 1926."

Kamika pursed her lips thoughtfully. "How about if we don't use paint? What if I get you a ten-by-ten sheet of sunflower yellow paper or, even better, cloth to tack up on the wall? You're allowed to hang pictures, aren't you? If you can hang pictures, you can tack up colored paper or cloth!"

Dr. Tremayne looked at Kamika in delighted surprise. "I hadn't thought of that. That would be perfect."

"Great. I'll send the material with Lea next time she's on campus to meet with you about her thesis."

"That will be Thursday," Lea said, her mind darting to the work she needed to do before the meeting. The previous spring, Dr. Tremayne came to Lea's rescue when her primary advisor, Dr. Mortimer Richardson, had published part of Lea's thesis, claiming it as his own work. Dr. Tremayne had filed a complaint against Dr.

Richardson with the research integrity officer on Lea's behalf. The results of the investigation into the theft of her work were due soon, and Lea had been worrying about the research integrity committee's findings. Accusing Dr. Richardson, a tenured professor who was well liked and respected, of stealing her work had been difficult. Some professors on the Graduate Studies Committee, of which Dr. Richardson was a member, still doubted her, making her visits to the history department tense at times.

Dr. Tremayne's eyes traveled around her office. "Until I met Montgomery and learned about the work you do for him at Bad Vibes Removal Services, it hadn't occurred to me that the claustrophobic sensation I get in my office might not be entirely from the fact that it's small. Maybe the emotional history of the room is weighing on me. Since I have to be in here for office hours, I've decided to try to make it as comfortable as possible. That starts with neutralizing the absorbed emotional history in the walls."

Kamika nodded approvingly. "I could add a calming scent like lavender in a diffuser or a small fountain for water noises too."

"I have music I can play, so I don't need the fountain, but lavender might help," Dr. Tremayne said.

Kamika stepped over to the window. "At least you have a window with a view. That's good."

Dr. Tremayne joined her looking outside. "I get natural light and a view. I'm lucky compared to some. A few professors I know have offices on campus that are below ground level. That would drive me crazy. By the way, I'm so glad you two came on a Saturday. Thank you. Montgomery told me it's your usual day off." She peered at Lea's long black hair, which was twisted into a knot on one side of her head, drooping down slightly in a loop

3

of intertwined strands. "I've been trying to place your hairstyle since you arrived, Lea. I've finally remembered where it's from. Is that a Suebian knot?"

"Yes." Lea patted her hair. "Germanic tribes, Iron Age to Roman period. I copied it from the bog heads found in Europe, though really my bangs should be in it too."

Dr. Tremayne nodded her understanding, impressed with the results. "Was it difficult?"

"A little. I have thicker hair than was typical in the men who wore their hair like this." Lea frequently tried out hairstyles, clothing styles, and makeup from the various ancient cultures she was studying. Her eyes flicked to the empty walls and neatly arranged books. "You cleared the walls, and you have no piles for us to trip over and almost no furniture. If we move the guest chairs and desk chair into the hall, we'll be done infusing some joy into these walls in no time."

Dr. Tremayne grabbed the desk chair and rolled it to the hall. Lea picked up a guest chair while Kamika lifted the other from in front of the desk.

In fifteen minutes, Lea and Kamika finished infusing the walls of the office with a sense of joy. Kamika plugged a lavender scent diffuser into the wall. As Lea and Kamika packed up their equipment, Dr. Tremayne returned the chairs to her office.

A knock sounded on the doorframe. Lea, Kamika, and Dr. Tremayne turned around to find a young woman wearing calf-length yoga pants and a burnt orange UT t-shirt standing in the open doorway of the office.

"I'm sorry to interrupt, Dr. Tremayne. I see you're busy. Could I make an appointment to come see you another time?"

"You're, let me think, um . . . Evie, aren't you?" Dr. Tremayne said with a welcoming smile.

"Yes, ma'am. From your Celtic history elective course." The girl nodded jerkily. She didn't smile, and her eyes were underlined with dark shadows. She stepped awkwardly into the office, clasping her hands nervously in front of her.

"Is it about the twenty-page paper due Tuesday?" Dr. Tremayne asked.

"Yes, ma'am." The girl's face flushed with embarrassment. Suddenly, her eyes filled with tears and her face crumbled in distress. She put her hands up and covered her face. "I'm sorry, so sorry. I'll come back later." She turned hurriedly to leave, slamming the side of her face into the doorframe. "Ouch!" she cried as blood began to ooze from a gash on her temple.

CHAPTER 2

EVIE STUMBLED AND WOULD HAVE FALLEN had Lea not grabbed one of her arms.

"Sit down, sit down. It's okay, dear. Take a deep breath," Dr. Tremayne said as she helped Lea lead Evie to one of the office chairs.

Kamika pulled several tissues from her equipment bag and handed them to the girl. "Put this on your temple and apply pressure."

Tears were sliding down Evie's face. A red welt with a gash in the center had appeared on her temple near her eye. She dabbed at the wound with the tissues, as blood dripped down the side of her face.

Kamika bent over Evie to examine the wound. "That's going to need a bandage and an ice pack for the swelling. Is there an ice machine in the building?"

Dr. Tremayne nodded. "Yes. It's upstairs."

"Tell me where, and I'll go get it," Kamika said.

Dr. Tremayne shook her head. "I'll go. Keep Evie company until I get back." She hurried out of the office and down the hall.

The instant Dr. Tremayne's footsteps had faded from hearing, Evie stumbled out of the chair to her feet and looked at Lea and Kamika with fearful eyes. "I'm making a fool of myself. I'm so sorry. I didn't mean to cause a scene. I'll leave." She started toward the door with one hand holding the tissues to the bruised and bloody side of her face.

Lea grabbed Evie's arm to stop her. "You're hurt. Sit down. Dr. Tremayne isn't going to fail you for bumping into a doorframe. Although, she will be annoyed with you if you leave before she comes back."

Kamika blocked the door, shaking her head, which caused her bronze, corkscrew curls to dance above her shoulders. "Uh-uh. Hon, you need to sit down. That bump had to hurt. I'd still be cursing if I banged into something that hard."

"Who are you? Are you teaching assistants of Dr. Tremayne's?" Evie asked, taking in Kamika's fashionable, coral-colored blouse and pale green leggings and Lea's hairdo before surrendering and allowing Lea to push her back into the chair.

Lea patted Evie's shoulder. "I'm Lea, and this is Kamika. I'm a graduate student, and Dr. Tremayne is my advisor."

"Actually," Kamika said winking one green eye conspiratorially, "our boss is dating Dr. Tremayne." She nodded at Evie, who was looking at her in surprise. "He sent us here to do some work for her."

"Kamika, this isn't the time for gossip," Lea said, rolling her dark eyes. She turned to Evie. "I'm studying ancient cultures and civilizations for a master's degree."

"So you're a student, but you're in Dr. Tremayne's office for your job." Evie looked from Lea to Kamika. "Are you a student too?"

"I'm not a student," Kamika said with aplomb. "I'm an interior designer. Lea and I are here to make sure Dr. Tremayne's office is free of ghosts and negativity. We work for Bad Vibes Removal Services."

Evie's eyes widened. "Ghosts! I've heard commercials for Bad Vibes Removal Services, but they don't say anything about ghosts! Of course, the whole service sounds fake to me, but—" She broke off suddenly, and her face flushed even redder.

"We aren't fakers!" Kamika said defensively, hitching one hip onto Dr. Tremayne's desk, her voice rising as she spoke. "Would Dr. Tremayne have us come here to improve the atmosphere in her office if we were frauds? Would she date our boss if she thought his inventions were bogus?" Her flawless, mocha face became the perfect mask of affronted beauty.

Evie shrank into her chair with downcast eyes. "Sorry. I didn't mean to be rude. I'm so tired that I keep saying the wrong things and tripping over myself. Could you tell me about what you do?"

Lea shot Kamika an exasperated look and replied in a calm, even tone. "It's okay. A lot of people are skeptical about what we do. Our boss, Mr. Montgomery, is a private detective. He owns Montgomery Investigations. He's also an inventor. He discovered a way to detect changes in wall board or wood at the molecular level, changes that are caused when sound waves move through the wall. At the same time, he discovered he could detect patterns left by bursts of emotional energy or even long-term, sustained emotion. He built scanners to detect and analyze those sound and emotional patterns to aid in solving crimes."

Evie checked the bloody tissues she was holding to her temple, folded them to expose a fresh area, and put them back. "Okay, that makes sense, I guess. But that's for investigations. You aren't here to investigate anything."

"Some of our assignments end up as investigations, but not all," Kamika said with a laugh.

Lea ignored Kamika. "Mr. Montgomery couldn't get the law enforcement community to accept his equipment for use in crime scenes because it hasn't been acknowledged by the courts yet as a valid method of evidence collection. So he thought of a way to get his work in the public eye. You see, once he figured out how to read the patterns, Montgomery also realized how to eliminate them. He decided to start a second company, and Bad Vibes Removal Services was born. We eliminate the old sound and emotional histories from rooms."

"And you do interior design too?" Evie asked. "The commercials mention that."

"That's my specialty," Kamika said, waving her hand. "I know how to place furniture to make the best use of space and to entice people into an area. I can use color to make a room happy or exciting or inspiring or calming. Then, with scent diffusers, I can arouse emotion through the nose, like some apartments use the smell of baking cookies to make people feel at home. Then, with sound—music, flowing water, waves, bird song—I can add to the whole experience. On top of that, we can infuse different feelings into the wall. We just blocked the claustrophobia in this room and added joy."

"Who hires you for all that?" Evie asked.

"Everyone," Kamika said with a satisfied smirk.

"Well," Lea interposed, "spas want to be relaxing. Car dealerships and casinos want to inspire risk-taking. Medical centers want calm and happiness to inspire faster healing and fewer medical errors, and they want to eliminate any sensations of panic or pain. Regular people want the previous residents' stresses erased from their houses and apartments. We keep busy."

Evie gave them both a curious look. "None of that has anything to do with ghosts. Were you speaking metaphorically, like the old history was a ghost in the room?"

"Yes, and no," Lea said, glancing at Kamika. She knew what Kamika would say.

Kamika elbowed Lea. "Lea's being modest. Sometimes she finds rooms haunted by more than emotion and sound history. Sometimes the room really is haunted by a previous resident. Usually Lea is the only one who can see ghosts. I saw a screaming ghost once, and it scared the pants off me. So I prefer that Lea is the only one to see them. She sees ghosts a lot."

Evie stared at Lea, "So you weren't kidding about the ghosts." Evie bit her lip and looked at her shoes.

Lea wasn't sure if Evie was in pain or if she wanted to say something else. "Is something wrong? Does your head hurt?"

"My head does hurt," Evie said. She looked at Lea with hesitance in her posture but speculation in her eyes and glanced quickly away.

Lea didn't want to pressure the girl. Then, quite suddenly, she got the impression that Evie was pleading for help with every fiber of her being. As Lea was about to ask Evie again if something was wrong, Dr. Tremayne returned. She entered the office carrying a plastic cup filled with ice.

"I'm glad I didn't send you in search of the ice, Kamika," Dr. Tremayne said as she handed the cup to Evie. "I was wrong about the location of the machine and had to search for it."

"Thank you, Dr. Tremayne," Evie said as she held the side of the cup to her injured face.

Lea caught Dr. Tremayne's eye over Evie's downturned head. She shot Dr. Tremayne a worried look, nodding toward Evie.

Dr. Tremayne raised one eyebrow, which vanished under her straight fringe of heavy bangs, and glanced at Evie. She sat down in the second office chair next to the injured student. Dr. Tremayne eyed the young woman sitting in front of her critically. "You're a freshman, aren't you, Evie? About eighteen years old?"

"Yes."

"I'm going to take a look at your wound. How many hours are you taking this semester?" Dr. Tremayne gently moved Evie's hand with the cup of ice away from the wound and examined the gash.

"Sixteen." Evie turned her head slightly to give Dr. Tremayne a better view of the injury.

"Hmm. Are you working anywhere? I mean other than doing classwork?" Dr. Tremayne got up, walked around her desk, and began rummaging in a drawer. She pulled out a first aid kit and put on a pair of disposable gloves.

Evie fingered the cup of ice nervously. "No, ma'am. My counselor reviewed my schedule with me. He said it wasn't physically possible to do my schedule this year and work too. At least, not if I wanted to get more than three hours' sleep a night."

Dr. Tremayne sat down next to Evie and opened a packet of gauze. "Where do you live, Evie?"

"In the dorms, in Dellonmarsh." She ran her free hand through her wavy brown hair, which frizzed more than smoothed it.

Dr. Tremayne raised the gauze and looked Evie in the eye. "Hold still while I clean the wound a bit. Evie, I know it's hard to leave family behind and come to school. Do you think you're adjusting okay?" Dr. Tremayne wiped the small gash with the gauze, cleaning away blood.

Evie sucked in her breath through her teeth as the gauze met the wound. "I'm fine. I call and text my family all the time. I enjoy my classes."

"Were you coming to request an extension on your paper?" asked Dr. Tremayne in a neutral voice as she opened the bandage and some clean gauze.

Evie watched her fold the gauze, then answered softly, "Yes, ma'am. How did you know?"

"You're a freshman, and you look exhausted. I see a lot of that. Are you having trouble sleeping, Evie? Or are you involved in too many extracurricular activities? Are you having trouble keeping up with your work?"

Evie hesitated. "Extracurricular activities aren't the problem. I'm keeping up with my work."

"Here comes the bandage and some gauze for padding and pressure. The wound isn't too deep, so it shouldn't need stitches, but it is still bleeding. Head wounds do tend to keep bleeding. I'm going to use the bandage to tape the gauze in place. Hold still." Dr. Tremayne carefully applied the bandage and gauze to the cut. "So are you having trouble sleeping?" she asked again.

Evie sighed softly. "Not exactly."

"What's going on?"

"We've had problems in the dorm. Vandalism and pranks. Someone broke into a few of the rooms and spilled shampoo on the beds. A bunch of people had rude notes shoved under their doors. Then my whole hallway was awakened by loud noises three different times this week. When the resident assistant investigated, she didn't find anything to explain the noises. And last night, there was a really loud explosion in the bathroom. Water went everywhere, we think from one of the bathtubs, but nothing else was damaged. The residents are getting worried and scared."

Kamika nudged Lea and whispered, "What's a resident assistant?"

Lea leaned toward Kamika and said in her ear, "Resident assistants are students who are paid to live on a floor in a dorm on campus. They keep peace, enforce rules, and deal with roommate conflicts and other problems."

Evie looked at Dr. Tremayne with tears in her eyes again. "I only got four hours of sleep four nights in a row. I'm having trouble concentrating. I'm so tired. I tried to nap, but during the daytime, it's too loud. My window overlooks the café, which is always full of people. I've tried to write my paper, but I'm only halfway done, and I don't know if I'll be able to finish it."

Dr. Tremayne pressed her lips together in a flat line as she collected the used tissue, gauze, and bandage wrapper, folded it all into her disposable gloves, and rose to throw it away in a trash can behind her desk. "Have the authorities been notified about all this trouble in the dorm?"

"The UT police came when someone broke in and spilled shampoo on the beds, but they didn't do anything but take down information," Evie said as her fingers traced the outline of the bandage on her temple.

Lea detected a note of fear under the exhaustion in Evie's voice. "Evie, did you get a note under your door?"

Evie nodded with a pained look on her face.

"What did it say?" Dr. Tremayne asked as she sat back down next to Evie.

Evie's red-rimmed eyes teared up. "Nothing important. It was just rude."

"Please tell me, Evie," Dr. Tremayne said, gently patting Evie's knee.

Evie shrugged. "It said that I was stupid and talked too loudly. It said that everyone knows I'm not smart enough to be in the honors dorms because I get lost coming out of the bathroom." Evie cringed, deflating before their eyes.

"You know that's not true," Dr. Tremayne said. "You're a very good student."

"The note was right, though. I got lost several times during the first week of class. If I have to meet someone in a building that I haven't been to before, I leave early in case I get lost on the way. I have to refer to my map of the campus all the time."

Lea looked at Kamika with concern and then looked back at Evie. "Do you think the person who wrote the note knows you?"

"They must." Tears leaked out of the girl's eyes again. "They knew that I got asked to keep my voice down by the RA. I was practicing a skit for Spanish with my partner from class, and we got a little loud. Only someone in the dorm would know about that."

"No wonder you aren't sleeping," said Dr. Tremayne, giving Evie a sympathetic glance.

Evie shuddered. "On top of that, everyone says the dorm is haunted, and I'm beginning to believe them."

CHAPTER 3

"WHY DO THEY THINK THE DORM is haunted?" Lea asked. "Did someone see a ghost?"

"I haven't seen any ghosts. But when we all moved into the dorms, we were given a tour and told the history of the dorm: how it was built in 1927, and how the Dellonmarsh family had it built for female freshmen. They told us that Olive Dellonmarsh was rumored to haunt the dorm, benevolently looking out for the girls, like she had for the nieces and nephews she helped put through the university when she was alive. They said she was a friendly ghost who loved students. One of the girls said Olive likes to move books. That she'd seen it happen."

Lea smiled. "They've probably been telling that story to the girls each year since Olive Dellonmarsh died. I know friends of mine were told the same thing years ago."

Dr. Tremayne nodded in agreement. "As far as I know, that tradition goes back a long way."

Evie started to shake her head, winced, and rubbed the side of her face. "Yes, but then all the trouble started. The girls began calling the vandal a ghost. It started as a joke. Someone suggested that maybe Olive was annoyed. But everyone stopped laughing after that explosion in the bathroom last night. No one was in there, and we didn't find any evidence of what caused it."

"Someone probably set it up as a prank," Kamika said. "I never lived in dorms, but back at my high school, the boys were always making something explode in the toilets."

Evie looked unconvinced. "But they probably left evidence. This ghost didn't. And it wasn't in the toilets. The water came from a bathtub."

Dr. Tremayne smiled suddenly. "I can think of ways to make small explosions in water without leaving evidence. Chemistry students take pride in knowing that kind of thing. I know a chemistry professor who enjoys waking his class up by dropping bits of sodium metal into water on the first day of class. A tiny amount would make noise and splash the water everywhere. No visible evidence would be found either."

Lea chuckled and said, "I think I had that class! The sodium reacts on contact with water." She paused in thought. "All the vandal would have to do is delay the reaction by putting the sodium in oil inside something that would eventually dissolve, like a pill capsule. That would prevent the water from touching the sodium for a little while, giving the vandal a chance to escape before the explosion occurred."

Kamika pursed her lips, thinking. "That would mean taking a big risk. Someone could have come into the bathroom after the prank was set up but before it went off! Depending on how they set up the explosion, someone could have gotten hurt."

"Sodium metal in water probably wouldn't have hurt anyone. But still, you're right. Somebody's willing to take risks to scare the others in the dorm. Why? What could they possibly gain from that?" Lea asked.

"Well, it's exam time," Dr. Tremayne said, sitting down in her desk chair. "Someone chose a week when the majority of the students have exams or projects or papers due that are worth a third of their final grades. Upsetting people and making them sleep deprived this week could affect grades for the semester."

Kamika crossed her arms over her chest and made a derisive noise. "What kind of perverse idiot gets his kicks from making people get bad grades? Sounds like a sadistic psychopath with a sick sense of humor!"

Evie looked at Kamika in shock. "You mean someone could be doing this for fun?"

Kamika gave her a perplexed look. "Haven't you watched enough television or YouTube to know that a certain percentage of the people in this world are pretty twisted? Why do you think our boss has such a booming investigation business?"

Evie paused, considering the idea with dawning understanding, "Oh. Now I'm mad!"

"Our boss could probably figure out who's behind the problems." Lea glanced at Kamika for agreement. "Montgomery Investigations handles all sorts of situations that the police can't solve."

"I wish he would come solve this!" Evie said wistfully. "This horrible person needs to be stopped. I won't let whoever it is bother me anymore, even if I have to go sleep at a friend's place for a few nights to get past the sleep deprivation."

"Good," said Dr. Tremayne. "Mad is much better than scared and worried. You have today, tomorrow, and Monday to finish your paper. I could give you an extension, but I'll bet you can finish it with time to spare."

"I'll get the paper done. Thank you!" She rose from her chair too quickly and winced. "Ugh. First, I'm going to get some ibuprofen for my head. Goodbye, Dr. Tremayne." Evie waved to Lea and Kamika and left the office.

As the sound of her student's footsteps receded, Dr. Tremayne turned to Lea and Kamika with a troubled look on her face. "Let's hope that situation doesn't escalate. That sort of harassment can drive a troubled student to the edge, if not over it."

"Is there anything else we can do?" Lea asked.

Dr. Tremayne pulled her phone from her pocket. "If memory serves, one of my graduate students lives in Dellonmarsh as the head resident in charge of all the resident assistants. I'll make some inquiries and see what else I can find out about this situation." She selected and called a number on her phone.

Lea and Kamika gathered their equipment bags while Dr. Tremayne talked on the phone.

"Dr. Tremayne doesn't look happy," Kamika said, observing the progression of the phone call.

"We'll find out soon enough," Lea said, watching Dr. Tremayne hang up the phone with a concerned look on her face.

"What's up?" Lea asked, sensing a growing level of tension coming from the professor.

Dr. Tremayne leaned back in her chair and said in a grim voice, "Evie doesn't know the whole of the problem. Apparently, some incidents were hushed up so most of the girls in the house didn't hear about them. My grad student who is the head resident at Dellonmarsh is quite concerned. She thinks the problem has been escalating since school started. The dorm residents are on edge."

Lea lifted her packed equipment bag up onto her shoulder. "Would the university allow a private investigation? The UT Police Department might only see it all as a series of pranks. I'm sure they're investigating the vandalism, but if they haven't arrested anyone or come up with any leads, maybe they could use Montgomery's help."

Kamika looked at Dr. Tremayne. "Would Montgomery be allowed to investigate?"

Dr. Tremayne drummed her fingers on her desk. "Well, if we go through proper channels and ask the housing department for permission, we might get an answer next semester. I have to make a few discreet calls. This might be a case where the residents themselves will have some latitude in handling the matter." She smiled at them and gestured for them to follow her out of her office. "You girls don't need to waste your Saturday sitting around. Go home. What I have to do could take days. You'll hear from me or Montgomery if I make any progress on the matter. Thanks for helping me with my office."

"Come on, Kamika," Lea said. "Let's go home."

"Fine by me." Kamika followed Lea down the hall and out of the building.

As they walked away from the building, Lea heard a voice calling after her. Turning, she saw Dr. Tremayne waving to her from the entry door. "Lea, wait. I forgot to tell you something about your thesis."

Kamika dumped her equipment bag onto the sidewalk. "You can go talk to her. I'll wait here."

Lea walked back to Dr. Tremayne.

"Lea, I reviewed your thesis. Because of the work you did this summer to prove that Dr. Richardson stole your thesis, you are ahead of schedule. Once the research integrity committee issues their findings in your favor, and I have no doubt that they *will* find in your favor, you will have almost nothing left to do but a final draft and your defense of your thesis. Everything else is done. You could graduate this semester instead of waiting until next semester."

Lea looked at Dr. Tremayne in surprise. "Finish this fall instead of in the spring? I hadn't realized." She was flabbergasted. "Will I be ready in time?"

"Yes! You've done a beautiful job of researching and putting together a cohesive theory on an ancient civilization based on the new archeological findings. You've provided a brand-new picture of the daily lives of the people who built geoglyphs and mounds in Kazakhstan eight thousand years ago. It's an excellent and eloquently expressed scholarly contribution to the field. Besides, if you graduate early, you would save money and time." Dr. Tremayne studied Lea's face. "I see I've surprised you, but I'm not sure it was a pleasant surprise. Is something wrong?"

"Wrong? Oh no." Lea bit her lip. "I had fixed in my mind to start looking for a new position, a job that uses my degree, in the spring before graduation. If I'm graduating early, I'll need to start now. I have to readjust my planning." Lea's brain was awhirl. The future where she stopped working with Kamika at Bad Vibes Removal Services had seemed so far away. Now it wasn't the future anymore. Changes were coming sooner than she expected.

Dr. Tremayne smiled at her. "I understand. This has always been your plan, though. You've done amazing work in the face of a terrible betrayal by your supervisor. It's time for you to reach for your dreams."

Lea nodded. "I guess." She glanced at Kamika, waiting for her on the sidewalk. "I should go."

"Okay," Dr. Tremayne patted her shoulder. "I'll see you this week for our thesis meeting. You'll see then how very little is left to do. I should have the research integrity committee's report by then too."

"Right. See you then." Lea hurried to join her friend. Her thoughts turned to the people she needed to tell about her early graduation: besides Kamika, there was her boss, Montgomery, and her boyfriend, Patrick. *I'll have to break the news to Kamika and Montgomery soon. But not today. I'll call and tell Patrick. He'll be surprised without being sad about it.*

Lea and Kamika began walking the few blocks down Guadalupe Street to where they had left their van in the San Antonio Parking Garage. Sweat was beginning to roll down Lea's neck as they approached the garage.

"Dang humidity," Kamika said, shifting her bag from one shoulder to the other for the third time. "I feel like I've been lifting weights in a sauna. Fall is taking its sweet time coming this year. Someone needs to tell Mother Nature that Halloween is coming."

"I can see the garage entrance. We're almost there," Lea said, brushing sweat from her eye.

"Thank goodness," Kamika said.

Lea's phone began to ring in her pocket. She stopped walking and put down her bag.

"That'd better not be Montgomery with another job for us." Kamika leaned wearily against the side wall of the parking garage with her equipment bag between her feet. "It's Saturday, and I want to go home and shower, or jump in a pool, or swim in an ice bath. And I need to work on my blog."

Lea looked at her phone as she answered it. "It's Montgomery, all right." She raised the phone to her ear. "Hello?"

Montgomery's voice came through, loud and vibrant. "Lea, you and Kamika haven't left the university yet, have you?"

"No, we're standing outside the parking garage where we left the van. Why?"

"Don't go anywhere. I spoke to Jenny—Dr. Tremayne, that is—and she said she might need you to stay there."

"Stay here?" Lea glanced at Kamika, who raised her eyebrows in query.

"Yes. Grab lunch, or coffee, or a snack on me. My tablet has the van parked near 25th and Guadalupe. It that where you are?"

"Yes."

"Good. That's not far from the Dellonmarsh Residence Hall. Tell Kamika I know she hates to work Saturdays, but that I'll pay you both double for working an investigation today."

Lea grinned at Kamika, who was looking at her with annoyance. "Does that mean someone wants us to investigate the incidents at the dorm?"

"The head resident wants us. I'm working with Jenny on the permissions. It shouldn't take too long," Montgomery said confidently. Montgomery's persistence and persuasive abilities were legendary.

"Okay. Call us when you're ready." She ended the call.

Kamika tilted her head to one side. "Well, now what?" she asked in a resigned tone.

"Now we go to lunch on Montgomery. He is going to persuade someone to let him investigate Evie's dorm's problems. And he said to tell you he'll pay us double for working an investigation today."

"He'd better! He knows this is my day off." She picked up her equipment bag. "Come on. Knowing Montgomery, persuading someone to let him investigate won't take long. He can talk his way into almost anything. We might not have time to eat. Let's dump these bags and grab some food. I saw plenty of places to eat down the street."

Lea picked up her bag and followed Kamika into the garage.

Half an hour later, as they were finishing pitas with a side of hummus, Lea's phone rang again.

"It's Montgomery," she said to Kamika as she answered the phone. "Hello?"

"Lea, once you finish lunch, walk over to the Dellonmarsh dorm on Dean Keeton Street. I'll meet you there shortly. Bring the scanning equipment."

"I take it you talked them into letting us investigate," Lea said, not the least surprised.

"Not exactly. You and Kamika are going to help me do that right now."

"What?"

"The hall government is going to meet, and you two are going to talk to them. I'll be there as soon as I can. See you soon." He disconnected the call.

"What's wrong?" Kamika asked, seeing the puzzled look on Lea's face.

"Montgomery says we have to help him convince the hall government to let us investigate."

"What? He wants me to convince someone to let me work on my day off? Has he lost his mind?" Kamika picked up the remains of her lunch and tossed it in the trash. "Montgomery better think twice before he asks me to speak."

Lea laughed as she collected her own trash, knowing Kamika would change her mind. "I'd better do the talking then. We're meeting Montgomery at the dorm." She nudged Kamika as they walked toward the trash can by the exit to the restaurant. "Now we get to see for ourselves if the dorm is haunted."

CHAPTER 4

AFTER RETRIEVING THEIR EQUIPMENT BAGS, LEA and Kamika walked several blocks and arrived at the back of the dorm. A drop-off driveway and stairs leading up to a door on the second floor were visible. Montgomery was nowhere in sight.

"That can't be the main entrance," Kamika said as Lea pointed out the building to her. "I don't see Montgomery yet. Where did he want us to meet him?"

"Let's go to the front of the building, inside the quad." Lea led the way past an outdoor café filled with students sitting at umbrella-shaded tables, eating, studying, and talking. "This is the Dellonmarsh Café. It operates out of the lower level of the dorm."

They followed the path to enter a green space surrounded by dormitory buildings on four sides, creating an enclosed, rectangular courtyard. Three of the four buildings were connected to each other. Only the Dellonmarsh Residence Hall stood independently, with wide sidewalks separating it from its neighbors.

Lea pointed at a tall, black, iron fence as they passed through it. "This gate and one on the other side are closed and locked at night, limiting access to the quad inside and to the buildings. Residents need access cards to get into the buildings. Given the security around here, whoever is causing trouble in the dorm must be a resident. The other buildings in the quad are also dormitories: Andrews, Blanton, and Carothers."

Kamika gazed around the courtyard. Unlike the crowded café, only a few students were using the open, green space. Two girls were sunbathing near Dellonmarsh's porch entrance, where an absence of trees allowed for a sunny spot. A few male students were playing Frisbee around a statue of Diana the Huntress in the middle of the quad. Giant oaks spread their branches over much of the courtyard, shading large areas. "It's quiet in here," Kamika commented. "Where should we wait for Montgomery? In the café? On one of these benches? Up on the dorm veranda?"

Lea nodded toward the girls who were sunbathing. "Let's see what the girls have to say about the vandalism."

Lea and Kamika walked up the front steps past the girls and set their equipment bags on the porch. One of the sunbathers gave Lea a curious look, but the other didn't even move.

"Hello," Lea called to the girls.

The curious girl sat up and openly inspected Lea's hair, casual jeans, and t-shirt and Kamika's chic clothes. Although it was mid-October, the student was wearing a string bikini. Her pale blond hair was knotted on top of her head in a hasty fashion, threatening to fall loose at any moment. "Hi," she said.

"I'm Lea. This is Kamika. We're waiting for a friend, but we're early."

"Oh," said the girl, straightening the towel on which she'd been lying.

"We heard y'all had some trouble with vandalism in the dorm. Did they catch whoever did it?" Lea asked, hoping to see how the girls would respond to the question.

The second girl bolted upright and turned toward Lea. "Where did you hear that?" she demanded. This girl wore a bandeau top and tiny shorts that exposed long, slender legs. Her auburn hair was French braided with the end of the braid pinned up off her neck.

"A friend was complaining about the rude note slipped under her door, and she mentioned that the dorm had some issues lately," Lea said in a placating, nonconfrontational voice.

The auburn-haired girl turned to the blonde. "Somebody talked! I told you we should have threatened a fine or something."

"I'll bet it was Allysia," said the blonde. "She wanted to do a segment on her YouTube channel about our situation for her followers. She thinks she's such an important influencer. Natalia told her to respect everyone's privacy, but I'll bet she didn't listen. She doesn't believe in privacy and she says keeping quiet isn't 'woke.'"

"No, wait," Lea said shaking her head, "I don't know who Allysia is, but she didn't tell us anything, and we didn't hear about it on YouTube. We aren't going to spread the information. We're actually here to help—that is, if we are allowed to help."

The girl with auburn hair looked at Lea suspiciously. "Are you with the police or from housing?"

"Neither," Lea said.

But before Lea could explain anything else, the front door to the dorm swung open, and a lanky young woman in slim Capri jeans and a burnt orange, peasant-style blouse came out. Her long black hair shimmered in the sun. "Matty and Corinna, we have an emergency meeting of the hall government in twenty minutes. Come on."

The two girls jumped to their feet. "What's up, Mei?"

"One of my professors contacted me with a possible solution for the issue we're having." The young woman's eyes strayed to Lea and Kamika. She lowered her voice and continued to talk to the two sunbathers.

Lea heard the young woman, Mei, tell the girls to send everyone a message in their chat group and to knock on doors to round up people if needed. The two girls, Matty and Corinna, collected their towels and water bottles and retreated into the building.

Mei started to follow them inside but paused by Lea and Kamika. "Do you need something?"

Kamika was seated on the porch, leaning her chin on her hand. "I think we're the reason you just called a meeting," she said with a knowing smile.

Mei looked at her in surprise, which swiftly changed to skepticism as she surveyed Kamika and Lea. "You're detectives?"

Lea laughed at the look of confusion on the young woman's face. "The detective with the license is our boss. We arrived before he did, so we're waiting for him."

Mei still looked puzzled. "Y'all really work for a detective? You look like you could be students here."

Kamika pointed at Lea. "She's a grad student studying history. I'm not a student. I went to a small liberal arts college to study interior design."

"You studied interior design, and she's studying history, but you both work for a detective. How does that work?" Mei asked with her arms crossed over her narrow torso.

"Well, Lea has a specialized skill that's useful in solving certain crimes, and I go along to keep her out of trouble when we help with investigations. But we don't do that full time. Most of the time, we work for Bad Vibes Removal Services. Our boss, Mr. Montgomery, owns Bad Vibes *and* Montgomery Investigations."

Lea approached Mei and extended her hand. "I'm Lea. I heard you say one of your professors contacted you. Was that Dr. Tremayne? She's my thesis advisor and a friend of our boss."

Mei shook Lea's hand, her eyes sizing Lea up as she greeted her, pausing only fractionally on Lea's Suebian knot hair. "I'm Mei, the head resident here at Dellonmarsh. Dr. Tremayne is one of my professors. I'm currently studying Celtic mythology for my master's degree in European history."

Kamika introduced herself too. Then Mei invited them inside the dorm and led them through the lobby, down a wide hall to an enormous common living room. The room contained stuffed chairs and couches that had been arranged in groups to make multiple conversation areas. Antique wooden tables with straight-backed chairs around them invited group work and studying. Mei led them to seats near the large fireplace.

"So what's the plan? You're going to have a hall government meeting?" Lea asked, dropping into a stuffed chair.

Mei nodded. "My supervisor in the University Housing Division told me that if the hall government approves, we can allow Montgomery Investigations access to all the common areas to see if he can resolve our vandalism problem."

"Only the common areas?" Kamika asked.

"Yes. Students would have to give you access to their individual rooms on a room-by-room basis." Mei glanced up as a few girls entered the living room. "Here come the members of the Advisory Committee, which is what we call our hall government. Are you willing to answer any questions that they have?"

Kamika and Lea both nodded, and Kamika answered, "Absolutely. But do you make the final decision, or do they? I don't understand who's in charge."

Mei frowned, concentrating as she explained. "I guess it's a two-tiered system. I'm the head resident, supervising the resident assistants living on each floor and helping them with problems that arise with the residents. I attend all the hall government meetings and ensure university housing rules are followed. However, the advisory makes decisions on events for the whole building. I can guide and suggest and let them know whether something they want to do is allowed under the university rules, but they vote on activities to hold for the dorm. They have a president, vice president, secretary, and treasurer, and the rest of the members are in charge of various things, like special events, or holiday decorations, or the newsletter."

Kamika watched the young women gathering on the other end of the room. "So you can recommend us, but they have to vote on it. I understand."

"I have to go start the meeting." Mei rose from her seat and hurried across the room to greet the young women who were arriving.

Kamika and Lea watched from their seats as the meeting was called to order. As Mei explained why the meeting had been called, Kamika whispered to Lea, "This place is supposed to be for female freshmen, right?"

"Yes," Lea whispered.

"Those girls look too confident and collected to be freshmen. None of them look as tired and overwhelmed as Evie did."

Lea thought for a moment. "I remember now. The hall government is made up of sophomores, girls who lived here last year and were elected to remain another year to advise the incoming freshman."

"That explains it," Kamika said, satisfied.

Lea counted the young women by Mei. "I see fourteen members. Plus each of the three floors has resident advisors who aren't freshmen, plus Mei. That makes at least eighteen residents who aren't new freshmen, maybe more depending on how many RAs per floor."

"How many girls live here?"

"I'm not sure. Around one hundred fifty, I think. The building isn't that big."

The students in the meeting were suddenly all speaking at once in a babble of voices. A loud girl with long brown hair sporting Kool-Aid-red highlights, called them to order. She said, "We all have questions. We have people who can answer them. Let's go to the source." Then the girl turned to Mei and said something.

Mei waved at Lea and Kamika, gesturing for them to come and join the group.

"We're up," Kamika said as she stood and shook her curls back out of her face.

"Yep." Lea stood and followed Kamika.

They walked to the other side of the room and stood beside Mei.

"What would you like to know?" Lea asked the group of waiting residents.

The loud-voiced young woman with the Kool-Aid hair spoke. "Hi, I'm Natalia. I'm the president of the advisory.

We would like you to explain what you do. Some of us think—" She paused. "That is, we don't understand how your equipment could possibly work." She smiled, trying unsuccessfully to take the disbelief out of her words.

Kamika raised one eyebrow and crossed her arms on her chest. "You think we're a bunch of liars here to cheat you?" Kamika glared at the girl.

Lea put a restraining hand on Kamika's arm. "I've got this. Take a deep breath."

Kamika nodded but still looked perturbed.

"Hi. My name is Lea Saroyan, and this is my colleague, Kamika. We work for Bad Vibes Removal Services and Montgomery Investigations." Lea launched into her explanation of the sound-pattern-scanning equipment and emotional-energy-scanning equipment that Mr. Montgomery had invented. She explained how the devices worked and what use they had in the real world. "From apartments to doctors' offices, people function better in a happier, stress-free environment. We at Bad Vibes Removal Services can improve well-being for people by eliminating built-up, negative emotional energy and improving the interior sensory signals in the building by changing color usage, layout of furniture, sounds, and scents. Montgomery Investigations uses the scanning equipment to aid in solving crimes. If a record of arguments, yelling, gunshots, and other loud noises can be detected in the walls, we can use that to identify participants and catch criminals. Do you have any questions?"

A girl's hand shot up. Lea nodded at her.

She glanced at the girl next to her. "I heard you guys have gotten rid of ghosts too. That seems like a trick to me. No one can prove ghosts exist. I don't believe they do."

"Whether you believe in ghosts is up to you. Ghost removal is not on our slate of services and neither Bad Vibes Removal Services nor Montgomery Investigations will promise to get rid of ghosts." She paused and met the girl's eyes. "However, we have encountered ghosts on cases. They can prevent the resetting of the emotional atmosphere in buildings. When that happens, we usually can't resolve the problems with the emotional atmosphere without resolving the problem with the ghost. Any other questions?"

Several girls started talking at once.

"Quiet down. One at a time. Raise your hand," Natalia called in her big, presidential voice.

The girls fell silent and several hands shot up into the air. Lea nodded at another girl.

"Have you actually encountered ghosts?"

"Yes."

More hands shot up. Lea looked around the room. "Does anyone have a question that doesn't relate to ghosts?"

All but one hand went down. A belligerent-looking girl held her hand defiantly in the air.

Lea nodded at her. "What's your question?"

"Are you the Lea Saroyan who got Professor Mortimer Richardson suspended from his position?" the girl asked in a strained voice.

Lea was surprised by the question. "How do you know about that?"

"I know everything. Dr. Richardson's daughter, Paisley, told me about you. How you falsely accused Dr. Richardson of stealing your work and publishing it under his own name. You're a liar. He would never do that."

Lea wanted to explain how Dr. Richardson had plagiarized entire sections of her master's thesis word for word, and about how he had been placed on administrative leave and suspended from teaching by the university pending an investigation by the committee that had been convened by the research integrity officer. But she wasn't supposed to talk about it yet. Lea swallowed and cleared her throat. "I can't talk about that until the committee finishes its investigation."

"Well, I can talk about it, and I'm going to tell everyone! You ruined his life! You ruined his whole family," the girl yelled with tears glinting in her eyes.

"He ruined his own life," countered Lea, fighting to remain calm but with some consternation in her voice.

The girl jumped up from her chair and fled the room.

Lea watched her go in disbelief. She glanced at Kamika, who looked as shocked as Lea felt. Lea cleared her throat and attempted to return the conversation to the business at hand. "Do you have any more questions about how we work?"

"Uh, no. Uh. Sorry about Cressida. She's upset." Mei shook her head as if to clear her mind. "Natalia, you need to organize a vote now." Mei turned to Lea. "Would you and Kamika mind stepping into the lobby? They need to discuss their options and take a vote. I think the girls would rather do that in private."

"Of course," Lea said. "Come on, Kamika. We'll go wait by the reception desk." She and Kamika left the room, walking back to the lobby.

As they reached the main lobby, Lea found Cressida fuming and pacing. When Cressida saw Lea, she stalked toward her looking distraught and irate. She marched up to Lea, stopping inches from Lea's face.

Lea stood her ground, preparing to block a blow if necessary.

Cressida yelled, "I hate you! You only think of yourself and your stupid work. People's lives are more important than the ancient history of Kazakhstan!" She turned on her heel and ran down the first-floor hallway that led to dorm rooms.

Lea looked at Kamika in stunned silence. The verbal attack left her feeling slightly sick to her stomach. She inhaled deeply, realizing that she'd been holding her breath.

Kamika was the first to speak. "What the hell is that about?"

"I have no idea," Lea replied, utterly flummoxed.

Kamika stared down the hall where the girl had vanished. "Is she really blaming you for the consequences the professor had to suffer as a result of stealing your work?" she asked in a tone infused with outrage. "Being suspended is appropriate. He's lucky. Most thieves go to jail, but he'll only lose his job. Blaming you is like blaming the murder victim for getting killed, or blaming identity theft victims for having their accounts hijacked. The person who committed the crime is to blame, not the victim."

"Maybe she's having a hard time accepting the truth. It's not as if Dr. Richardson was a terrible human being entirely. Maybe she was inspired by his teaching or his philanthropy or she knows him as a good father because she's friends with his daughter, Paisley. People have a hard time accepting that someone they like and admire may do something wrong. I chose Dr. Richardson as my advisor because he inspired me in class. He was a phenomenal teacher. He is known for being charming and considerate of others. He organized charity events within the department. He also volunteered at one of the local elementary schools. I had trouble wrapping my brain around what he did, so imagine how hard it must be on someone who wasn't involved."

Kamika's green eyes popped open wider as if a thought had occurred to her. "You don't think he killed himself or something, do you? If he was despondent over losing his career and reputation, could he have . . ." Her voice trailed off.

The suggestion made Lea shudder in horror. "I haven't heard anything like that. If he'd committed suicide, I'm sure someone would have told me." Lea's face went pale as she swallowed the lump of anxiety in her throat. "At least, I hope someone would have told me. I'll ask around the department. See what I can find out." Lea tried to put Kamika's question to the back of her mind and focus on the dorm problems, but she could feel the tension building in her body.

"Lea! Kamika!" called a voice behind them.

They turned to find Mei beckoning them from down the hall by the living room.

"The girls' vote tied, so they have a request," Mei said as they approached her.

CHAPTER 5

LEA AND KAMIKA WALKED INTO THE large living area to find the advisory group watching them. Some were smiling. Others were frowning or looking anxious.

The president of the group, Natalia, stood up and shook her red hair from her face. "We've decided we need help. Not everyone is completely comfortable with having you here, but this problem is escalating, and we need to act before it gets worse. Anyway, could we get a demonstration of your equipment before we hold a final vote on the matter?"

Kamika said, "Sure! We've got the equipment. We could scan a wall." She looked around the large room. "Or, at least, a section of a wall."

Lea asked Natalia, "Which would you prefer to see, a sound-pattern scan or an emotional-energy scan?"

About six voices sounded at once, "Sound!"

Natalia surveyed the group. "Sound?" Seeing nods, she shrugged and turned back to Lea. "Sound scan, please."

"Okay," Lea said.

Lea and Kamika retrieved their equipment bags from the lobby. Kamika initiated the necessary programs to receive the incoming data on a tablet computer. Lea turned on the sound scanner and looked around the room for a good place to scan. She selected an area between two windows on the far side of the room.

Turning to the girls, Lea explained what she would do. "I'm going to slowly guide the scanner in overlapping strips over this section of wall. The data will be received on the tablet in Kamika's hands. Once the scan is complete, we'll run the analysis program to identify the patterns we find." Lea proceeded to scan the section of wall. Once she finished, she joined Kamika to review the results.

"Coverage looks good for the scan," Kamika said. "It's compiling data now."

Lea watched and then announced to the group of watching girls, "This building is really old. The data may go back decades unless something really loud obliterated earlier data completely or the wall board was replaced more recently. Fortunately, we can set the parameters of our analysis to show recent sounds."

A girl with naturally red hair called out, "How loud would a sound have to be to obliterate earlier sounds?"

Kamika replied, "Gunshots at close range, fireworks, sounds that are painfully loud."

"Over one hundred forty decibels," Lea said, looking up from the data. "I can tell you that I see evidence of a live band featuring a trumpet playing in this room in about 1950. On the most recent layers, I see a bunch of popping noises. It looks like balloons, lots of them. And, at the same time, someone—a female voice, based on the register—yelled, 'On your mark, get set, go!'" Lea could see amazement on the faces of the young women.

"What's wrong? Didn't you have an activity popping balloons in here?"

Natalia nodded with a pleased look on her face. "We did. We had a silly game night. In that area, we had a game where girls raced to sit on and pop balloons." She paused. "Then you can find noises and words with that scanner?"

Kamika held up the tablet displaying the results. "Yes. The louder the voices, the easier it is to figure out what people said. Softer conversations may leave little or no pattern while shouting or arguing leaves a clearer pattern. This program is especially good at identifying cursing, since people tend to curse when they are upset or yelling."

The murmur of voices in the advisory group grew loud as the girls talked among themselves.

Natalia waved her arms, collecting the group's attention. "I'm convinced, but we need to take a final vote. All in favor of allowing them to investigate in the dorm say 'aye.'"

A chorus of "ayes" rang out.

"All opposed, say 'nay.'" Natalia looked from face to face, checking for opposition. No one spoke.

Natalia clapped her hands. "The ayes have it."

The girls began talking excitedly among themselves again as Natalia and Mei approached Lea and Kamika.

"When can you start?" Natalia asked. "And how long do you think it will take to find our vandal ghost?"

Lea shrugged. "We'll do our best to resolve the situation as quickly as possible. When we start is up to our boss, Mr. Montgomery, who will be here soon. He'll probably want to talk to as many residents as possible who've had any trouble with the vandal or been victims of pranks."

Mei said, "I'll have the resident advisors on each floor call meetings tonight to explain to our residents what's going on. We'll ask anyone with information about the incidents or who's been a victim of a prank to speak to Mr. Montgomery."

The meeting broke up and advisory members began to drift out of the room in small groups. Lea caught a few girls looking over at her. She suspected they had something to say, maybe information about the incidents that had occurred, but more likely questions about ghosts. She sighed, wishing they hadn't asked about ghosts. Whenever she had to talk about ghosts, she felt like people were looking at her as if she had sprouted two heads. Her stomach clenched as she caught a glimpse of Cressida joining a group of girls.

"Mei," Lea said in a quiet voice, "that girl, Cressida, is really upset about Dr. Richardson being suspended. She yelled at me during the meeting and again in the lobby. I thought she was going to hit me."

An appalled look came into Mei's eyes. "I'm so sorry about that. Cressida's roommate was Paisley Richardson, Dr. Richardson's daughter. Cressida and Paisley went to high school together. I think Cressida has known the Richardson family her entire life. When Dr. Richardson was suspended at the beginning of September, Paisley decided to move out of the dorm to be near her family. She was a sophomore on the advisory, like Cressida. Last I heard, Paisley was considering withdrawing from the university altogether. Cressida was heartbroken at losing her roommate and distraught over the turmoil in Paisley's family. She told me that the entire Richardson family is falling apart. Mrs. Richardson filed for divorce, and a younger sister was hospitalized on a psychiatric hold for depression and suicidal thoughts."

Lea turned to Kamika with dismay. "I had no idea. The sins of the father really did fall on the family. That's terrible." Lea's shoulders drooped as the sinking feeling in her stomach worsened. She felt nauseated by the news.

"*It's not your fault* that he stole your work," Kamika said in a bracing voice, emphasizing her words. "Dr. Richardson made his choices. He has to live with the consequences for himself and his family."

Mei patted Lea on the shoulder. "I totally agree. I'll speak to Cressida. She has to understand that the Richardson family's situation isn't your fault, and that she can't yell at you like that."

Kamika pointed out a nearby window. "I see Montgomery arriving. Let's go meet him in the lobby."

The three women walked to the lobby and opened the door for Montgomery, who came in wearing his typical khaki slacks and white button-down shirt. The buttons strained a little across his wide midriff and his large belt buckle was hidden beneath his drooping belly. Montgomery was over six feet tall, and bulky, near three hundred pounds, but surprisingly energetic and active. What remained of his blond hair formed a ring around the top of his balding head.

"Lea, Kamika, thanks for coming ahead of me," he said. "Traffic on I-35 was terrible!"

"It was nothing," Lea said.

"Yeah," Kamika said. "These girls need our help. Some twisted nut job is making life miserable for them." She gestured to Mei. "This is Mei. She's the head resident here in the dorm, which means she's sort of in charge of guiding the hall government and enforcing rules."

Montgomery extended his beefy hand and shook Mei's thin hand. "Pleased to meet you. Did your hall government make a decision yet?"

"Yes. Lea and Kamika explained what your company does and then did a sound reading on a small section of wall as a demonstration for some of the skeptics in the group. In the end, they all agreed to ask you to investigate." Mei grinned up at Montgomery, who stood head and shoulders above her.

Montgomery glanced around the lobby. "Great! Can we sit down and talk? I'd like to get a full description of every incident that has occurred in the dorm this semester. I understand that some of these pranks were suppressed, found before the whole dorm could become aware of them."

Mei opened her mouth to answer but then paused and watched as a few residents, laughing and talking among themselves, came through the lobby and walked out the doors to the quad. "Let's go to my rooms. I have a sitting room that we can use." She led them across the lobby toward the dormitory wing of the first floor.

She stopped by the first door off the lobby. "This is my place. Come on in." She unlocked the door and allowed them to enter in front of her before closing the door behind them.

Lea looked around. Although containing modern furnishings, the rooms were clearly of an older architectural style. Windowsills and doorframes showed many layers of paint, built up over decades. Chipped spots on the doorframe gave telltale hints of the many colors the room had been painted in the past. A transom window over the door had been painted shut, but pieces of the mechanism to open it remained visible. The sitting area contained a small, pastel-print loveseat and two other chairs, a wingback and a rocker, arranged in a conversational group. A built-in bookshelf full of books filled one wall. Pale yellow, lace curtains hung over wooden blinds on the window overlooking the quad outside.

Lea sat down on the loveseat while Montgomery chose the sturdy-looking, pale blue wingback chair.

"This is a lot bigger than any dorm room I've ever seen," Kamika said as she joined Lea on the loveseat. "I like how you've decorated it."

"I'm lucky," Mei said as she sat down in the remaining empty chair, a gliding rocker with a pale yellow cushion tied to the seat. "This suite was built for a house mother who lived in the dorm and was in charge of the girls in the early to middle 1900s. I get full walk-in closets, this sitting room, and a bedroom. Plus, it has a sense of history to it."

Montgomery pulled out his tablet and opened a file, preparing to take notes. "Okay," he said, "tell me how this whole business got started. Can you pinpoint a start date for these incidents? What was the first thing that happened?"

Mei's brow wrinkled as she considered his questions. "Let me grab my phone. I need to look at my calendar. I can give you an exact date." She removed her phone from her pocket and tapped on the screen. "Yes. Here it is. September 20. We were a few weeks into the semester, and we had an advisory meeting that evening. Right as the meeting was ending, around eight-thirty p.m., Anjali Singh came running into the living room looking for me. She'd been at the library studying, and, when she returned to her room, she found her door was open, and the room was a wreck. Papers were scattered everywhere. Clothes were dumped out of her dresser. A bottle of shampoo was dumped out on her and her roommate's beds. She lives here on the first floor. As I was going to see the damage to her room, two more girls, Jonna and McLayne, came up to me. The same thing had happened in their rooms. Jonna Livingstone lives on the second floor and McLayne Provence lives on the third floor. All three girls had left their rooms to go to dinner by six p.m. Anjali went from dinner to join a study group at the library. Jonna went from dinner to intermural soccer practice. McLayne went from dinner to the first meeting of the Premedical Students Association."

"What about their roommates?" Lea asked. "Where were they?"

"Two of them, Allysia and Erin, were in a biology lab from six to ten p.m., and the third, Gwen, was in a six-to-ten p.m. chemistry lab. They'd all gone to dinner at five to eat before class. And all six girls' belongings were vandalized. We called the police, who verified three of the girls were in labs working with partners or in groups. They all had alibis, not that I think they would have vandalized their own beds. All six girls were furious." Mei sank back into the rocker dejectedly.

Montgomery took notes on his tablet. "What are the room numbers for the damaged rooms?"

Mei rose from her seat. "Let me get the report I had to fill out for the housing department. The numbers are on there." She crossed the room and opened the door leading to her bedroom. She returned with a laptop computer. Sitting again, she said, "I'll send you a copy of the incident reports."

Montgomery gave her his email address, and, in a moment, he had received the files. "Thank you," he said. "What happened next?"

"Next came the anonymous letters. I had to fill out reports when eight girls got threatening or disparaging notes shoved under their doors. That happened around October 1."

"Send me those as well," Montgomery said.

Mei forwarded the reports to Montgomery.

Lea asked, "How about the banging noises waking girls up at night?"

"Those didn't involve specific rooms or residents, and we never located the source or found any damage caused to the building, so I don't have a report on them," Mei said. "That happened three nights in a row, Tuesday through Thursday of this week, and woke the entire west side of the building. A lot of us have been running on caffeine and sugar to stay awake in class since we've lost so much sleep."

"We heard that there was an explosion that splashed water all over one of the bathrooms," Kamika said. "Was that the most recent event?"

A look of annoyance and chagrin passed across Mei's face. "That happened last night less than an hour after I walked the whole building looking for trouble. After all the noises the previous nights, I decided to do a walking patrol, but I didn't prevent anything. A loud explosion in one of the third-floor bathrooms woke everyone up. I have a report for that one because of the flood it caused. Some of the water leaked out of the bathroom into the hall. Janitorial staff had to clean up the mess."

"Send me the report," Montgomery said.

Mei complied.

Montgomery verified he received the files. "Now, tell me about these rude or threatening notes. Did any of the girls who got shampoo on their beds get a note?"

45

Mei checked her records. "Umm, no. Different girls were targeted."

"And were they delivered in the evening or at night too?"

Mei shook her head. "No. The first resident reported finding a note mid-afternoon. The rest reported them later in the afternoon as they came back to their rooms after being out for classes."

"Okay. Then the notes would have been left under the doors earlier in the day, but not the night before because girls would have found them in the morning when they woke up." Montgomery frowned thoughtfully. "We have no consistent time for the various incidents then. So we're looking for someone with access to the dorm at all times, most likely a resident or someone getting access from a resident."

Lea asked, "Could the vandal have decided daytime stunts were too dangerous? If this person almost got caught vandalizing those three rooms or putting notes under the door, he or she might have switched to night-time out of caution."

"It's a possibility," Montgomery agreed. "But at this point, all we can do is speculate." He glanced at his notes. "Next, I was told that some other incidents were hushed up, kept from the residents, and not reported. Can you tell me about them?"

Mei grimaced and nodded. "It was only one other incident. A resident advisor found something and woke me up. No permanent damage was done, so we didn't report it." She leaned closer to Montgomery. "Someone wrote in ketchup on the stairwell wall, 'Cheaters live here.' The second floor RA found it around two a.m. She was coming downstairs to look for something she thought she left in the living room." Mei's eyes dimmed at the memory, and she shivered lightly. "I cleaned it up."

"Did you document that? Take a picture?" Montgomery asked.

Mei nodded. "At first, I thought it was paint. But then we noticed the smell and saw that it was dripping down the wall. I realized it was ketchup, and we wiped it off before any of the residents saw it."

"When did that happen?" Montgomery asked.

"About two weeks ago. A week before the loud noises started."

"Try and pinpoint a date for me."

Mei took out her phone. "Let me think." She stopped. "No, wait! I know when it was. It was my brother's birthday. I called him later that day. He noticed I was tired on the phone. I told him I'd been up late cleaning up a mess. That was October 3."

Montgomery typed out notes, pausing to ask questions. "And no one reported seeing strangers in the dorm or someone who didn't belong?"

Mei sighed and leaned forward in her chair. "No. I'm afraid that whoever is responsible for these incidents lives in the dorm."

Suddenly, a loud banging shook the door. A voice outside called, "Mei, come quickly, we need you."

CHAPTER 6

M EI JUMPED FROM HER CHAIR AND flung open the door. "What's wrong?" she asked breathlessly.

Natalia stood there with a frantic look on her face, her red-highlighted hair falling over one eye. "Someone destroyed the study nook at the end of the third-floor hallway!"

"Destroyed? What do you mean?" Mei asked, sounding aghast.

Montgomery, who was standing behind Mei, interrupted, "Show me the damage."

"It's this way. Follow me!" Natalia said as she trotted across the lobby and turned by a bank of mailboxes to get to a stairwell. She bounded up the stairs.

Mei, Lea, and Kamika ran up the stairs after her with Montgomery behind them. At the second-floor landing, Kamika stopped. "Doesn't this place have an elevator?"

"Yes," Mei said as she continued jogging up the stairs. "It's an old Otis model that was installed when the building was built in 1927. You have to manually close both a gate and the door to operate it. It's slow too. Walking up the stairs is faster. We only use the elevator when someone is injured and can't use the stairs."

Kamika grunted and continued her climb.

They arrived at the third floor and made their way toward the end of the hall.

A crowd of teenaged girls stood blocking Lea's view. Whatever had happened, many of the residents had turned out to gawk.

Montgomery announced in a booming voice, "Make a path, please. Stand back, now!"

The crowd of female freshmen split apart and lined the walls of the hallway, revealing the nook at the west end of the hall.

Lea stared at what had been an upholstered loveseat. Someone had dug into the seat cushion, ripping it open in several places, making long, deep gouges. Stuffing tumbled from long rents in the seat back. Bits of glass covered the floor where a study lamp had been smashed.

"Did anyone see what happened?" Montgomery asked, turning to face the crowd.

Mei turned from the mess to eye the watching girls. "Anyone? Please answer if you heard or saw anything. That lamp didn't shatter silently."

A girl with thick blond hair called out, "I heard the sound of breaking glass about five minutes ago."

Another voice said, "So did I."

"Did anyone *see* anything?" Mei asked.

No one answered.

Mei stood with her hands on her hips, waiting. When no answer came, she turned back to Montgomery. "We have to call the campus police." She pulled out her phone and dialed.

Montgomery put on shoe covers and disposable gloves that he carried in his pockets. Being careful not to disturb the scene, he inspected the damage.

A few minutes later, campus police arrived and took over.

"What do you want us to do, boss?" Kamika asked as she watched the officers start to take down names. "We could scan that big living room."

"I'm going to wait here and catch a word with the officers once they're done with their investigation. I need to let them know that I've been engaged to work in the dorm anyway. You two go ahead and start scanning the common areas: halls, bathrooms, living room, lobby." He opened his tablet and clicked through his notes. "Hang on. Here it is. The third-floor bathroom on the east side. Start there. That's the opposite end of the floor from this study nook. The emotional energy scan might give us an idea of motivation in that incident."

"Okay," Lea said. "We'll let you know if we discover anything interesting." She and Kamika returned to the lobby to retrieve their equipment.

As they were walking back to the stairs, Mei appeared in the hallway, returning from the upper floors. "The police are finished taking pictures. Now they are interviewing the residents who heard glass break. What are you going to do?"

"We're going to scan the bathroom where the explosion occurred," Lea said.

"Good," Mei said, running a hand through her straight black hair in annoyance. "I have to go file another damage report. I'll be in my rooms if you need me."

Lea and Kamika climbed the stairs up to the third floor. Lea mused out loud, "So much for the idea that the vandal switched to nights to avoid being caught. It's only two o'clock now."

"Mid-afternoon, like when the notes were shoved under the doors. And it's Saturday. No one is on a set schedule, so anybody could decide to come down the hall at any time. Vandalizing the study nook was risky." Kamika reached the third-floor landing and opened the door.

They walked down the hall and entered the bathroom. Looking around, they discovered half of the room contained toilet stalls. The other half had showers and bathtubs with shower heads.

Lea studied the room, puzzled. "Lots of showers, lots of toilets, but where are the sinks?"

Kamika walked around. "Here's one! That's really weird. What's with that?"

"Not sure. We'll have to ask a resident."

Kamika opened her tablet. "I'll start the analysis programs; you can start sound scanning anytime."

Lea removed the sound scanner from its bag and turned it on. "Okay. Here goes." Lea slowly scanned the walls of the room, moving the scanner up and down in overlapping strips. She skipped tiled areas, backsplashes, bathtub surrounds, and other materials not soft enough for sound waves to penetrate, concentrating on wood and wall board most likely to contain records of the passing sound waves.

"Good coverage," Kamika said, giving Lea a thumbs up.

The whole sound-scanning process, with Lea maneuvering the scanner in and out of stalls and around windows, took an hour. When at last she finished, she glanced around at Kamika and asked, "Did I miss anything? Do you see any areas I didn't scan that might hold a pattern?"

"Nope!" Kamika said, shaking her head. "You did great. We need to narrow this analysis, though. This building is so old, the scanner found lots of layers from years and years of sound."

Lea approached and looked over Kamika's shoulder at the data as it appeared on the tablet. "I see what you mean. The program will take forever to complete the analysis if we don't give it some parameters. Let me see the initial scan data."

Kamika handed the tablet to Lea. "Have at it."

"I see the explosion in the top layers. It obliterated a bunch of the previous layers in the nearby area," she paused and studied the room, "around that bathtub with the window over it." She pointed across the room, then reset the analysis settings. "Let's focus on the last two months of data, since all the problems relate to this semester. It's October and the girls moved into the dorm in August. Anything before that is irrelevant."

"Sounds good to me," Kamika agreed. "While the program runs through the data, I wanted to tell you about my blog. It's crazy what's happening."

Lea looked up from the tablet. "What's crazy?" She knew that Kamika had been putting a lot of time into her website, blogging about how colors, scents, sounds, and furniture arrangement affect mood and emotion.

"My blog is going viral! I went from two thousand readers six months ago to a million last month. I'm getting emails from all these paint and furniture and flooring companies wanting to pay me for advertising space and asking if they can send me samples to review."

"Oh wow! What are you going to do?"

"Well, I researched the financial side of it, and monetizing the blog seems fairly straightforward. I've got skills for the finance end, and I can hire the technical end. In fact, I've already hired a guy to be responsible for the technical end of the website and to handle placing the advertisements. Running everything as a company has been keeping me busy for the last couple weekends. It's what I'd be doing right now if we weren't here."

"What are you calling your company?"

"It's only a DBA right now, but I'm doing business as Kamika's Interior Design for Emotional Atmosphere, or Kamika's IDEA for short."

"What a fabulous name! I like it," Lea said.

Kamika's green eyes shone with pride as she grinned at Lea, her lovely mocha face aglow with excitement. "I've got people begging to throw money at me, all for doing something I love to do anyway."

"That sounds like the best kind of work. Do you think it will keep growing? Are you planning on switching to working on that full time? I mean, I'd miss you if you left Bad Vibes, but I'd understand."

Kamika laughed. "The money is barely coming in right now, so I'm not leaving my day job until I know if I can make the company function in the long run. Most startups fail in the first five years. And blog-based businesses can be in the fifteen-minutes-of-fame category. I'm going to analyze the heck out of this thing before I make any big decisions. In any case, handling a few advertisements doesn't take that much time right now. As long as I have enough hours in the day to get everything done, I'm good where I am."

Lea gave Kamika's arm a squeeze. "You've got a good head for business and the best head for finance of anyone I know, other than Montgomery. You'll know if you can make it work. I'm glad you aren't leaving me yet."

"Besides," Kamika said, "who's to say you won't leave me first? Aren't you graduating with your master's degree in the spring? This is your last year of graduate school, isn't it?"

Guilt washed through Lea. She realized she needed to tell Kamika that she was graduating early. "About that. Dr. Tremayne says I can finish up this fall, graduate a semester early. It would save me money too."

Kamika grabbed Lea by both shoulders and hugged her. "Wow! Graduating early! Congratulations! Then you'll be looking for a new job soon. And . . . wait a minute. Did you and Patrick make any plans? You've been dating for a while now. I remember something about you getting engaged when you graduate." Kamika released Lea and stood looking at her with her eyebrows raised expectantly.

Lea hesitated and her face reddened. "We've talked about the future. Some. I haven't told him that I could graduate early yet. Dr. Tremayne told me this morning. Oh, look, the analysis is finished." Lea turned her attention back to the tablet, pushing the questions about Patrick to the back of her mind.

"Saved by the bell," Kamika said. "Don't think you're off the hook. What used to be 'someday' is coming up fast."

Lea resolutely refused to look at Kamika, studying the data analysis instead. "Uh-huh. Sure. Look at this. We've got a few conversations in the analysis." She pointed at the tablet.

Kamika read the results. "I see a conversation about borrowing shampoo, a lot of laughter over a month ago, and, ooh, here's an argument."

Lea studied the analysis. "I'm not sure that helps. It looks like typical roommate problems. Somebody used somebody's dishes and didn't wash them."

"Yeah, but the owner of the dishes was mad enough to come in here and find the roommate to yell at her while she was in the toilet." Kamika's nose wrinkled. "That seems a little over the top to me."

A voice came from the doorway behind them. "That's Joella and Rena arguing. When they argue, it's always crazy loud. And they argue a lot."

CHAPTER 7

LEA AND KAMIKA TURNED TO FIND Evie in the doorway behind them.

"Hi, Evie," Lea said. "How's your head? Are you still in pain?"

Evie touched the bandage on her temple. "I'm okay. I took some ibuprofen, but the side of my face is sore. Did Dr. Tremayne send you here?"

"Partially. She contacted the head resident. Then your dorm advisory group voted to let us investigate."

Evie's face brightened. "That's a huge relief for me!"

Kamika asked in a low, conspiratorial voice, "What's with these girls with the loud arguments?"

Evie shrugged and walked closer to Lea and Kamika. "They're identical twins! Sometimes they finish each other's sentences and move in tandem like a single unit. It's amazing how in sync they are. Then, other times, they scream at each other. But the screaming doesn't seem to bother them. It's like they're either in perfect unison or complete dissonance, nothing in between. Rena said to blame their loud Italian ancestry for it."

"Oh, so it's not serious?" Kamika asked, disappointed.

"It sounds serious to everyone else, but not to the twins, apparently." Evie yawned and shook her head. "Sorry, I'm still tired. I think Rena and Joella need counseling to teach them more effective communication techniques."

Lea nodded, noticing as she looked around that she could feel the atmosphere of the dorm seeping in around her, with tension and fear dominating.

Kamika tapped Lea's arm. "Earth to Lea! Come back to the present."

Lea focused back on Kamika. "Sorry. I guess my mind was wandering."

Kamika eyed her. "Are you lost in thoughts of the future, or is something here distracting you? Wait, don't tell me. Here, look at the tablet. I don't see anything else of interest in the analysis. We know the explosion noise came from that central bathtub, but anyone could have told us that. Sound reading's a bust. Let's try the emotional energy scan."

Lea glanced at the analysis and nodded. "Okay. I'll get the scanner ready." She looked at Evie. "We have more scanning to do. We can talk again when we're done." She paused. "By the way, where are the sinks? We only found one." She gestured around the bathroom.

Evie laughed. "That's one of the quirks of the dorm. All of the dorm rooms have sinks, so some of the bathrooms only have one or none."

"That's bizarre," Kamika said, pausing in her work on the tablet screen.

"Yeah," said Evie, "but even with the quirks, I still like it here."

Lea put away the sound scanner and got out the emotional scanner. "Montgomery, our boss, is here. If you have anything you can tell him about the problems in the dorm, he'd love to hear it."

Concentration lines formed between Evie's eyes. "I don't know what I could tell him. I don't know anything at all! I wish I did." Her mouth drooped.

Kamika said, "You know lots of stuff that could be helpful! You know about the arguing twins. I'll bet you know a lot about the girls who live here: who keeps to themselves, who's talkative, who's nosy, or who's overly sensitive or always irritated. You could help us get a picture of life here in the dorm. Montgomery will need that information to narrow down who could be responsible for the trouble."

Evie brightened. "Really? Well, I know about this floor, but not much about the first or second floor." A look of doubt crossed her face. "I wouldn't want to put suspicion on someone just because of their personality. I haven't seen anyone do anything wrong."

Lea shook her head. "Don't worry. Montgomery needs a picture of dorm life. He won't suspect someone for no reason at all. Go talk to him."

Evie looked at the scanning equipment curiously. "Can I watch you scan the room first? I would like to see how you do it."

Kamika waved her over. "Come stand with me. Lea will scan and we can watch the data as it comes in to make sure she doesn't miss anything."

Evie moved next to Kamika. "Fantastic."

Lea started scanning the walls, moving the scanner in carefully overlapping lines as she had with the sound scanner. She could hear Kamika explaining to Evie the overlap margin and data appearing on the tablet as she worked. After she finished the room and turned off the scanner, she asked, "Did I miss anything?"

"No. Looks good. I've started the analysis."

Lea walked over to see the tablet in Kamika's hands. "I see tension. Not surprising given the pranks and vandalism. I can feel tension in the air."

Evie nodded. "I've been stressed out and tired. I'm sure a lot of the other girls are too."

"Look, near that bathtub. Do you see that?" Kamika pointed at the screen.

Lea pursed her lips in a flat line. "Anger, self-righteousness, and a desire for vengeance."

"Wow." Evie looked at the screen with awe.

"Do you know anyone like that? Angry and vengeful, but also self-righteous?" Lea asked.

"Most of the people here are used to getting good grades, being smarter than everyone else, being right. But self-righteous? I don't know."

"With so many smart people in one area, they must learn quickly that someone else is always smarter than they are," Lea said.

"I suppose some of them expect to be taken down a notch when they arrive at the university, but even so, I know a lot of arrogant people. They feel like they're better than other people because they get good grades, as if academic ability were the only standard to measure one's character."

"Do any of those people live on this floor?" Kamika asked.

Evie looked at Kamika thoughtfully. "I know a few really confident people. You know, people for whom everything goes right. The only angry person I know is Gwen. She's been mad since someone poured shampoo on her bed. But self-righteous and vengeful? I'm not sure."

Lea packed the scanners back into their bags. "While you think about it, we can go find Montgomery and tell him what we found."

As they exited the bathroom, Lea felt the hair on her neck rise. She turned quickly to look back into the bathroom, but it was empty. She wondered briefly what she had felt, but the sensation vanished before she could identify it.

Evie and Kamika were ahead of Lea, walking toward the stairwell that led to the lobby.

"I've been thinking about what you said earlier, and I had an idea," Evie said to Kamika.

"What'd I say earlier?" Kamika asked.

"You said that some twisted psychopath might be trying to upset people for the fun of it, that someone enjoyed throwing people off so that they would get bad grades."

"Oh yeah. I did say that. What about it?"

Evie stopped walking and beckoned Lea and Kamika closer. She leaned in to them and said in a whisper, "I think whoever is doing this isn't doing it for the fun of it. I think they have a purpose, an academic purpose."

Lea and Kamika looked at Evie with matching puzzled looks.

"What do you mean?" asked Lea.

"Well, the competition to get into the top seven percent of the senior class in my high school was fierce. Only the top seven percent get automatic admission into this university. Right?"

Lea nodded knowingly.

"Huh?" Kamika said.

Lea explained, "The competition to get automatic admission into the best colleges in Texas is crazy. This university is one of the best in the world, and one of the least expensive for Texas residents. So you get a lot of bang for your buck coming here. High school kids work their butts off to get automatically accepted. It's a state school, so current state law says some top percentage of students graduating from high school get automatic admission."

A flash of annoyance passed over Evie's face. "At my high school, people would do anything to get perfect test scores and a high GPA. It was practically no holds barred, all's-fair-in-love-and-war kind of stuff. I saw people cheat, share answers, and try to get copies of test questions early. In one really awful instance, I saw someone tamper with another student's physics project to try and eliminate competition for the top score in the class. Luckily, the cheater was caught."

Kamika looked stunned. "Are you saying people were cheating, not to pass tests, but to get perfect scores on the tests? To get perfect grade point averages?"

Evie nodded. "All the top ten students had better-than-perfect GPAs at my high school. We had to get perfect scores in our classes and get extra points for taking advanced-level classes to get GPAs that high."

Kamika frowned thoughtfully. "No Bs or Cs allowed on the report card. How did you do that? Did you cheat to get accepted here too?"

"No!" Evie replied indignantly. "I studied and read all the time. I'm lucky, I have a really good memory for things I read, what you could call a photographic memory. I can see the words written on the pages in my head. I get good grades because I'm wired this way. Other people, well, they have the drive, the ambition, and, frankly, the lack of ethics needed to get what they want. I know students whose parents told them to cheat to get those last few points because their futures depended on it. I used to joke with a friend that if we were at Hogwarts, most of the top ten percent of the class would belong in Slytherin."

"Achievement by any means necessary," Lea said.

"Yes," Evie agreed.

"Weren't they worried that they'd get caught? That someone would tell?" Kamika asked.

"No. Sometimes it felt like everyone was cheating around me," Evie said with a sigh. "When so many people are cheating, no one sees it as wrong. Who was going to tell? Only me. And I could see that the teachers knew what the students were doing most of the time and were trying to counter it as best they could. I tried to ask a counselor about it once, but she was too busy to talk to me unless it was about a life-or-death crisis."

Lea led the way down the stairwell. "Surely, the cheaters can't get away with that here?"

"I don't know what they can get away with. I hope cheaters get caught. But I haven't been here long enough to see how that will play out. This is still my first semester."

"Come on, let's talk to Montgomery about this," Lea said, exiting the stairwell at the lobby level. "Evie, I've been in school here for a while now. Believe me when I say that they have procedures for ethics violations like cheating."

Kamika put up one index finger. "Hang on. All these kids in high school were cheating and trying to outdo each other in order to get automatically accepted to college. Why would they keep it up once they got here? What would be the reason? They're already here."

Evie smiled sadly at Kamika. "A lot of the students are still competing academically. They need high scores to get into graduate schools, law schools, or medical schools. Or maybe they need to keep scholarships."

Kamika looked at Evie. "So this mess in the dorm could be an extreme competition for grades? I hope not."

"I hope we catch this person soon," said Evie tiredly. "I don't know how much longer I can go without regular sleep."

Lea gave Evie a look of sympathy. "Montgomery is as persistent as they come. I'll be surprised if he doesn't come up with something pretty quickly. Right, Kamika?"

"You bet! We're on this," Kamika said.

As they walked toward the lobby, their ears were filled with the babble of voices. As they entered the lobby, Lea spotted Montgomery surrounded by a crowd of young women, all talking at once.

"What the heck is going on?" Kamika asked, looking at Lea.

"Let's find out," Lea said. "Evie, any ideas?"

Evie studied the crowd of residents around Montgomery. "I see the first-floor resident assistant and some advisory members. I don't know most of those girls by name, although I've seen them around. They don't live on the third floor. I'll bet they all live on the first floor."

Montgomery looked up and saw Lea and Kamika. At over six feet tall, he could see above the crowd of residents in front of him. "Lea! Kamika! I need a word with you." He turned his attention back to the crowd. "Ladies, I will look into the matter. Please put your name and room number on my tablet, and I will speak to you all in turn." He pulled out his tablet, opened a document, and handed the device to the first girl he saw. "Pass this around," he said. Then he extricated himself from the crowd and ambled over to where Lea, Kamika, and Evie stood.

"What's going on?" Lea asked.

"We may need your expertise on this one, Lea. Three residents are claiming that they saw a ghost in the first-floor hallway. They all say that it vanished outside Mei's rooms before it reached the lobby. They are spooked."

CHAPTER 8

L EA GLANCED ACROSS THE LOBBY. SHE could see Mei's
door, the first one in the hall leading from the lobby to
the first-floor dormitory wing. "I don't see anything there
now. I can check it out." She called out to the group of
girls adding their names to Montgomery's list. "Can any
of you tell me exactly what you saw and where you saw
it? I want someone who actually saw something. Don't
tell me what you heard from your friend or roommate."

Two hands went up. Lea recognized the girls who
had been sunbathing in the quad when she and Kamika
arrived. Lea glanced at Montgomery. "I'll talk to the
girls. Can you talk to Evie?" Lea gestured to Evie. "She
has some insight on how things work in the dorm and
a theory you need to hear."

"Okay," Montgomery said. "Pleased to meet you,
Evie. Let's go to the living room and talk." Montgomery
turned to the crowd of residents. "Ladies, I'll be in the
living room. Bring me my tablet when you've finished
putting your names down."

Lea and Kamika walked over to the girls who had raised their hands.

"We met earlier," said the blond girl. "I'm Corinna."

"And I'm Matilda, but call me Matty," said Corinna's slender, auburn-haired friend.

"You're in the hall government, so you're sophomores, right?" Lea asked.

"Yes," said Matty. "We're roommates. We live on the first floor." She clasped her arms around her body, as if she were cold.

Lea studied the girls. Both radiated fear. "Montgomery said three girls saw the ghost. Who was with you?"

"Another girl on our hall. She had someplace to go and she was scared. She ran out of here," Corinna said.

"Okay. What were you doing when you saw the ghost?" Lea asked.

Both girls started to talk, then stopped and looked at each other.

"You tell it," Matty said to Corinna.

"Fine." Corinna drew a deep breath and glanced back down the hall past Mei's rooms to the east wing of the building. "We came out of our room and knocked on Josie's door to ask her if she wanted to go to dinner."

"Can you show me where your room is?" asked Lea.

"Why?" Matty asked with fear in her eyes.

"We need to retrace your steps and see if we can figure out what you saw," Lea said in a soothing voice.

"Do we have to?" Corinna asked quietly, glancing nervously over her shoulder toward the hall.

"It would help me figure out what you saw. Please," Lea said. "We can all walk together. Kamika will come too. You have nothing to be afraid of."

"Okay." Matty shuddered but started walking toward the first-floor dorm wing. "Come on."

Lea, Kamika, and Corinna followed her.

Matty led them down the hall to a T intersection where they had to turn either right or left. Matty turned left toward the north side of the building. She stopped halfway down the hall. "This is our room." She pointed to a door colorfully labeled with the names Corinna and Matty.

Lea stood next to Matty. "You came out and locked the door, right?"

"Yes. I locked it," said Corinna. "Matty went to Josie's door." Corinna pointed back down the hall in the direction from which they'd come.

Matty walked toward a room four doors down on the same side of the hall. "I knocked, but no one answered. Josie and Rosalia weren't there. We thought they'd already left for dinner. So we walked down the hall toward the lobby. We were going to eat in the cafeteria in Kinsolving Hall."

"Let's walk," Lea said. "Was anyone else in the hall?"

"Yes," said Corinna. "A freshman from the other end of the hall. I think her name is Lucinda."

"Where was she?" Lea asked.

Corinna pointed to the south end of the wing. "She came from down there and turned toward the lobby at almost the same time as we did. Then we all froze, because we saw the . . . the . . . whatever it was. A ghost, I guess."

They all rounded the corner to the lobby and stopped.

"Is this where you stopped?" Lea said. "Where was the ghost?"

Matty gestured down the hall. "It was outside Mei's door, just, I don't know, hovering." Matty hugged herself again.

Lea walked toward Mei's door, swiveling her head to see the walls and ceiling as she went. She stopped in front of the head resident's room. "I don't see anything that could have created a shadow or projected anything. Can you describe the ghost?"

Corinna nodded. "It was a woman in a long dress that went down to her feet."

"If she had feet," said Matty, "I couldn't see them."

"Right," agreed Corinna. "I didn't notice a color to her dress. She was see-through."

"Transparent," Matty corrected her roommate.

"Yeah, whatever." Corinna frowned in concentration. "I think she had gray hair pulled back, like in a bun on her head."

"Did you see her face?" asked Lea.

"No, I saw her from the side," said Corinna.

"In profile," said Matty. "It looked like she was knocking on the door."

"For some reason, I got the idea she wanted to find someone. No, she *needed* to find someone." Corinna shook her head. "I don't know what made me think that."

"Yes, you're right," said Matty. "I remember I got the impression she needed help too, until I realized I could see right through her. Then I freaked out."

"There's no need to freak out," Lea said. "We can scan the hallway for residual emotional energy and see what we find."

"What do you think we saw? Was it really a ghost? Was it Olive Dellonmarsh?" Corinna asked, her eyes rounded in fear.

"If it was, don't be afraid. She wasn't here to hurt anyone. As you both said, you thought she needed help. Sometimes I see echoes in time. When something emotionally intense or traumatic happens in a place, sometimes it marks that place. I've seen echoes of soldiers standing guard, awaiting attacks. They aren't really there. I think of it as the history of the place bleeding through. You may have seen an echo of a time when someone needed help and ran to the head resident to get it."

"But maybe it really was Olive," Matty said, her eyes widening with excitement. "When we moved in, they told us that Olive watches over the dorm. That she's a benevolent ghost who keeps an eye on the girls."

"I suppose it's a possibility," Lea said. "You ladies can go to dinner. It's Saturday night. You probably have things to do. Don't let this worry you. Whatever you saw, it won't hurt you."

"Okay. We're going to see a play on campus and it starts at seven." Matty grabbed Corinna's arm. "Come on. If we don't get going, we won't have time to eat."

The girls hurried across the lobby and out the door toward Dean Keeton Street.

Lea and Kamika found Montgomery sitting in the living room typing rapidly on his tablet at a dark wood table with six straight-backed chairs around it. Evie was gone. He looked up as they approached him. "Hello. What did you find out?"

Lea answered, "They definitely saw something. But they both got the sense that the ghost wanted to get help or needed help, which is interesting. The girls are all stressed out in the dorm. All is not well here. A ghost who's rumored to watch protectively over the place and appears to be looking for help doesn't seem unreasonable given the situation."

Kamika pulled out a chair at the table and sat down. "You mean that the ghost knows something is wrong, and she wants to help?"

"Or maybe she's trying to get help. She went to the head resident's door. That could be seeking to help someone in authority or asking for help."

"Do you want to scan the hallway?" asked Montgomery.

"Yes," Lea said.

"Today or Monday?" asked Montgomery. "No need to work tomorrow."

Lea looked at Kamika. "I know, it's Saturday. You probably have plans. Hot date?"

Kamika rolled her eyes. "Actually, I was going to go work on my blog business, but we could scan that hall. It's only five o'clock."

"All right," Lea said. She picked up the bag with the scanners. "Let's get this done."

Montgomery rose from his seat. "I'm reviewing the records on the incidents that occurred here. I'm going to run background checks on a few people too, but I need to get back to the office. I've already told Mei that we'll be back on Monday. Please send me the scan results for the hall and the bathroom and your comments on the findings."

"Will do," Kamika said, saluting him.

"Have a good evening," Montgomery said, and he walked out the door into the quad.

Lea and Kamika returned to the first-floor dorm hallway by the lobby. Lea turned on the emotional energy scanner and walked toward Mei's door. "I'm going to scan the door first."

"Go ahead," Kamika said. "I'll get the analysis program ready."

Lea scanned the door and then scanned the surrounding hallway walls. "Let's start with that and see what we find." She walked over to stand by Kamika as the analysis program began.

"We've got the overall tension and stress in the building, some fear too," Kamika said.

"Look at this, centered on the door. Frustration and desperation. Together that's someone who needs help. No wonder the girls thought the ghost needed help."

Kamika gave Lea a worried look. "Is she frustrated and desperate for help because of some old problem or because of the stuff happening here today? If she's desperate because of what's going on now, then something must really be wrong."

Lea's mouth turned grim. "We need to solve this fast. Dr. Tremayne said pranks like the ones happening here could push an unstable person over the edge. There are about a hundred fifty residents in the dorm. How are we going to figure out who's responsible?"

"I don't know," Kamika said. "All we can do is catch this idiot quickly. Then maybe that will relieve everyone's stress."

Lea and Kamika scanned the rest of the hallway for residual emotion and sound but found nothing useful. They returned to the lobby to repack their equipment to go home.

As Lea tucked the scanners back in their bag, she paused. "What's this?" she asked, as she pulled a folded piece of loose-leaf paper from the bag. She unfolded the paper and read the rounded, girlish print on the page.

"What is it?" Kamika asked, leaning forward to see the paper.

"It's an anonymous note." She handed the paper to Kamika.

"'The girls in room 220 have a secret. Ask them what they are hiding,'" Kamika read aloud. "What do you think? Check it out now or wait until Monday?"

At that moment, Mei walked into the lobby. Lea nodded toward her. "Let's ask Mei. Hey Mei," she called out, "could you come see this?"

"What's up?" asked Mei, hurrying toward them.

"We found a note shoved into our bag. Take a look." Kamika handed the note to Mei.

Mei read the note with a frown. "Ugh, this could be spite. This could be tattling on any little breach of the rules. Or this could be about the pranks." She stared silently at the note. "I'm all for being direct. Let me see who lives in 220." She walked over to her room and let herself inside. In a moment she returned. "Raven and Amalie, two freshmen, are in that room. I haven't had any problems with them. They didn't get notes under their doors or any damage to their room. Let's go see if they're home." Mei led Lea and Kamika to the stairs and up to the second floor.

When they reached the door to room 220, Lea looked up and down the hall. It was approaching six p.m. on a Saturday night, and all was quiet. Most of the girls appeared to be out.

Mei knocked on the door and waited.

A voice called, "Who is it?"

"It's Mei, the head resident," Mei answered loudly. "I need to speak to you for a moment."

"Oh, um. Just a second," called the voice.

Lea heard a door slam. She looked at Kamika. Kamika raised one eyebrow.

A moment later the door opened, and a girl's head popped out. "What's up?" she asked, a little breathlessly, her eyes widening as she noticed Lea and Kamika.

"Are you Amalie?" Mei asked.

The girl, who was almost six feet tall with green eyes and light brown hair, shook her head no. "I'm Raven."

Kamika gave the girl a confused look.

"I know. I don't look like a Raven. My hair was black when I was born, so my parents thought it would stay dark. It didn't. It could be worse. They almost named me Pixie because I was tiny, only five pounds, with kind of pointy ears. I didn't stay tiny either. Given the options, I'm glad they chose Raven." She shook her head at the stupidity of parents. "What did you need?"

Mei held up the note. "Do you have any idea what this is about?

The girl took the note. "Umm, no," she said, as a dark red flush slowly climbed her neck and filled her cheeks.

Mei stared at the girl, giving her a look of disbelief. "Then what did you hide in your closet?"

A thumping noise came from the closet, making them all jump. Raven's shoulders drooped.

"What was that?" asked Mei in a tone of authority that demanded an answer.

CHAPTER 9

"I'M SORRY. I KNOW IT'S NOT allowed, but I couldn't leave him to die." Raven walked over and pulled open her closet. She reached in and scooped up an orange kitten. "He's only a baby."

Kamika squealed happily.

Mei's face fell. "A kitten."

"He was in a tree between the Main Building and the 'Six Pack,' on the South Mall."

"It can't stay," Mei said, shaking her head in exasperation.

"Oh, how adorable!" Kamika said. "I love kittens. Can I hold him?"

Raven handed the kitten to Kamika, who allowed it to nuzzle into her neck.

"What a sweet baby!" Kamika crooned softly.

Mei stood with one hand on her forehead as if her head ached. "We have girls with allergies. University housing rules forbid pets other than fish. The handbook says if pets are found in the dorm they have to be removed immediately. You have to get rid of it. You're facing possible disciplinary action for having it in your room. I really don't want to have to report this. We've had enough trouble in this dorm already this semester. But it has to go now!"

Tears filled Raven's green eyes. "I can't dump him outside. He'd get run over or eaten!"

Mei closed her eyes and shook her head. "Ugh. This semester sucks. Okay, look. Don't you have any family or friends who can come pick him up and take him to their place?"

Raven's face crumbled and a tear leaked down her cheek. "I'm from Fort Worth. I don't have any family here. I moved to Austin in August when the semester started. All the friends I've made since classes started live in the dorms too." Raven turned to Kamika, who was still snuggling the kitten. "Can you take him? Do you have a place you can keep him?" she pleaded desperately.

"I have an apartment. Cats are allowed under the lease." Kamika looked at the kitten thoughtfully. "You won't be too much trouble, will you?" The cat mewed softly. "Does he have a name?"

"I've been calling him Jasper."

"Jasper! That's a great name for a cat," Kamika said. "Looks like you're coming home with me, Jasper."

"Oh, thank you so much," Raven said. She shot a look of condemnation at Mei. "Some people have no heart."

Mei narrowed her eyes to angry slits. "You know the rules. I have to enforce them. It's my job. Do you know how much trouble I'd be in if I walked away and let you keep that cat in your room? What if some poor girl had a severe allergic reaction because of it? We have these rules for a reason!"

Kamika interrupted. "No worries! I got this. You have to do your job. We wouldn't want anyone sick from allergies." Kamika winced as the kitten began to climb up onto her shoulder, digging its claws into her as it went. "Ouch. Watch the claws, buddy." She detached the cat from her coral blouse and held him in front of her as she examined the snag he'd made. "I can see you are not going to be good for my wardrobe. We'll have to get you a scratching post."

A few minutes later, Kamika and Lea left the dorm with the kitten. Lea gave the kitten a gentle scratch behind the ear and said, "I think we're going to find more secrets not related to the vandalism when we come back on Monday. A dorm with so many people living in it could have jealousy, personality conflicts, and a well-oiled rumor mill. With stiff academic competition on top of that, we may be getting more notes or whispered accusations. We're going to have to sort through all the false leads to find the real culprit."

"I suppose," Kamika said. "But that's true in a lot of our investigation cases. When we go digging through people's lives, secrets spill out all over the place." The kitten mewed in her arms, and she hugged it closer to her chest.

Lea stopped and glanced back at the dorm building behind them, sensing that she was being watched. A face peered down at her from a third-floor window. The face vanished in an instant.

"What is it?" Kamika asked, stopping a pace ahead of Lea.

"Someone was watching us."

"Probably that girl, Cressida. I'm pretty sure she hates your guts. She told you so to your face, remember?"

"Cressida? Maybe. That reminds me: I have to find out what's happening with Dr. Richardson."

"Later!" Kamika said. "It's Saturday night. Let's get some food, and then you can tell me about what plans you have for your future with Patrick. Don't think I've forgotten that you haven't answered." She paused with Lea at a traffic light, waiting to cross Guadalupe Street, the main street on the edge of campus.

Lea started walking when the crosswalk sign indicated they could go. "Patrick is in Dallas, hiring and training people for the new branch office of Montgomery Investigations. He's almost done with all the hiring since it will be a small office to start with—only a couple investigators, a receptionist, and an office manager/bookkeeper. He already trained the senior private investigator, who will be in charge of the office, on how to use the scanning equipment."

Kamika nodded. She was familiar with the process since Patrick had already set up a similar office in Houston. "So then he'll train the less-experienced investigators who will work under the senior guy. He'll make sure the tech guys set up the computer systems properly, and he'll oversee a case or two to get the ball rolling."

"Yes. So he'll be there a while still."

"Humph," Kamika said with a frown as they skirted the edge of a large group of students walking together. "He's on the road a lot. I know he enjoys his work, but that must be tough on you two."

"He comes back to his house in Killeen most weekends. We talk and text every day. It's fine. And I'm taking care of Wally for him." Wally was Patrick's German shepherd, a retired, military, bomb-sniffing dog.

Kamika moved the kitten, which was trying to crawl up her shirt again, "'Fine' is not 'good.' It's also not 'great.' Besides, where is he today? It's Saturday. Shouldn't he be home?"

Lea hefted the equipment bag she was carrying higher up on her shoulder. "The first case came in, and Patrick is riding along with the lead investigator to make sure he doesn't have any trouble with the scanners or software." She looked up the street in front of them. "The parking garage is up ahead. Let's get out of here. Are we taking the kitten to your place before we eat?"

"We'd better." Kamika nuzzled the kitten's ears. "I wouldn't want to leave him alone in the van."

"Do you want to order a pizza and eat at your place? I'd offer my place, but Wally might eat the kitten. I don't know how he responds to cats."

"Pizza at my place works. Half mushroom and olive and half pepperoni, or do you want something else on your half this time?"

"No, pepperoni works for me." Lea turned up a drive into the parking garage where they'd left the van earlier that morning.

⁑

Later that evening, after eating their fill of pizza and spooning some tuna into a bowl for the kitten, Kamika showed Lea the changes she had made to her blog site.

"This looks great, Kamika. You're getting a lot of questions and comments on each blog. It must take a while to answer them." Lea sat on a couch in Kamika's exquisitely decorated living room with Kamika's laptop on the coffee table in front of her, scrolling through the blog.

"That's what I've been doing in the evenings. I have a handful of people to answer via the contact page form too. I guess they're too shy to post in the comments section." She paused. "And some are too foulmouthed to comment in public. I've got one troll who likes to send me bullying emails about twice a week."

Lea glanced sharply at her. "Uh-oh. Threatening you?"

"Not so far. Mostly telling me that I know nothing, that I'm making it all up, and that everything I write is fake and doesn't work. He ends each email by telling me to stop spreading lies and shut up."

"Have you responded?"

"No. You know what they say, 'Don't feed the trolls.'"

"If it gets worse, you'll let Montgomery know, won't you?" Lea knew Montgomery could probably track down the troll and issue a cease-and-desist letter quoting the appropriate cyber-bullying statutes.

"I hope it doesn't come to that," Kamika said. "Probably, if I ignore him, he'll go find someone else to annoy."

"I hope so." Lea's cell phone rang in her pocket. "Maybe that's Patrick." She glanced at the phone. "I don't recognize the number."

"Don't answer. It's probably a scam or a robocall."

Lea clicked the button silencing her phone. "Probably." She turned her attention back to Kamika's blog. A few seconds later, her phone beeped to let her know she had a message. "That's odd, most of the telemarketing calls don't leave messages. I'm going to see who called." She picked up her phone and listened to the message.

"What is it?" Kamika asked. "Is it that scam where they tell you that you won a vacation to the Bahamas?"

"No," Lea said with a puzzled look. "It was a reporter from the *Daily Texan*, the university's student newspaper. They want to talk to me about Dr. Richardson."

"Are you going to call them back?"

Lea stared at her phone. "No. I'm not sure I can say anything. When Dr. Tremayne and I reported the matter to the university, she told me not to talk about it until they had finished investigating. It's all confidential. She said that the research integrity committee's initial report is due this week. Maybe after that comes out, I can talk about it."

"Well, the university suspended Dr. Richardson, which should tell the reporter that your accusations have merit. Can't you tell them what happened to you? You know, your side of the story?"

"I don't think so. The investigation has to be totally done. Besides, what's the worst that can happen? The paper has to publish an article without a quote from me. So what."

Kamika gave Lea a worried look. "I don't know. If the reporter is a supporter of Dr. Richardson, they could publish a pretty one-sided story."

Lea handed the laptop back to Kamika. "Even if it's one-sided, the basic facts still remain the same. He stole my work. What else could they say? Anyway, you have comments to answer, so I'll head home."

"I'll see you Monday at work. Or are we going straight to Dellonmarsh?"

"Montgomery will let us know."

⁜

Monday morning Lea, Kamika, and Montgomery met up at the Bad Vibes Removal Services Offices in Georgetown, per Montgomery's texted instructions. They piled into Montgomery's car for the drive down to the University of Texas in Austin.

Lea asked Kamika, "Is Jasper behaving for you?"

"He tried to sleep on my face last night, but he's so sweet that I forgive him." Kamika sighed happily.

"Who's Jasper?" Montgomery asked, looking at Kamika in surprise.

"My new kitten, courtesy of a girl who was hiding him in her dorm room." Kamika told Montgomery about finding the kitten on Saturday.

Montgomery listened as he drove, finally commenting, "The dorm is full of girls with secrets. We'll probably uncover a few more secrets before we hit on something relevant to our case."

Lea laughed. "We may turn up some more illegal pets." She turned to Kamika. "Did you finish what you needed to do for your blog yesterday?"

"I answered all my comments and prepared a new post for today. It's about using scent in businesses: cinnamon, peppermint, lavender, baking smells. I even did a section on how some grocery stores disseminate the smells of bacon and eggs near the refrigerated sections where they sell bacon."

"I've noticed that," Montgomery said. "My mouth waters as I walk by the area."

"Yeah, well, how better to subliminally suggest that you buy some? Did you buy it?" Kamika asked.

Montgomery shook his head. "No. I'm trying to lose a few pounds, and bacon is not on the menu at the moment."

"The temptation of the scent didn't work?"

"Oh, it worked," Montgomery said, "but Jenny, er, Dr. Tremayne, was with me, and she stopped me from picking it up. I think she's immune to that kind of suggestion."

"Lucky you. She helped you stay on your diet."

"Yeah, lucky me." Montgomery rolled his eyes.

Lea and Kamika laughed as Lea's phone began to make pinging noises. Before she could get it out of her pocket, it pinged again four more times.

Kamika shot her a curious glance. "That's a lot of texts at once. What's up?"

Lea looked at her phone. "Oh no! Damn it!" A now-familiar sinking feeling engulfed her, and she fought back panic.

"What's wrong?" Montgomery asked in a concerned voice.

"Apparently, I need to read the opinion section of the *Daily Texan* right now!" Lea replied as she typed rapidly into her phone. "I found a link to the article. Hang on while I read this." Lea paused, reading rapidly.

As she read, her phone began to beep steadily, announcing texts as the phone received them.

"I think everyone I know is texting me to tell me about this article," Lea said, looking up from her phone with distress. "It's awful!"

CHAPTER 10

MONTGOMERY GLANCED AT LEA AS HE drove. "What does it say?"

"In short, I'm being accused of lying about Dr. Richardson to further my own career." Lea choked up with emotion and had to clear her throat. "Most of the article focuses on Dr. Richardson himself: his charity work, his efforts over the years to help struggling students, how many students he's mentored and advised on research projects. The writer suggests that a man who did all that good work wouldn't suddenly steal from one student. The writer says that to steal from me would be out of character." Lea's dark eyes filled with tears. "They say that, given his track record, he should be given the benefit of the doubt and be considered innocent until proven guilty. And that his accuser—that's me—is an unknown with no track record and that I should be considered an unreliable witness with ulterior motives."

Kamika rubbed Lea's shoulder. "Oh, hon, I'm so sorry! That's so not fair to you."

Lea bit her lip and took a deep breath. "The sad thing is, I understand why they don't believe me. I know the decent and kind Dr. Richardson that the writer is describing. I never thought he would steal my work. It was a shock to me too! Everyone loved Dr. Richardson. And the university's review of the situation is a closed process, so no one can review the evidence supporting me until the committee releases its findings."

Montgomery's brow wrinkled, and he shook his head. "Now hold on a minute. The writer is assuming that Dr. Richardson never crossed a line with any of his other students. I'll bet he's done this before. To steal all your work like he did, whole sections word for word, even knowing that your secondary advisor had died and couldn't speak on your behalf, was a huge risk. He thought you wouldn't fight back. He thought that you wouldn't know how to fight him. He was wrong because you had Dr. Tremayne in your corner. But he got the idea that you wouldn't fight from somewhere, probably previous experience."

Lea frowned. "You mean, you think he's done this before but didn't get caught because the victim didn't speak up?"

"That's exactly what I mean. And I bet if I dig, I'll find dirt."

Kamika nudged Lea. "That's because worms like Richardson hide in dirt." She leaned forward in her seat toward the front. "Hey, boss, are you going to investigate? Look for other victims?"

Montgomery turned his serious blue eyes on Lea, all trace of his normal good humor gone. "I can locate other students of Dr. Richardson's who've moved on. Someone else may have a tale of their own to add to yours. Do you want me to do that?"

Lea hesitated. "What if no one else had a problem with Dr. Richardson?"

"I'll bet you a bottle of scotch that someone else has a story similar to yours," Montgomery said with the sparkle returning to his eyes.

"No bet!" Lea replied. "Okay. You're right. I'll help you. Where do we start?"

Kamika giggled. "Oh, hon, I know the answer to that one. You look up who else had Dr. Richardson as a thesis advisor."

"That's right," Montgomery said. "I especially want to know if anyone didn't finish their thesis while working with Dr. Richardson."

Lea sat up straight in her seat and considered the situation. "I can look up old papers and get you a list of people from them. But if a thesis wasn't completed, it won't be on file. I'll have to ask around the department. People may not want to answer any questions, but I'll try." She scrolled through her phone looking at her text messages. "Oh! Here's a place to start! A friend of mine, Parker Poulsen, another graduate student in the history department, sent me a message of support. He says that he knows Dr. Richardson is a two-faced liar and thief who was good at fooling people."

"Good! He may have information that would support you. When we've found more stories like yours, Lea, we'll present them to the press, with the victims' permission, of course," Montgomery said as he pulled his car into a parking spot in the San Antonio Parking Garage on the edge of the university. "Well, ladies, we're here. Let's see if we can identify our vandal/prankster."

Lea's phone continued to send notifications of new texts received, so she silenced it. She decided to ignore the messages and focus on the case at hand.

After walking a few minutes to get from the garage to Dellonmarsh Residence Hall, Montgomery, Lea, and Kamika were greeted by Mei in the lobby at ten a.m.

"Welcome back," Mei said. "I've been on edge since you left Saturday." She led them to the living room.

Montgomery looked at her in concern. "Did something happen after we left?"

"No, no. It's something else. I'm not sure how to explain it. Everyone is nervous, jumpy. A lot of girls are cramming for tests or working on big projects that are worth a third or more of their grades, so it's been quiet. But at the same time, I feel like I'm holding my breath waiting for another incident."

"That seems to be what your vandal wants: to get everyone upset and tense," Montgomery said. "Try not to let it interfere with your classes."

"That's easier said than done, I'm afraid," Mei said with a tired sigh.

"How are the residents holding up?" Lea asked. "The resident assistants on each floor are supposed to keep an eye on the girls, try to deal with conflict, and help girls adjust. Are they reporting more problems?"

Mei looked crestfallen. "I'm hearing more reports of arguing and disagreements, especially over laundry, but over all kinds of little things. Lots of discord and distrust. It's probably what the vandal wants: everyone to be miserable."

Montgomery's eyes briefly blazed with anger before being replaced by a look of determination. He looked at Lea and Kamika. "Then we need to put this situation to rest as soon as possible. Lea and Kamika, scan the living room and the vandalized third-floor study nook this morning. We'll do the stairwells, starting with the one that was vandalized with ketchup, and the lobby later. I'm going to make myself available to anyone who wants to talk." Montgomery turned to Mei. "All the girls have been informed of the investigation, right?"

Mei nodded. "We held 'all hands' meetings on each floor. A few residents might have skipped, but we reached the majority."

"And you told them that anyone with information could come talk to me in the living room today at any time?"

"Yes. Girls will be coming and going all day for classes. Hopefully some of them will stop to see you."

"Good," Montgomery said. "While I'm waiting, I'll be reviewing the police reports and the reports you gave me. I've also initiated a few background searches based on information I already have. Those searches should yield results today."

Mei gave Montgomery a confused and troubled look. "What? Who are you checking on?"

Montgomery grinned. "Don't worry about it. No information on anyone will be released. I won't even tell you anything, unless it becomes necessary."

Mei's troubled expression didn't abate. "Okay. I suppose I have to trust you." She glanced at the time on her wrist. "Natalia should be here any minute. She'll be your escort for a couple hours this morning. The advisory girls will trade out so that someone is with you in the building most of the time."

"That's part of the housing rules for visitors, right?" Lea pointed to a sign on the door that read, "All visitors must be escorted at all times."

"That's the rule, and we're going to try to follow it, but I'm making an exception for you. I tried to get some of the girls to stay with you the whole time you're here, but we couldn't get enough people. My boss in the housing office isn't thrilled about it, but she's agreed that you can walk around unaccompanied." Mei turned her head anxiously looking toward the hall. "I have class this morning. I'll check in with you when I get back this afternoon. Also, my boss said you have to leave when guest hours end."

"What are guest hours?"

"Sunday through Thursday ten a.m. to eleven-thirty p.m., Friday and Saturday ten a.m. to one-thirty a.m."

"We have no desire to be here after eleven-thirty p.m.," Montgomery said. "I'd be paying Lea and Kamika some serious overtime if I kept them that late."

"Not to mention I've got things to do after work this evening," Kamika added with a bright smile.

Mei hefted a backpack onto her slender shoulders, her lanky body flexing under the weight. "I have class in half an hour, and it's all the way over by the stadium. I have to go." She looked up as Natalia entered the living room. "Oh, good, you're here. They are all yours. Bye everyone." Mei waved as she pushed open the door into the quad.

Montgomery settled himself into a deep chair in a seating area near the fireplace.

Lea and Kamika unpacked their equipment and left Montgomery to his work. They moved to the far end of the room.

Lea nodded at the piano. "Let's start in the corner near the piano."

"Fine by me. You want me to scan while you monitor results this time?"

"Okay," Lea agreed. "We'll switch when your arms get tired."

Kamika looked around the room. "I can do this room. With so many windows and glass doors, there really isn't much wall space to scan."

Lea glanced at the long, rectangular room. "It was built in a time before air conditioning, so the doors and windows would be opened to allow for cross breezes. I like it. You get a lot more natural light with all the windows."

Kamika looked up and pointed. "I bet those ceiling beams could tell some tales. Look at that painted pattern of flowers and greenery on the beams. And the wood floors! And those giant red carpets! And the antique benches and furniture! This place is gorgeous. I feel like I fell into a movie set."

Lea laughed as she looked up. "It's Spanish Renaissance style. Did you notice that the ground-level windows along the café side of the building have ironwork over them?"

"Yeah. I wonder who thought of putting iron bars with a row of heart shapes in them over windows. Is that because it's a women's dorm?"

"I have no idea. But the attention to detail in the design is amazing."

"It's a lot nicer architecture than Jester," said a quiet voice behind Lea.

Lea turned to see a student, a young woman in leggings with a long t-shirt falling down over her hips, standing behind her. The girl's long black hair was in a ponytail. Her skin was a deep brown. She held a folder under her arm. "Hi. I'm Lea. This is Kamika. We're here to—"

"I know. To investigate." The girl's brown eyes found Montgomery and Natalia in conversation near the fireplace.

Lea followed her glance. "Did you want to talk to Montgomery? Do you have questions? Information you want to share? Maybe we can help you. What's your name?"

"Izabeta Rueda. You can call me Izzie."

"Are you a freshman?" Kamika asked.

"Yes." Izzie clasped her hands over her folder in front of her hesitantly. "What are you doing?"

Kamika held up the sound scanner. "I'm going to scan the room for residual sound deposits while Lea monitors the data collection and analysis."

"Oh." She glanced at the piano. "Then I'll come back later. I was hoping to get some practice in on the piano, but I don't want to interrupt you." She turned to walk away.

"Wait," Lea called after her. "Could you talk to us for a minute?"

Izzie turned and looked at her guardedly. "About what?"

"Have you had any trouble from the dorm prankster? Notes under your door? Vandalism? Anything?"

Izzie gave her an appraising look, pausing on Lea's black hair looped in its lopsided knot before deciding to answer. "I got a note. It was rude, but no worse that the texts on the group chat when we have laundry wars."

Kamika asked curiously, "What are laundry wars?"

"That's when someone does laundry and then forgets it in the washer or dryer. When the next person comes along and wants to start a load of laundry, they can't. The person who wants to start their laundry will post something like, 'Some idiot forgot their laundry on the third floor! Move it or I'll dump it out!'"

Kamika's eyebrows shot up. "And do they dump it out?"

Izzie frowned. "If it's in the dryer, most girls will stack it on top of the dryer, and it will sit there until the owner claims it. If it's in the washer for hours, well, that can get unpleasant. But the worst was the time someone's pen exploded in the dryer."

Kamika shuddered. "Let me guess. Did ink get all over everyone's clothes?"

"Yes. And no one would claim responsibility and clean it up. Finally, the resident assistant took rubbing alcohol and cleaned the inside of the dryer. The group messages got pretty ugly that time."

"I can imagine." Lea set down the tablet she was holding. "Did anyone get blamed for the ink problem?"

Izzie nodded. "Me, at first, and then my roommate. Someone said they saw my laundry basket in the laundry room on the third floor where I live, but I don't even do my laundry here. I take it to my cousin's apartment. She lets me wash my clothes for free. I posted that, and then everyone started blaming Juliet."

"Juliet is your roommate? Was she upset?" Lea asked.

"She doesn't let that stuff bother her. She can give you a look like daggers going through your soul, so no one messes with her. They still think she did it, though." Her eyes wandered to the piano again.

Lea noticed Izzie's lingering look and asked, "What's your major?"

Izzie's eyes snapped back to Lea. "I have two, music and math."

"Wow! What kind of music were you going to practice? Something classical?"

"No, ragtime. Scott Joplin. I need to practice. I've got a performance coming up. Besides, playing relaxes me."

"Oh, can we hear a little?" Kamika asked. "I'd love to hear you play. One song?"

"Well, okay." Izzie moved to sit down at the piano. She opened her folder and extracted sheet music. Settling herself on the bench, she placed her hands on the keys and started to play.

Lea noticed that Izzie seemed to be missing some notes as Izzie stopped playing abruptly.

"Something's wrong!" Izzie stood up from the piano and looked at Lea in alarm. "A bunch of keys aren't working. They're sticking down."

Chapter 11

IZZIE LEANED OVER AND EXAMINED THE keys. "There's something . . . something sticky, jammed in between the keys!" Tears filled her dark eyes. She walked around the piano and lifted the lid to view the strings. "The strings are fine. But I won't be able to practice."

Lea walked over and bent to study the keys, "The vandal has struck again." She turned and called across the room, "Montgomery, we have something you need to see."

Montgomery set his tablet aside. Natalia jumped up from her seat and walked over to join Lea, Kamika, and Izzie. Right then, Evie walked into the living room carrying a laptop. She deposited the computer on a wooden table before walking toward the piano to see what was going on.

"What's up, ladies?" Montgomery asked, standing by the piano with his hands on his hips.

Izzie started to speak, got choked up, cleared her throat, and tried again. "It's the piano. When I played yesterday morning, it was fine. Now someone's messed with the keys. There's something sticky between them. I can't play! First my favorite study nook is destroyed, and now the piano!" Tears leaked out of the corners of her eyes and dripped, leaving trails down her dark brown cheeks.

Natalia rushed to put a comforting arm around Izzie. "It will be okay. We'll report the damage. Someone will come to fix it."

"But I need to practice today!" cried Izzie. She put both hands over her distraught face. "I'm so tired. Why do these stupid pranks keep happening? Why won't they stop?! They destroyed my favorite place to study, the nook on the third floor, and now the piano."

Natalia muttered soothing noises and led Izzie to sit on a nearby upholstered chair.

Montgomery was examining the keys. "I'm not sure what this substance is, some kind of rubbery, slimy stuff."

"Rubbery, slimy stuff?" Kamika's green eyes focused intently. "Let me see." Montgomery stood back and let Kamika examine the slippery substance. She bent over the keys and came up smiling. "I know what this is. It's slime."

Montgomery gave her a blank look, then turned to Lea seeking an explanation.

Lea shot him an equally confused expression, then turned to Kamika with raised eyebrows.

"Come on," Kamika said. "You know. Slime. The stuff that kids like to make in the kitchen with glue and borax and something else, I can't remember. They add food coloring or glitter to make it different colors. Then they play with it." She shook her head as Lea and Montgomery still gave her uncomprehending looks. "Look it up. It's a thing."

Evie, who was standing off to one side, spoke up. "Oh, I know what you mean. We had Girls in Engineering

Day on campus last week. Tables were set up all over the place with activities for kids to get them interested in the sciences. One of the chemistry tables had ingredients for slime. The students running the tables had the kids put the ingredients in a Ziploc bag and shake it up."

"Yeah!" Kamika said, nodding her head knowingly. "It's easy chemistry for kids."

Montgomery grabbed his tablet and began to take notes. "So chemistry students would be familiar with this?"

"Everyone would be," Evie said. "I made slime in elementary school." She paused. "I think I played with it in kindergarten."

A memory clicked in Lea's brain. "Wait. That sounds familiar. I think I made that in a high school science lab."

"I've never heard of the stuff," Montgomery said.

Evie considered him appraisingly. "You're older. Maybe they didn't make slime when you were a kid. And if you don't have any kids, you wouldn't know about it."

Montgomery looked like he was about to protest her evaluation.

Evie turned red with embarrassment. "I'm sorry. I didn't say that right. I say the wrong thing sometimes."

Lea stifled a laugh as Kamika caught Montgomery's attention by holding her phone out to him. "Here, look. I've got multiple links on how to make slime."

Montgomery accepted the phone and perused the list. "Three-ingredient slime. School glue, baking soda, and either borax or saline solution with borate in it. Here's one recipe that uses shaving cream." He looked up at Evie. "This is easy to make in any dorm room without making a mess?"

Evie nodded, her cheeks still red. "During activities aimed at kids, like the Explore UT weekend or Girls in Engineering Day, hundreds of kids will be running around with baggies of it."

"All those ingredients are easy to get. You can mix them in a plastic cup or baggie," Kamika said. "And it could be dumped onto the piano keys without even touching the piano. No fingerprints, no DNA evidence."

"I have work to do." Evie pointed to her laptop computer. "I'll be at that table if you need me." She turned hastily, as if in a hurry to get away from Montgomery.

Izzie rose from the chair where Natalia had been trying to soothe her. "We need to report this and get it all cleaned out of the piano." Izzie gave a distraught look at the piano. "I need to practice. Now I'll have to go sign up for time in a practice room."

Montgomery pulled out his phone. "Well, Mei is in class, so we'll have to tell her about it when she gets back. We can report the damage to the police." He started dialing.

Izzie looked around anxiously as Montgomery talked on the phone. "I want to report this to the university. We have to get the piano fixed."

Natalia, standing supportively by her side, nodded in agreement. "I'll let my RA know. She'll know who to contact in housing to get this fixed."

"That sounds like a good idea." Lea noticed a prickling sensation in the back of her neck. She sensed she was being watched, but no one else was in the room. She sensed disappointment and concern pervading the air. Izzie was disappointed, and they were all concerned, but the depth of the emotion seemed stronger. It seemed to fill the air around Lea. She shivered as a cool breeze hit her arm. Lea turned to examine the doors and windows and then the air vents. All the doors and windows were closed, and she wasn't standing under an air vent. She couldn't determine where the cool air was coming from.

Kamika tapped Lea's arm. "What's up? You've got a look on your face that says trouble."

"Trouble? What do you mean?"

"I mean that look you get right before you tell me that you see something that no one else can see. Something like a ghost." Kamika glanced around the room.

Lea laughed half-heartedly. "I don't see anything at all. I felt cold. I *feel* like we're being watched, but I don't *see* anything unusual."

"Good!" Kamika said. "Though maybe a ghost could identify our vandal for us." She held up the scanner. "Shall we scan the room?"

Montgomery heard her and looked up. After completing his call to police, he had been talking to Izzie and Natalia. "You two keep scanning. Maybe we can find something useful around the piano. I'm going to sit down over here on the couch with Izzie and get her perspective of the incidents in the dorm while we wait for the police. Natalia is going to find a resident assistant to file a report with housing to get the piano fixed."

Lea picked up her tablet. "Okay. Go ahead and start your scans, Kamika. I'm ready."

Kamika scanned the area around the piano for sound patterns. Lea watched the data collection on the tablet.

Kamika paused. "Should we do the whole room in one sweep?"

Lea looked up from the data on the tablet. "Hold on. I'm reviewing the sound patterns left in the last few months. I see lots of piano music and an array of other noises, singing, and games from that event they had in here with the balloon-popping activity. I've found an argument."

"What are they arguing about?" Kamika walked over to look at the tablet over Lea's shoulder.

"Somebody yelled 'be quiet.' And someone else yelled that they 'need practice.' Let's ask Izzie about it." Lea walked toward Izzie and Montgomery.

"Montgomery, we found something in the scan near the piano." She held the tablet out to him.

Montgomery read the results quickly, then looked at Izzie.

Izzie looked from him to Lea questioningly. "What did you find?"

Lea answered. "Do you know anything about someone yelling for quiet while someone else was playing the piano? Was there an argument?"

Izzie's mouth dropped open. "I forgot about that! Yes. That was me. I was practicing one evening when Gwen yelled at me to be quiet." Izzie turned around and looked at the room. She pointed to a table with six straight-backed chairs around it. "She was sitting at that table, typing on her laptop. She got mad and stomped out of the room after an RA told her that I was allowed to practice until quiet hours started."

"Who is Gwen?"

Izzie frowned anxiously. "She lives on the third floor near me."

Montgomery asked, "Do you think she could have done this?"

She paused, thinking. "I don't know. That was over a month ago. I know she was annoyed at me, but surely she'd have gotten over it by now. Besides, she stopped coming here to study."

Montgomery took notes.

Izzie stared miserably at the damaged piano. "I feel like someone is targeting me. First I got a rude letter, then we all got awakened night after night, then the study nook I love to use was destroyed, and now the piano is vandalized. I know a lot of other people have been affected. At least no one poured shampoo on my bed, but this feels like a personal attack."

Montgomery patted Izzie's shoulder, "We'll solve this as quickly as we can. Try not to take these pranks personally. We have no evidence that any single person is the target."

Lea and Kamika went to finish scanning the room.

"After I finish the sound scan, we can do the emotional residue scan by the piano." Anger flashed in Kamika's green eyes. "If somebody is doing this to hurt Izzie's grades, I want to shake them and tell them to grow up!" She glanced at Izzie, still clearly upset, seated with Montgomery, and pursed her lips. "Izzie will have to find a new place to practice outside the dorm and a new place to study. That stresses her out and cuts into her practice time. Given that she got a letter under her door too, maybe she is one of the vandal's targets."

Lea rubbed her nose thoughtfully. "Maybe. But other girls might use that study nook and the piano. Izzie may be one of many targets or not the target at all. Come on. Let's get this done. Maybe we can find something else useful."

They returned to scanning the wall in careful, overlapping segments.

Lea and Kamika were almost done scanning when a uniformed University of Texas Police Department officer walked into the room.

The officer examined the piano, spoke to Izzie, and then came to take statements from Lea and Kamika. He looked skeptical when Lea explained what they were doing with the scans. She had to explain the equipment and the entire process. Montgomery ended up taking the officer aside and reviewing the sound scan data from around the piano with him.

Lea and Kamika proceeded to the emotional energy scan, starting by the piano. As Kamika finished the immediate area, Lea called out to her, "Hey, Kamika, look at this!"

"What is it?"

"I see deceit, narcissism, superiority, and vengeance."

Kamika grimaced. "Whoever is doing this thinks they can get away with it and probably thinks they are better than everyone else."

"That's what I think too. Let's show Montgomery." She took the results to Montgomery, who was still talking to the UTPD officer.

"That doesn't help identify the suspect very well," said the officer.

"It does if you think of it as a profile. Our suspect is narcissistic with a superiority complex and looking for vengeance. Someone living in the dorm probably knows who fits that description."

The officer shook his head doubtfully. "We'd need more than that to charge someone with damaging property."

"I realize that," Montgomery said, "but it's a place to start."

The officer shrugged. "So far all I see is a typical dorm disagreement over noise. That happens hundreds of times a year around here. As for your emotional energy scan, show me a criminal who isn't arrogant, deceitful, and narcissistic. That's all of them." He paused then amended his statement, "Okay, maybe not all of them. Some are just stupid."

"In a jail, an arrogant narcissist might not stand out, but one might in a university dorm," Montgomery countered good-naturedly. He was always ready to talk about his inventions and debate with law enforcement.

A few moments later, the officer left. Lea and Kamika finished their sound and emotional energy scans of the living room, with no useful results. Izzie left to go to class.

Mei returned from her class and was dismayed when told about the damage to the piano. "I'll put in a maintenance request."

As Mei left, Montgomery suggested Lea and Kamika scan the vandalized study nook on the third floor and the area of the stairs where the ketchup writing was found. He would remain in the lobby in case more girls wanted to speak to him.

Lea and Kamika had Mei show them where the ketchup writing had been. A scan showed rage in the area but no useful conversations. After that, the two trudged up the stairs to the third floor carrying their scanning equipment.

"Once we finish the nook, let's get some food," Kamika said, pausing on the third-floor landing. "It's time for lunch."

"Sounds good to me." Lea pushed the door open to the hallway and realized she was walking into the middle of an argument.

"You cheated!" yelled a red-faced girl with blond hair in a ponytail. She was standing in the hallway, blocking the door to the stairs.

"You're a sore loser," shouted a girl with blue hair. She stood almost toe to toe with the blond girl. Glancing over the blond girl's shoulder, she saw Lea.

The blue-haired girl turned on her heel, marched to a door down the hallway, opened it, went inside, and slammed the door behind her. Seeing the blue head vanish behind the door left Lea with the impression that an angry mermaid had fled the scene.

CHAPTER 12

THE BLOND GIRL BURST INTO TEARS.

Kamika came out of the stairwell behind Lea with a look of concern on her face. She touched the girl's shoulder. "Are you all right? What was that about? Oh, and hi, I'm Kamika. What's your name?"

The girl wiped the tears from her face with the back of her hand and sniffled as she took in Lea's dark hair in its lopsided Suebian knot. Instead of calming down, she became angrier. Her face became pinched with rage, turning even redder than it had been. "I'm Belinda Guerrero-O'Hara. The girl with the blue hair is Gwen Carter. She's a lying cheater, and it's messing with everyone's grades!"

"What do you mean?" asked Lea. "How?"

Words tumbled out of Belinda in a torrent of sentences. "We're in the same chemistry lab class, and her results in lab are always perfect! Always exactly what they're supposed to be! Nobody's experimental results are that perfect. She's finding out what the results are supposed to be before each lab, and if her results on her labs don't come out right, she turns in prepared results that she brought with her. She must have two lab notebooks: a perfect one and an actual class one."

Kamika waved her hand to interrupt, looking perplexed. "How does that affect everyone else's grade?"

"The whole class is graded on a curve, and she's a curve buster. Normally, the highest grade would be in the low nineties, and the whole class's grades would be curved off the highest grade. A 93 would be equal to 100. On a seven-point curve, an 83 would be a 90 at the end of the semester. They know perfection isn't possible. The class, a chemistry lab, is made to be a weed-out course, really tough to pass, so that people who can't handle the higher levels don't move up. If you work really, really hard, you'll get around a 90. People who don't prepare will fail. Everyone else falls on the scale in between depending on how hard they work. But the teaching assistant told the whole class that there would be no curve this semester because someone had a 100 in the class, with perfect labs each time. That's never happened before in the history of the class!"

Lea took her bag of equipment off her shoulder and put it on the floor. "However unlikely a perfect grade is, it isn't impossible. How do you know she's cheating?"

"I was at the lab station next to her. I saw her results! They were the same as mine! When we got our graded labs back, she got a 100 and I got an 89. She changed the results before turning in the lab." Tears slid out of Belinda's eyes. "It isn't fair!"

Kamika's brow furrowed and she squinted at the girl. "Wait a minute. You're passing the class fine without the curve, aren't you?"

The girl sniffed. "Yes, but that's not the point. The point is I'll end up with a B instead of an A as a final grade, which will lower my grade point average!"

Kamika blinked twice in disbelief and stared at Belinda. "So you're already in college. Why does your GPA matter?"

The girl answered sarcastically, as if stating the obvious. "Because I need a high GPA to get into medical school. All my grades matter. Getting into medical school is really competitive. Unlike that cheating witch, I'm not willing to be dishonest to get better grades." She sniffled loudly. "But sometimes I think I'm one of the few who won't cheat."

Lea interrupted, "It can't be as bad as that, but I understand your frustration. And you are the second person we've talked to today who had a disagreement with Gwen. By the way, I'm Lea. We're here to investigate the vandalism incidents in the dorm."

"I know why you're here. I think everyone on the third floor has had an issue with Gwen. And you're wrong. The cheating is that bad. I know a guy with a network of people to trade information. For example, if he has a chemistry class and a calculus class, he finds someone with the same teachers at different times and trades information on test questions with them. If he takes the morning test or a test the day before, he tells the other person what's on the test. In exchange, that person tells him what's on the calculus test when they take it before him. It's cheating."

Lea moved out of the doorway to the stairwell as another girl emerged from her room and walked toward them. Lea waited until the girl had vanished down the stairs before she answered. "Cheating like that shouldn't work too well at this level. Professors make different versions of the test to give on different days and times to prevent that kind of cheating."

Belinda shook her head. "Sometimes all they do is rearrange the question order. The cheaters still know the questions to expect."

Kamika tilted her head to one side. "I'd send a note to the professor or teaching assistant explaining what was going on. You don't have to name any names if that makes you uncomfortable. But if the professor is aware of the issue, maybe he'll change the questions completely. And as for the lab witch down the hall, report her. Though, I'll bet the teaching assistants in the lab have already noticed her and are watching. If they've never had a curve-buster like her before, they are probably suspicious."

The grim expression left Belinda's face and she asked hopefully, "Do you think so? I hadn't thought of that." She glanced down the hall toward the blue-haired girl's room. "I hope they catch Gwen in the act of cheating on a lab." Her jaw set stubbornly for a moment before relaxing. "I'm not normally so easily upset. But I've been sleep deprived and stressed out recently."

"Because of the pranks and vandalism in the dorm?" Lea asked.

"Yes, mostly the issues here in the dorm. I saw worse cheating in high school. Heck, in high school it was like an epidemic—so common it was the norm for most people, copying work and sharing answers and test questions, plagiarism to get papers done, buying and selling essays. I thought it would be different at the university level, but it's the same people playing the same stupid games." Belinda glanced around the hallway with bleak eyes. "It felt so safe here when I moved in. Such a pretty, historical building. Not like some of the other dorms. Now every night as I go to bed, I wonder if I'll be awakened by some new, hellish noise. Or if the vandal will up the ante and set a fire or something. It feels like each time the prank is worse and the damage more severe."

Lea gave Kamika a worried look and then asked Belinda, "What do you think is driving the pranks in the dorm?"

Belinda shrugged. "I haven't really thought about it. You mean, if this person had a reason for why she's doing this stuff, what do I think it could be? I don't know what drives crazy people. Isn't it just stupidity or enjoying upsetting people?"

"Well," Lea said, pausing to look up the empty hall at Gwen's room, "you're the second person to tell me that the drive for academic success has gotten out of control. Another girl told me that it felt like everyone is a Slytherin, trying to win by any means necessary, fair or foul."

Belinda's mouth formed an O., "I hadn't thought of that. That's a great way to describe the problem!" She scowled down the hall. "Gwen is definitely a Slytherin!"

"Do you think it's possible that the prank-playing vandal could be trying to upset people's sleep and studying to make other people's grades go down? Academic competitiveness to the extreme?"

Belinda hesitated, concentrating her focus inward before nodding in agreement, "That makes perfect sense! It's all one with the other idiotic stuff I've seen, from trying to psych people out before tests to hiding their laptops." She pushed stray, blond hairs out of her face and glared down the hall. "It's the kind of thing that witch down the hall would do."

Kamika leaned forward and asked softly, "Could the witch have damaged the study nook at the end of the hall?"

Belinda chewed her lower lip thoughtfully. "Based on her personality, yes. But she can't be responsible for all the pranks! She was in a chemistry lab when someone dumped shampoo on her bed. She's been pissy and unfriendly ever since. She suspects everyone." Belinda glanced down the hall and watched another girl walk to the bathroom wearing a bathrobe and flip-flops. When the girl vanished, Belinda said in a low voice, "If I had to point out someone who is behaving oddly, I'd have to point to Jolene."

Lea asked in an equally soft voice, "Why do you suspect her?"

"Her roommate never showed up, and the girl they reassigned to be her roommate is never there. Jolene says her roommate moved in with her boyfriend and didn't want her parents to know, so they think she lives in the dorm. However, I've heard Jolene talking to someone in there. And she never lets anyone in her room. She never lets anyone see inside her room. She's jumpy and nervous when you knock on her door. She's hiding something."

Kamika leaned toward Belinda and whispered, "Like what? You think she's crazy? Talking to herself and plotting against people? That crazy?"

Belinda shuffled her feet in discomfort. "She slips out of her room like she doesn't want anyone to see inside, barely opening the door. She never lets anyone go inside. She goes to class, comes home, and shuts herself in there. I've only seen her talking to one person, some guy. What do you think?"

"We can check her out," Kamika said. "Who knows, maybe she's only hiding a pet in there like one of the other girls was."

Belinda's mouth opened into a delighted grin. "That would explain it. Who was caught hiding a pet? Who was it? Tell me. What kind of pet did she have? Was she on this floor?"

Kamika said, "It was an orange kitten, and I took it home with me. Mei said the rules required instant removal of the animal."

"Please, tell me who it was," Belinda begged.

"It's not important," Lea said. "No need to spread gossip."

"Give me a hint. Was she on this floor? Which room?" Belinda pointed down the hall. "West wing? East wing? In the middle? Please, give me a hint."

Lea picked up her equipment bag. "Show me which room belongs to the girl you think is acting weird, and I'll tell you if we found the kitten in that room."

"Okay." Belinda made a beckoning motion. "Follow me." She turned and trotted down the hall, around a corner, and stopped in front of room 304. "This is it. Collette and Jolene. Was Jolene hiding the kitten? Collette doesn't really live here. She pretends to live here when her parents visit."

The names were taped to the door, identifying the occupants of the room.

Lea shook her head. "No, it wasn't this room. And, truthfully, it wasn't this floor."

"Oh darn. Then, I'll have to go ask around on the other floors," Belinda said, more to herself than to the others.

"Let's go," Lea said. "We shouldn't just stand here. Kamika, let's scan the damaged nook area. Then we can report the results to Montgomery and tell him about this girl, Jolene."

They walked down the hall to the small study nook by a window. It had contained an overstuffed loveseat and reading lamp. The remnants of the smashed lamp had been removed, and maintenance staff had taken away the damaged couch. A blue wingback chair from the living room downstairs had been brought in as a replacement, but no new lamp had appeared yet.

Lea and Kamika quickly scanned the walls in the nook while Belinda, whose curiosity was piqued, watched the process.

"Did you find anything?" Belinda peered over Lea's shoulder as Lea and Kamika analyzed the data on the tablet.

Kamika manipulated the tablet to analyze the data. "A couple arguments over who was here first. An argument about someone moving someone's things and taking the space. A fight over leaving clothing on the floor. Someone crying that their boyfriend dumped them. Typical dorm stuff. The vandal seems to be working alone and silently. She isn't having helpful conversations with an accomplice that we could use to identify her."

Lea flicked her finger across the screen. "Let's see the emotional energy scan. Desperation and frustration, sadness, anger, running the whole gamut of emotion. Ugh. Everyone sits here, don't they? And overlaying it all, fear and worry." Lea turned to Belinda, "Thanks for your help. If you notice anyone else acting oddly, let us know. This vandal is arrogant and vengeful and is working hard to disrupt life in the dorm. She may show contempt for other girls, act like she's better or smarter than everyone else. Do think Jolene fits that description?"

A speculative look crossed Belinda's face. "I don't know. Jolene avoids interacting with anyone, so who can say what she's like? As for people with a superiority complex, I can think of a couple. Gwen's vengeful and arrogant and cunning. She would do well in class even if she didn't cheat. She only cheats because she thinks she has to be perfect."

Lea and Kamika packed up their scanners and equipment and tramped back down the stairs to the lobby.

They found Montgomery deep in conversation with Mei.

Montgomery greeted them in a low voice. "We've received permission from the university to put hidden cameras in the common spaces. The halls, stairs, library, kitchen, living room, and lobby. For well-lit areas, I have color cameras. For dimly lit areas like the stairs, black and white cameras work best. I'm going to place them today after lunch, but we don't want the girls to be aware of them."

"Good," Kamika said. "This vandal is working like a ghost, totally silent. We got nothing from the scan of the third-floor study nook or the stairwell with the ketchup message on it."

Lea said in a lowered voice, "We do have another name of a girl behaving suspiciously. Belinda, on the third floor, who by the way confirms the extremes people are willing to go to get high grades around here. Says a girl named Jolene doesn't interact with any of the other residents and won't let anyone see into her room. She has a roommate in name only. The other girl assigned to the room moved in with her boyfriend right after school started but doesn't want her parents to know. The parents think she lives in the dorm. Jolene is in room 304."

Kamika twitched her mouth doubtfully. "I'm betting she's got an illegal pet, like that girl Raven. I'm not taking another kitten. If it's another cat, somebody else will have to take it."

Mei flicked her eyes upward as if trying to see through the ceiling to the floors above them. "Okay, let's see if she's home. I can ask to see her room if I suspect a rule violation."

They all marched back up the stairs to the third floor. Lea and Kamika stood back while Montgomery and Mei approached the door and knocked.

A girl with her hair in a braided pigtail on each side of her head looked out the door. "What is it?"

Mei replied, "I need to do a room check for rules violations. Please open the door."

The girl's eyes widened with fear, turning swiftly to anger. "What? No. You can't just barge in!" Anger blazed in her eyes.

"Yes, I can. You are Jolene, right?" Mei said, reaching forward to push the door open.

"I'm Jolene, but you can't come in." She stepped out and closed the door behind her. She stood with her arms crossed over her red t-shirt and her chin up. She looked down her nose defiantly at Mei.

CHAPTER 13

Lea heard sounds of feet crossing the floor behind the door. A glance at Montgomery and Mei told her that they had heard the noises too.

Mei narrowed her eyes and glared at Jolene. "Look, we know your roommate isn't here. Overnight guests have to be signed in, and you didn't sign anyone in. Open the door now."

An anguished look came across Jolene's face. "Please, no."

Mei pushed the door open to reveal the narrow room, which contained a set of bunk beds. Both beds' sheets were rumpled as if they had been slept in recently. No one else was in sight.

Mei turned on the light, marched across the room, and flung open the door to the first walk-in closet. No one was in it. She moved to the second closet and opened the door.

A dark-haired, teenaged boy, barefoot, wearing khaki shorts and a white undershirt, stood against the wall. He looked past Mei and saw Montgomery, then panic filled his eyes.

"I know it's against the rules," the boy said, his eyes glued to Montgomery. "I'll leave, just let me get my stuff together."

Lea and Kamika stood in the doorway behind Montgomery. Lea could see plenty of evidence that the boy wasn't merely a guest. The room showed signs that two people were living there. Both closets contained clothing, but the one containing female items was bursting with apparel while the one with male items was mostly empty.

"Well, that's no kitten," Kamika said softly into Lea's ear.

Montgomery had noticed the signs of double occupancy as well. "You're not visiting, are you? You've been staying here."

Jolene spoke up. "I had room, and he needed a place to stay. It wasn't fair that they kicked him out with nowhere to go!" Her face flamed red in anger again. "How was he supposed to finish school without a place to live? It was cruel!"

"Quiet, Joey. It's okay. It's not your fault," said the boy.

"What's your name?" Montgomery asked.

"Wade Johnson."

"I take it you can't go home to your parents?" Montgomery asked.

Wade gave a hollow laugh. "I haven't seen my parents since Child Protective Services removed me from their care when I was six. I barely remember them. I don't think anyone knows where they are. I aged out of the foster care system when I turned eighteen in September."

"Are you a student here at UT?" Mei asked.

Wade looked at her and shook his head. "No, I need to finish high school. I've been staying here and doing online classes, trying to finish so I can get my high school diploma. I need to finish the classes I would have had this semester and in the spring semester if they'd let me stay where I was living with my foster family. But I couldn't afford to live in the district for that high school by myself. The rent was too high. So I found an accredited online program run by the state, and the counselor at my old high school helped me get started on it when she realized I wouldn't be able to stay and graduate."

Jolene went and stood next to Wade. "He was a junior last year at my high school while I was a senior. I graduated and came here. He didn't realize that the state would kick him out of his foster family when he turned eighteen, even if he hadn't finished high school. When that happened, he had no place to stay. He tried staying in a park, but he couldn't do his homework, and drug dealers threatened him one night. Then it stormed the next night. When I realized my roommate wasn't going to be here, it seemed like the easiest thing to do was offer him her bed. I didn't want him to die on the streets." An angry tear rolled down Jolene's face.

Mei stood with one hand under her chin, shaking her head. "Well, he can't stay here. You know that!"

Jolene stomped her foot and turned away from Mei. "It isn't fair! He doesn't have a diploma, so he can't get a job that earns enough to pay rent. And even if he could get a job, he can't work full time and go to class. Plus, he's too smart to quit school. He wants to be a doctor. His test scores are better than mine. He'd be eligible for scholarships and could get into college and a dorm himself if only he could finish his senior year!"

"Joey," Wade said as he walked over and hugged her from behind, "it's okay. It's not your fault. We knew this might happen. I'll try the homeless shelter." He kissed the top of her head.

Montgomery studied the unhappy duo. "Wade, are you sure you have no other relatives who might be able to help you?"

Wade looked at Montgomery through bleak eyes. "Wouldn't you think they'd have shown up sometime in the last twelve years to claim me if I did?"

"You never know. That depends on whether they know you exist, don't you think?" Montgomery answered. "If your parents didn't provide background information, the state may not have been able to find relatives to notify, especially since you have such a common last name."

Wade shrugged out his indifference to the idea. Clearly, he didn't think searching for extended family was worth any effort.

Lea stared at the young couple. "Jolene, did you consider asking your parents if they might let Wade stay at your house?"

Jolene stared at her feet for a moment. "Why would they do that? They were looking forward to traveling now that I'm out of the house. I'm the youngest child. They made tons of plans for what they were going to do now that they are 'empty nesters.' They were going to turn one of the bedrooms into a sewing room for my mother. She was so excited about redecorating."

"You didn't even ask them? Given the stakes here, don't you think it's worth a shot?" Lea said. "Your mother might think Wade's life is more important than redecorating. Besides, it would only be for a little while, until he gets into college. Your parents might be willing to help out for a few months."

Jolene and Wade looked at each other. Neither looked hopeful. At last Jolene sighed and said, "I'll call my parents. All they can do is say no, and we'd be no worse off than we already are. What have we got to lose?"

Wade nodded.

Mei looked relieved. "Start packing. He needs to be out of here by the end of the day."

"Okay," Wade said politely. He turned toward the closet, as if he was going to start packing immediately.

Montgomery looked at Wade. "Hang on a minute, Wade. Were you here Saturday when the study nook down the hall was damaged?"

Wade paused, then nodded. "Yes. I was here."

"Did you see anything? Anyone? Have you noticed anyone acting strangely?" Montgomery asked.

"I didn't see anyone that day, but I did see something strange earlier. I usually sneak in and out of here in the afternoons when lots of people are coming and going. But there was one day that we went to a late movie. By the time it ended, visiting hours were over, so I couldn't just walk into the building. We decided to wait until everyone was asleep and then sneak inside. We cut through the Andrews Dorm into the quad and came in through the living room. Jolene came in first to make sure the coast was clear. Then she let me in, and we snuck to the stairs. We both heard someone on the stairs, but when Joey went ahead to check, she didn't see anyone, so we kept going up. At the top of the stairs, Jolene went into the hall first to check if it was empty. While she was checking, I heard someone else on the stairs below us. It was late, after one o'clock in the morning. I was afraid whoever it was might come up to this floor, but instead they went down. I peeked over the rail and looked down. I saw a tall girl. She had on a zipped-up, dark purple hoodie jacket, with the hood over her head. I remember thinking it was strange that she had the hood on inside the building."

"Other than the hoodie, why was that strange?" asked Montgomery.

"She was acting weird, creeping along. She moved slowly down the stairs, like she didn't want anyone to hear her. And then, twenty or thirty minutes later, that explosion sounded in the bathroom down the hall and water went everywhere."

"Wade, would you help me figure out exactly how tall this girl was?" Montgomery asked.

"I'd like to help, sir," Wade said. "What do you need me to do?"

Montgomery looked at Mei. "I'm going to need Wade to show me where he was standing when he saw this girl in the hoodie. Then maybe we can get an estimate of how tall she was. If he can give us a good description of her clothes, that would be useful too."

Mei nodded. "That's fine. He needs to be moved out by the end of the day." Mei looked at her phone to check the time. "I need to go to class. I will be back to check the situation here this evening," she said, looking directly at Jolene.

Jolene glared at Mei but nodded that she understood.

Montgomery and Wade retreated to the stairwell.

Kamika patted Jolene on the shoulder. "Go ahead and call your parents. You never know. They may surprise you. Don't you think your parents are basically good people?"

Jolene sank forlornly down onto her bed and shrugged. "I guess."

"Well, they obviously raised you to care about people, didn't they?" Kamika pressed.

"Um, yeah, they did." Jolene sat up straighter.

Kamika sat down next to her. "So call them. No time like the present. The clock is ticking, and Wade needs a place to stay other than an all-female dorm."

Jolene located her cell phone on her desk where it was plugged in to charge the battery. She unplugged it. "Can you give me a minute?" she asked, looking at Lea and Kamika.

Lea grabbed Kamika's arm and pulled her toward the door. "Sure. Come on, Kamika. We can wait outside." Lea closed the door to Jolene's room behind them.

As they stood in the hall, a door nearby swung open. Cressida appeared. When she caught sight of Lea, an exultant look came across her face. She waved a copy of the campus newspaper at Lea. "See! Now everyone will know you're a liar! Professor Richardson is innocent. No one should trust a word you say against him! His track record speaks for itself." She laughed contemptuously and pushed past them down the hall toward the stairwell.

Lea stared at Cressida in shock but didn't respond. Kamika, on the other hand, was ready to explode in defense of Lea.

"You don't know anything about it!" Kamika shouted after Cressida. "Don't you dare call my friend a liar!"

CHAPTER 14

Lea grabbed Kamika's arm to restrain her from following Cressida.

Jolene's door swung open, and Jolene appeared with her phone still in her hand. "What was all that shouting?" she asked.

Kamika blurted out angrily, "It was—"

"Nothing important. What did your parents say?" Lea interrupted.

Jolene's face lit up. The crushing despair from earlier had lifted, and she stood tall, almost dancing with energy. "They said yes! Can you believe it? They said he can have a room at my house! He'll be able to finish high school."

Kamika gave Jolene a side hug, squeezing her shoulder to shoulder. "That's fantastic. See? Parents can surprise you! But I'm not surprised. Caring parents raise caring daughters. And you are clearly a caring daughter."

Lea mustered up a smile, trying to push Cressida's words aside. "That's great news!"

"I can't wait to tell Wade!" Jolene almost skipped down the hall toward the stairwell in search of Wade.

Kamika watched Jolene skip away then turned back to find Lea staring blankly at her phone. "Are you reading more text messages about that hit piece in the news?"

"I shouldn't have looked at them. Some of them are vile and insulting." Lea turned off her phone and put it back in her pocket.

"I know how you feel. My blog troll is vile and insulting too. What do you want to do?" Kamika gave Lea a sympathetic squeeze.

"I need to speak to Parker, the grad student who said he believed me. I need to know if Dr. Richardson stole from other students." Lea's mind was churning. *What if I was the only one? What if Dr. Richardson's behavior with me was an aberration? Will anyone believe me?* The news article was right about all Dr. Richardson's good qualities. Lea desperately hoped Parker had news that would support her.

"Okay," Kamika said, hooking her arm through Lea's. "Let's tell Montgomery that we are going to lunch and to find Parker. You can contact him before we eat. If he's available, we'll go see him right after. You look like you require sustenance! Or caffeine and sugar! Besides, it's one o'clock, and I'm starving."

Lea exhaled her pent-up frustration. "Caffeine would be good. A soda, maybe, with lunch."

Kamika grinned. "One soda? Ha! You look like you need refills!"

They entered the stairwell and found Jolene and Wade hugging happily on the landing.

Montgomery trotted up toward them from where he had been standing on the second-floor landing. He grinned at the young couple. "Good news?"

Jolene stopped hugging Wade but retained a hold on his hand. "My parents said Wade can live at my house! Isn't it wonderful?"

"That is good news." Montgomery glanced at Wade. "Wade, most people aren't totally without relatives. It does happen. However, when it comes to unstable young parents who get in trouble with the law, sometimes they've made choices that disengaged them from their families. Sometimes families lose track of people, particularly if they move to different states. You could have people out there who might be happy to know you exist—uncles, aunts, grandparents. A simple ancestry genetic test would probably find them. If you ever want to look into that option and need any help, give me a call." He handed Wade a business card.

Wade accepted the card. "I hadn't considered ancestry tests." A thoughtful look came into his eyes. "Thank you for the suggestion! I might try that." Wade stepped down the stairs with Jolene, where they sat down, deep in conversation.

Montgomery turned to Lea and Kamika. "Well, ladies, taking into account the possibility that hair could have added to her height, our suspect is between five feet nine and six feet tall."

Kamika, who topped out at five feet seven inches, whistled. "That should decrease the suspect pool for us. Most of the residents are nowhere near that tall."

"Yes," he agreed. "I think we can easily eliminate anyone five feet eight and under. Wade remembers the girl was wearing black yoga pants and sneakers with her dark purple hoodie jacket. She wasn't particularly overweight or underweight as far as he noticed, which should also eliminate a few people. Whoever she is, wearing a hoodie to disguise her hair was a smart move. She remembered to think about possible witnesses, even in the middle of the night."

"Our profile is getting better," Lea said. "Between five feet nine and six feet tall, smart enough to preplan and plot these pranks ahead of time as well as cover her tracks, angry, vengeful, and self-centered. And from what we've been hearing, she might have a desire to ruin other people's grades in order to help her own."

Kamika said, "Wait, something doesn't make sense. This vandal wrote in ketchup that the dorm was full of cheaters. And we've talked to girls who are mad about cheating and suspect others of trying everything to cause other people's grades to drop. So is our vandal mad about the cheating too, and trying to get even? Or is our vandal a cheater, and others are trying to get even? What if the vandal isn't responsible for every incident here?"

Montgomery leaned against the wall. "You think the problems might be caused by multiple students striking blindly at each other because they feel under attack? It's possible given the differing times for the incidents. Some of the incidents have similar tactics. Though I suppose it's reasonable for multiple students to know basic chemistry. The water explosion likely involved sodium metal, and the slime involved a minor chemical reaction." Montgomery paused as Wade and Jolene approached him.

"Wade needs to pack his belongings and get ready to leave," Jolene explained. "My parents will be here to pick him up in an hour."

Wade asked, "Do you need me for anything else, sir? Or can I go?"

Montgomery smiled at him. "Thank you for your assistance, Wade. Good luck with everything." He extended his hand to Wade, who shook it before walking away.

As the stairwell door swung closed behind the couple, Montgomery observed the troubled expression that had returned to Lea's face. "Is something wrong?" he asked.

Lea sighed and leaned back against the wall by the door. "Cressida came by to gleefully rub that stupid newspaper article in my face, and I'm getting some pretty ugly texts on my phone. I need to find out if anyone else had issues with Dr. Richardson. I need to contact that other grad student, Parker, who said he knew Dr. Richardson was two-faced."

Kamika added, "And she needs food and caffeine!"

Montgomery glanced at his watch. "Lunch sounds good to me, ladies. Can you be back in two hours? Is that enough time?"

Lea smiled, grateful for his understanding. "Thanks. It shouldn't take that long. We'll be back as quickly as possible."

Montgomery turned to go back down the stairs. "Well, I'm going to get some lunch too—at this lovely patio café attached to the building. While I eat, I can start some inquiries into your professor too. I'll see what I can dig up."

·:·

Forty-five minutes later, Lea and Kamika sat on a bench in front of the Main Building, holding very large drinks and waiting to meet Lea's graduate school colleague.

"See, you perked up nicely now that you've got some food and Dr. Pepper in you," Kamika said as she sucked a large amount of sweet iced tea through her straw.

Lea gulped another large mouthful from her cup and smiled. "I feel better. Soon maybe we'll have some more incriminating information on Dr. Richardson."

"You shouldn't let Cressida or the nasty text messages get under your skin."

Lea raised one eyebrow. "Me? What about you? You looked like you were going to follow Cressida and push her down the stairs if I hadn't stopped you."

Kamika swallowed some more tea. "I wouldn't push her. I'd trip her. Make it look like an accident." Kamika winked playfully at Lea.

Lea shook her head and suppressed a smile. "Remember, she's upset at losing her friend and witnessing her friend's life falling apart. No one wants to believe that a person they trusted and respected would commit a crime. She's in denial."

"She needs to accept the truth and leave you alone! By the way, what does this guy that we're waiting for look like? Is he cute?" Kamika asked as her eyes scanned the hordes of backpack-wearing students swarming past them on their way to class.

"His name is Parker Poulsen. He's tall and lean with thick, dark-rimmed glasses and longish, ash-blond hair that looks like he trimmed it himself. I suspect he's so busy that he forgets to go get his hair cut, and then the length bothers him, so he snips off the area around his ears and over his eyes himself until he can get to a barber. He's nice looking." Lea studied the crowd.

Kamika checked the time on her phone and slid it back into her pocket. "Poulsen. That's Scandinavian in origin, like half of my family. However, he's going to be late if he doesn't appear soon. We haven't got all day." She crossed her arms over her chest and tapped her right foot impatiently as she swiveled her head from side to side watching the crowd.

"There he is." Lea nodded toward a young man approaching them through the now-thinning crowds on their left. Classes were about to start and students were disappearing into buildings.

Kamika nudged Lea and whispered, "Ooh, nice. I see he's the studious type." Her eyes moved from his brown loafers to his slim khaki slacks and up to his plaid, short-sleeved, button-down shirt.

Parker Poulsen spotted Lea and waved as he ambled over, his long strides covering the distance in a few steps. He carried his backpack slung loosely over one shoulder. Arriving in front of them, he shook hands with Lea. "Good to see you, Lea. I hope that piece in the *Daily Texan* didn't upset you too much. It was barely short of libelous toward you, in my opinion." His distinct Louisiana drawl and low, rumbling voice made him sound like a classic southerner. His eyes looked large behind his thick glasses.

"Thanks for meeting me. You don't know how relieved I am to find someone who believes me," Lea replied. "This is my friend, Kamika."

Parker smiled swiftly and offered Kamika a large, bony hand. "Pleased to meet you, ma'am."

"Likewise." Kamika accepted his hand daintily with a giggle and a toss of her bronze, corkscrew curls.

Lea watched as Parker reluctantly dragged his eyes from Kamika's lovely mocha face and back to hers. She'd seen many young men become mesmerized by Kamika's wide, green, sparkling eyes and flawless face.

"What can I do for you, Lea?" Parker asked, politely keeping his eyes solidly on her.

"Well, you are one of the few people to come forward with total support for me in this situation with Dr. Richardson. You called him two-faced in your text. We were wondering if you had a problem with him as well."

Parker looked down at his shoes for a moment. When he looked up, his polite expression had melted into a look of disdain. "In Texan terms, Dr. Mortimer Richardson is a born con man, a snake in the grass, and a low-down, no-good, lyin' bastard. Or, if you prefer, in Shakespearean terms, 'a most notable coward, an infinite and endless liar, an hourly promise-breaker, the owner of no one good quality.'"

CHAPTER 15

PARKER SLID HIS BACKPACK FROM HIS shoulder and placed it between his feet. "I'm glad you had the proof to go after the SOB."

Kamika's mouth dropped open in surprise. She laughed and gave Parker a look of admiration.

Lea grinned widely at him. "I'm glad I had the proof too. And the support and advice I needed from Dr. Tremayne. She initiated the complaint to the research integrity officer, so I didn't have to. I take it that you didn't have enough proof? What happened?"

Parker looked around. "It's a long story. Shall we sit?" He gestured toward the bench.

Kamika hastily nudged Lea to one end of the bench and then sat on the other end, leaving space for Parker between them.

He took his assigned seat and leaned back in the bench, looking up at the clouds in the sky. "The story isn't really mine to tell. My former roommate was the one with the issue." Parker's mouth turned down, and a somber darkness filled his eyes. "But Cam isn't here to tell the tale, so I will. Dr. Richardson was Cam's supervisor for his master's thesis."

"Like he was for me," Lea said.

"Yep. Cam was into ancient civilizations and languages, especially translating ancient materials. He loved that they were finding new ways to read burned and damaged scrolls found in the ash of Mount Vesuvius over in Italy. And as for carved tablets like the Rosetta Stone, he could talk for hours about those things."

"It's fascinating work," Lea said.

"Yes, my area is the history of science and technology, but I loved to hear him talk about it. Cam was obsessed with his work. He'd found a translation error in a tablet on display in a museum in Britain. It was one of those things where one word changed the meaning of the next, changing the meaning of the line of text entirely. He was almost finished with his thesis when his secondary advisor got stomach cancer, took medical leave, and then moved out of state to be near relatives. He had a third advisor, who left when she was offered a new position in California. Anyway, shortly thereafter, the secondary advisor died. The next thing Cam knew, Dr. Richardson had published Cam's research as his own, without mentioning Cam's work."

"That's exactly what happened to me. Only my secondary advisor died suddenly, and I never had a third because of a mix-up! I'll bet that's why Richardson targeted me and Cam. He thought no one was left to stand up for us."

"Probably. Cam was in disbelief at first. Shock. He didn't know what to do. He went to Dr. Richardson to see if there had been some mistake, to see if his name was left out inadvertently."

"What happened?" Kamika asked, leaning attentively toward Parker.

Parker swiveled his head toward her. "Dr. Richardson laughed in Cam's face and said no one would believe Cam had done the work without his guidance and assistance. He said Cam should be glad he was 'letting' Cam work on the project. Richardson took all the credit."

Lea huffed angrily. "Wow. I almost did that. I almost went to him to ask him if it was a mistake too. I couldn't believe that a guy who seemed so decent and trustworthy would stab me in the back either."

Parker shifted his long legs and his shoulders slumped a little. "Cam was distraught, utterly devastated. He reported the matter to the research integrity officer, who conducted an initial inquiry. But the inquiry found a lack of evidence to proceed with a formal investigation. Richardson showed the research integrity officer some falsified documents that made it look like Cam had only been assisting in the work under Richardson's direction, not initiating the project and doing it by himself. Cam's confidence was shattered, not to mention his belief in humanity."

Lea's throat tightened. She gripped her hands together in her lap and forced herself to breathe normally. "I wonder if Richardson created the documents after Cam asked him about the situation. If I'd gone to Richardson instead of to someone else, he might have had time to fabricate evidence in his favor. By not going to him, by going to Dr. Tremayne, I got my evidence in first. I don't know what Richardson gave the integrity officer, but conflicting documents would have required the inquiry to proceed to a full investigation by the committee. I won't know what Richardson told the committee until a report is issued later this week and sent to Dr. Tremayne for comments before it's finalized."

Kamika shook her head with a knowing cynicism. "I think it's worse than that. Maybe you got a full investigation because you weren't the first accusation. Cam's complaint was dismissed because no one could believe a great guy like Richardson would do a thing like that. Maybe your complaint, made under similar circumstances, got more attention because you weren't the first accuser. Because one complaint may seem unlikely, but two makes a suspicious pattern."

Parker gave Kamika a respectful half smile. "You may be right about that. Cam was simply unlucky to be first."

"What happened to Cam after the inquiry failed to proceed to investigation?" Lea asked.

Parker answered in an even and carefully matter-of-fact tone, just tinged with sadness, "Cam tried to keep working, but Richardson made it clear that he wouldn't pass Cam's thesis unless he started over on a new topic. Cam refused. Richardson failed him." He paused to clear his throat and blinked his eyes several times. "Poor Cam. He had his project stolen from him. He had to leave the program. He'd been working toward his doctorate. No other program would accept him after he was forced out of here."

"Oh, that's awful." Lea hesitated but had to ask, "Where is Cam now?"

Parker Poulsen leaned back as if exhausted, the subject matter apparently taking an emotional toll. "Last I heard, he was working retail at a mall. It's a waste of his talent. He's got an incredible gift for seeing meaning in symbols and for translating hard-to-decipher texts." Parker shifted uncomfortably, leaned forward, and clasped his hands between his knees. "Richardson ruined Cam's career plan, maybe his life. I don't know if Cam'll ever recover. He was in a downward spiral mentally when he left here."

Lea could sense the feelings of frustration and helplessness emanating from Parker. "We need to contact Cam. This may be his chance at vindication. Dr. Tremayne says the committee report will be in my favor. My boss is a detective; he owns Montgomery Investigations. He said he thought if we looked, we would find more victims of Dr. Richardson's, and he was right. We found Cam. Montgomery wants to bring other victims' stories forward to the press as we find them, to support me by showing a pattern of misbehavior. Maybe if we publicize it, we can undo some of the damage Dr. Richardson did to Cam as well."

Parker sat up straighter, a glimmer of hope in his posture. "I don't know where Cam is. I have his email, but he hasn't returned my calls in months. I don't know if the phone number I have for him is still good. I'll try and track him down."

"If you can't find him, Montgomery can. We'll need his full name, birth date if you know it, phone number, and that email address."

Parker pulled out his cell phone. "I've got his email here somewhere. Give me a second." He tapped on the screen for a moment, searching. "Here it is."

Lea had Parker email her the information, which she forwarded to Montgomery. "Thanks for talking to us, Parker. I really appreciate the support."

Parker shrugged off her gratitude with an embarrassed smile. "A few of the other grad students are still starry-eyed over the man, but when anyone tries to put Mortimer Richardson on a pedestal in my presence, they get a piece of my mind and Cam's story. I think I've convinced a few people that you aren't lying."

The tower clock above them bonged twice, sounding out the hour of two o'clock.

Parker stood up from the bench. "I have to go. Contact me if you need anything. I'll be happy to talk to your boss if it would help." He extended his hand to Lea.

Lea shook his hand. "Thanks for your help and your support. It's a relief to know that someone is on my side."

Parker turned to Kamika. "It was nice to meet you. Lea has my number. Call me sometime, if you're free. Maybe we could get a meal." He shook her hand slowly, looking hopefully into her eyes.

Kamika fluttered her eyelashes at him and held his hand a moment longer than necessary. "That sounds like fun."

Parker grinned at her, then loped off. His long strides carried him rapidly away from Lea and Kamika, across the campus.

Kamika watched Parker until he disappeared from sight. "Now's there's a guy with some integrity who's willing to stand up for what he believes. And he seems pretty smart too."

Lea narrowed her eyes at Kamika. "If I give you his number, will you try not to break his heart?"

Kamika pointed one index finger at her own sternum. "Who, me? Are you suggesting I intentionally leave a trail of broken hearts behind me? It's not my fault if things don't work out. How am I supposed to know who's right for me unless I date a lot of different types of guys? I've never dated an actual 'gentleman and a scholar' like that. Maybe he's the one I've been looking for. We both have Scandinavian ancestry."

"You're Finnish, Japanese, and Nigerian. Since when have you cared about ancestry in your dates? Besides, that line about trying different types is what you say before every single one of your first dates. How many make it to a second date? Hmmm?"

"Not many," Kamika conceded. "That doesn't mean I should stop looking. You've found a great guy. I know there's one out there somewhere for me. I have to keep looking until I find him. I haven't tried sorting my dates by ancestry before. Scandinavian ancestry connected my parents. Maybe it will work for me too." Kamika's half-Japanese and half-Finnish mother had met her half-Nigerian and half-Finnish father at a Scandinavian students' meeting in college.

Lea put her hands up in defeat. "You're right. Maybe Parker can curse in Swedish or Finnish as well as you can."

Kamika flashed Lea a knowing grin and looked around the campus. "I like this place. Everyone seems so intent on learning and accomplishing something. Even in line at that taco truck for lunch, I heard people discussing philosophy and talking about medical research. Everyone is thinking deep thoughts."

"Not everyone and not all the time, but I understand what you mean. We should get back to work. Come on." Lea and Kamika started walking north across the campus, between the library and the Main Building.

As they walked, Lea heard a snatch of an argument about the value of modern art as a pair of students passed close by them, animatedly arguing differing points of view. Lea looked at Kamika and saw that she had caught the conversation as well. Lea said, "This whole push for perfect grades at any cost that the girls in the dorm were discussing kills actual thinking and learning. It results in clones with identical answers to questions copied off each other and regurgitated. It's not real learning. College life is meant to teach people to think, to challenge them to expand their minds and examine their beliefs. When someone challenges how you think, you're forced to analyze what you believe, forced to defend what you believe, and, sometimes, forced to see someone else's point of view. If people only care about perfect scores, debate dies. The process of learning to think dies with it."

Kamika pointed to students seated by the pond, reading. "I see too many people working hard for everyone to be cheating. I think the girls in the dorm are wrong. It's not everyone cheating. It's a certain type, a small group of bad eggs. Bad eggs make the biggest stink and make everything around them seem rotten, even when it isn't."

"Probably. Every class syllabus includes a statement on the importance of academic integrity. A university's reputation rests on academic integrity. These freshmen girls in the dorm may not know how important it is, and they haven't seen cheating punished yet. It's only October. They'll learn that cheating isn't tolerated here. Give it some time."

"I hope so." Kamika nudged Lea with her elbow. "You'd sense if the overwhelming vibe in this place was deception and self-interest, wouldn't you?"

Lea paused to consider. "I think so. All I'm picking up right now is the usual mix of emotion from such a large group of people. Not *everyone* is out to win by any means necessary. We need to catch this prankster so life in the dorm can return to normal. The vandal has gone from writing nasty notes to causing small explosions and destroying furniture. If this keeps escalating, someone may get hurt, especially since this vandal likes chemistry." Lea picked up her pace, walking faster toward Dellonmarsh, a sense of urgency growing in her mind.

CHAPTER 16

THE REST OF THE DAY MONTGOMERY discreetly placed hidden cameras in the public spaces of the dorm. Lea, Kamika, and Mei acted as lookouts, allowing Montgomery to install the cameras without residents observing him.

After they installed the last camera, they all retired to Mei's rooms.

Montgomery showed Mei how to gain access to the camera feeds on her laptop. The screen, divided into nine squares, showed different stairwell sections and hallways on each floor of the building, as well as the lobby and living room.

Mei toggled through the various camera feeds. "Wow. This is great. If this vandal strikes again, we'll have her caught! If I see something happening, I may even be able to catch her red-handed." She looked up at Montgomery with satisfaction.

Montgomery frowned at her. "I don't know if you should confront this girl alone. She may be dangerous. That chair from the third-floor study nook was ripped apart with something sharp, probably a knife."

Mei looked at him with widening eyes. "You think she may be violent? I hadn't considered that." Her confidence deflating, she asked, "So what should I do if I see something happening?"

"Don't approach her alone. If she's damaging something, call the police. Then get another resident assistant or, better yet, two others to go with you to stop her." Montgomery patted her shoulder in a bracing manner. "I don't mean to scare you, but I want you to be careful. I'd hate to see you get hurt."

Mei watched students walking down the second-floor hall on the screen while contemplating Montgomery's words. Then she clenched her jaw resolutely. "The safety of these girls is my responsibility. I'm here to make sure rules are followed. This is my job, and I'm going to do it. But don't worry. If I see something, I'll get help. I won't go alone."

Montgomery collected his tablet from the table and smiled slightly. "I can see you are made of sterner stuff than some. The university hired the right woman for the job."

"Thanks," Mei said, turning away from the screen. "I've also decided I'm going to hold another all-dorm meeting tomorrow night. I'll notify everyone tonight via the dorm chat group and put up signs on the doors tomorrow for everyone as a reminder. We have a basic description of this criminal: tall; wearing yoga pants, sneakers, and a purple hoodie; willing to use chemistry; and angry or driven enough to vandalize and play pranks. One of the residents may recognize the clothing."

"Okay. Don't be surprised if no one steps forward immediately with information. Give the residents a way to contact you privately." Montgomery glanced back at the video feed on the screen showing more young women moving through halls and stairwells. "For tonight, I have access to the camera feed, as well as to the stored copy. I'll be able to review it, so you don't need to watch it constantly. If something happens, we'll review the video to find our culprit. In the meantime, I'm going to sort through what we know about the various victims to see if I can find a common thread. Call me if the residents come up with a suspect or if anything new happens." He raised his eyebrows in inquiry to Lea and Kamika. "Are you ladies ready to go?"

Kamika jumped out of her seat by Lea. "We were born ready for anything. Even for going home."

Lea smiled at Kamika's corny joke and stood up from the pastel loveseat. "Let's go."

As they walked back to the van, Lea and Kamika updated Montgomery on the information they'd received from Parker Poulsen.

"I can find Cam," Montgomery said, looking at Lea thoughtfully but with his forehead wrinkled in concern. "He may be the silver lining in this. If you hadn't been attacked, we would never have gone looking for other injured parties. As it says on the front of the Main Building, 'Ye shall know the truth, and the truth shall make you free.' Perhaps the truth can free him to return to his studies."

Lea knew Montgomery was trying to comfort her. He wouldn't quit until he'd resolved things satisfactorily. Still she was nervous. "I hope so. It would be a relief to my friend Parker too. The sooner the truth comes out, the better for everyone involved. I feel like everyone is staring at me when I go to history department events."

Kamika flung her arm around her friend's shoulder. "Don't let the bastards get you down! We'll show them all that you and Cam are the victims here, not that rat Richardson. And speaking of Parker, I need his number. I'm free for dinner on Friday night." She gave Lea a wide grin.

Lea managed a smile for Kamika's sake. "Fine. I'll text his number to you."

⁂

The next morning, Tuesday, Lea sat at a table in the Bad Vibes Removal Services breakroom with black coffee in a giant mug decorated with a Texas flag and the words "Everything is bigger in Texas." She had to use both hands to lift the soup-bowl-sized mug and sip the hot, aromatic liquid.

Kamika appeared in the doorway in a fashion-forward, bright-green, one-piece linen jumpsuit. "I have a dinner date with that handsome, long-legged Parker Poulsen on Friday. And Jasper the kitten likes the litter box I got him, so I shouldn't have to clean up any more kitten poo. That's the good news. The bad news is that stupid troll who was emailing me through my blog contact page has upped his game. I had to delete a bunch of his obscene comments and block him from commenting on my blog." She sighed and shook her head. "What is wrong with people? He had to know I won't stand by and let him attack innocent people asking for decorating advice."

Lea carefully set down the heavy mug. "You aren't responding to his emails, are you?"

Kamika walked into the room and sat down at that table next to Lea. "No. Except for blocking him and not allowing his comments to post, I'm ignoring the troll." She glanced at Lea's enormous mug of coffee and grinned at Lea. "Needed a caffeine fix this morning, did you? Up too late? Thesis or boyfriend?" She studied Lea. "Bags under the eyes. And you didn't do your hair in that knot you've been wearing. Just a ponytail today. Definitely up too late."

Lea smiled and sipped her coffee again before answering. "I can't get anything by you, can I? Up late, yes. Mainly working on my thesis, but Patrick did call, and we had a video chat. Then I realized I hadn't walked Wally. I took him out for about half an hour. I worked on my thesis, fixing formatting issues and proofreading until after one in the morning."

Kamika nodded with satisfaction. "Glad to know it wasn't all work and no play. How's Patrick?"

Lea glanced at the door to the breakroom and lowered her voice. "He ran into an issue at the office he's starting in Dallas. He had to fire one of the new investigators he hired."

"Uh oh. Why?" Kamika scooted her chair at the table closer to Lea.

"The guy did a, and I'm quoting here, 'half-assed job' at reading a room. This guy took 'fake it 'til you make' it to a new level. Rather than being thorough, he scanned half the room and figured that was good enough. He missed an entire conversation. A conversation that showed two people arguing about skimming off the cash registers at their place of work."

Kamika's eyebrows shot up. "Idiot. How did Patrick catch him?"

"Patrick reviewed the scans and noticed the area scanned wasn't large enough. He looked at the guy's written report and found that the guy said he scanned the whole room. The guy lied in the report that he made for the client. Patrick was furious. He had to go back to the client and ask for access to rescan the location."

"Another guy looking for shortcuts in life." Kamika paused thoughtfully. "This guy didn't want to do the work needed to succeed. He just wanted it to look like he did. What is that? Stupidity? Greed? Laziness?"

Lea took a gulp of the now-cooler coffee. "I'd call it a lack of integrity. Same as Gwen, the blue-haired girl who was cheating on her lab work, though she was actually doing extra work to figure out what the answers should be. It's all dishonesty."

Montgomery's huge framed filled the breakroom doorway as he entered the room. "Good morning, ladies. What's dishonesty?"

Kamika turned in her chair to see Montgomery behind her. "Hi, boss. Cheating at school is dishonest. Stealing other people's work is dishonest. Only doing a job half-way and saying you did the whole thing is dishonest."

Lea said, "We've been encountering a rash of dishonest people lately, people who lack integrity in their decision making."

Montgomery lowered his bulk into a chair. "I heard from Patrick. He did a great job catching that report before it went to the client. And I assume we're talking about Dr. Richardson as well."

Kamika nodded with a look of disgust. "Yes, that jerk, and some of the girls in the dorm were complaining about students so driven to succeed that they were willing to cheat to get the highest grades."

Montgomery put his tablet on the table. "Ahh, academic dishonesty. Speaking of the dorm, I want to show you video from the cameras we set up." He tapped on the screen opening files.

Lea moved over to see the tablet. "Did something happen overnight?"

"Yes. Someone released a stink bomb on the third floor at three-thirty a.m. It was so powerful that they had to evacuate the second and third floors."

Lea tapped her fingers on the table. "The third floor again. The study nook, the bathroom explosion, and now this. Could someone on the third floor be the main target of this malicious behavior?"

"I don't know, Lea. Remember, girls on all floors got notes, and one room on each floor had shampoo spilled on the beds. The piano was damaged in the lobby. Plus, all the loud noises in the nights before the explosion were never pinpointed for location. I'd like to think we could narrow this down to the third floor, but I'm not sure we can."

Kamika wrinkled her nose in distaste. "A stink bomb. How nasty! Did we at least get the culprit on video so that we can identify her?"

"We do indeed have video." He angled the screen for Lea and Kamika to see.

On the screen in black and white, a tall girl in a dark hoodie carrying a backpack crept up the stairwell to the third floor. She stopped on the landing and surreptitiously peeked into the hallway. A new camera angle appeared, this time in color, showing the stairwell door from the well-lit hall side. After a moment's pause, the door to the stairs cracked open and the girl peeked out, revealing a face half hidden by large aviator-style sunglasses.

"Darn those sunglasses," Kamika said. "At least we know she doesn't live on the third floor, which rules out our dishonest, blue-haired resident. And she's wearing that purple hoodie Wade mentioned."

The video continued. The girl opened the door from the stairwell with a gloved hand and tiptoed down the hall. Reaching the west end of the hall, she paused and opened her backpack. She removed a jar from the backpack and placed it on the floor. With quick, deft movements, the girl opened the jar and swiftly retreated back through the hall to the stairwell. Here the camera angle switched again. They all watched as the girl ran down the stairs, taking the lid to the jar with her.

"Why did she take the lid?" Kamika asked.

Montgomery shifted in his seat. "The chemicals in the jar react with water in the air to create a nasty smell. Maybe she didn't want anyone putting the lid back on to cover the smell."

"Where did she go?" Lea asked. "The first floor? Is that where she lives?"

"No," Montgomery said. "Watch the rest of the video from the other cameras." He tapped the screen. "Here is what we caught on the first-floor cameras."

Video began to play again. The girl in the hoodie peeked out into the hall near the mailboxes on the first floor, right by the lobby. Seeing no one, she proceeded out across the lobby and left the building by the back, down the stairs toward Dean Keeton Street.

Lea and Kamika looked at each other in disbelief and then at Montgomery.

"Wait a minute," Kamika said, waving her hand. "She doesn't even live in the building? How did she get inside? How did she get access?"

Chapter 17

MONTGOMERY GRINNED. "YOU'LL NEVER GUESS. I traced her back to the basement area. I think she found a way in from the patio café. Or maybe the offices in the basement. My bet is on the café."

"She has access to the café?" asked Kamika, leaning back into her chair.

"Or she hid inside after it closed," Montgomery said. "I've looked at records. Years ago, the stairs allowed access to the basement for the girls to go to dinner. The café was the dorm cafeteria once upon a time."

Lea took another swig of coffee. "So the areas are probably still connected, possibly by a locked door. That means either our vandal got a key, or she picked the lock."

"I've already spoken to Mei. She was planning the all-dorm meeting this evening to give this girl's description to the residents and see if anyone recognizes her. I've emailed her the stitched-together video from the various cameras." He pointed at his tablet. "She can show the residents the video."

Kamika leaned back in her chair. "I guess it doesn't matter if all the residents know about the cameras now since the culprit doesn't live in the building."

Lea finished her coffee and looked at Montgomery. "Okay, so what do you want us to do?"

Montgomery heaved himself out of his chair. "We aren't going to wait for the meeting or for someone to get around to looking at messages to see the photo of our prankster and identify her.

I want you to take a still-frame image of the girl and knock on all the doors in the dorm and ask each resident if they know her. If no one identifies her, I want you to show the image to the café employees. Someone knows this girl. We need her name."

Lea asked, "You don't want to talk to them yourself?"

"I trust you two to handle it. I'm going to be following up on another avenue. That stink bomb used chemicals, probably some kind of sulfide since Mei reported that it smelled like rotten eggs. However, I'm going to visit the campus police and see if they identified the exact chemicals in the stink bomb. The explosive noises in the bathroom last week used a chemical reaction of some sort too. Dr. Tremayne guessed sodium metal reacting with water. The sodium metal and the chemicals for the stink bomb had to come from somewhere."

"Ahh," Lea said, "the chemistry department."

"Exactly. I'm going to trace the source of the chemicals. I'm betting one of the chemistry storerooms is missing a few items. I'm going to locate the person in charge of inventory, ask if anything is missing, see what sort of security that they have in place, and see who has access to the materials in storage for use in labs, and see if anyone recognizes our suspect. If I can locate the room the chemicals came from, I'll call you to come in and help me scan the room."

Lea fingered her empty mug. "So if no one in the dorm does identify the girl, we might be able to find her through the chemicals she used."

"Yes," Montgomery said as he collected his tablet from the table. "Now, if you've finished that ridiculously large cup of coffee, we can leave. How that amount of caffeine doesn't have you bouncing off the walls, or at least give you jitters, I don't know."

Lea laughed as she stood up to rinse her mug in the breakroom sink.

Kamika put her hands around her mouth and said to Montgomery, in a loud stage whisper, "Coffee runs through her veins instead of blood."

⁑

Later, after arriving at the university, Montgomery set off to meet with the chairman of the chemistry department while Lea and Kamika returned to the Dellonmarsh dorm to meet with Mei.

Lea, Kamika, and Mei knocked on doors inside Dellonmarsh asking the residents to view the image of the perpetrator. They were halfway through the second floor, having finished the first, but so far no one had been able to identify the girl in the video. The odor of rotten eggs still hung unpleasantly in the halls but not to the point of being nauseating. Lea dabbed peppermint-scented lip balm on her lips and under her nose to cover the odor.

Kamika knocked on a door and paused waiting for an answer, her hand over her nose and mouth. "I wish I had some perfume to put under my nose. This smell is awful. Besides, a lot of these girls are in class this time of morning. We're going to have to go back and revisit eight rooms already."

"Try putting this stuff under your nose." Lea tossed the peppermint-scented lip balm to Kamika.

Mei moved down the hall and raised her hand to knock on the next door. "The smell was unbearable last night. This is nothing. Anyway, we'll get the residents we miss tonight at the meeting. That's why we hold all-hands meetings at nine p.m. Most of the girls are home then, though a few residents may still be in a six-to-ten-p.m. science lab." She knocked on the door.

Lea knocked on another door and heard movement inside. She knocked again.

"I'm coming," called a sleepy voice.

The door opened to reveal a tousle-haired girl in pajama shorts and a t-shirt, rubbing sleep from her eyes. "It's early, and I didn't get much sleep last night thanks to that stupid stink bomb. What do you want?"

Lea held up her cell phone showing the image of the girl in the hoodie. "This is the girl who left the stink bomb last night. We're trying to identify her. Do you know who she is?"

The girl blinked rapidly to focus her bleary eyes. "Let me see." She took the phone from Lea's hand.

As the resident examined the image, zooming in on the face, Lea said, "This girl is tall. Based on the video we got this from, she's about five feet eleven inches."

"I don't know her. Let me ask my roommate." The girl turned back into the darkened room behind her and called out, "Marley, wake up. You need to see this."

Lea heard a groan and creaking noises as a girl climbed down from the top of a set of bunk beds. Soon, the second girl, Marley, appeared in the doorway.

"Marley, do you know this girl? She's the one who set off the stink bomb." Her roommate pointed to the photo.

Marley looked at the image and shook her head. "I don't know her. If you catch her, please strangle her for me. She's messed with my sleep too many times. Did that detective get this video of her?"

"Yes, he did," Lea said.

The girl nodded with satisfaction. "Good. That's more progress than the police have made in over a month since this nonsense started."

"Thanks for your help," Lea said.

The girls vanished back into their room.

Lea glanced down the hall to see Kamika talking with two more girls and Mei talking to another girl. She moved to the next door and knocked.

The door, labeled Jonna and Allysia, opened to reveal two girls that Lea recognized from the advisory meeting—one with naturally red hair and the other with short, thick, blond hair.

Lea smiled and held up her phone. "Sorry to wake you, but do you know this girl? She's the one who left the stink bomb last night."

"Hi. Let me see the picture. This might be the one who spilled shampoo on our beds!" The redhead took the phone and examined it. "She looks familiar, but I can't tell anything for certain because of the sunglasses. What do you think, Allysia?" She handed the phone back to the blonde.

Allysia enlarge the photo with her fingers on the screen. "No. No idea. Sorry." She turned to her roommate. "Why would someone we don't even know target us?"

"Maybe she follows you online!" Jonna answered in a peeved voice. She turned back to Lea. "I hope you guys catch this person soon!"

Lea accepted the phone back from Allysia. "There's going to be a dorm meeting tonight. They'll show the image to everyone again then. Hopefully, between knocking on doors and the meeting, all of the girls will see the picture. We're hoping someone knows who she is." Lea thanked them. As Allysia closed the door, Lea glanced down the hall. She was going to ask Kamika if she had already knocked on the next door, but the words died in her throat. She gasped slightly and blinked, staring hard. An older woman in a long dress stood outside a door down the hall. She was semi-transparent. And she was beckoning Lea.

Kamika and Mei were talking to girls. Lea moved past them slowly, walking toward the woman. As Lea got closer, she could see the woman's face held an expression of concern or fear.

"What's wrong?" asked Lea softly. "Do you need help?"

The woman pointed at the door. Then her hand went to the knob as if to open the door.

"Something is wrong with the girl who lives here? Does she need help?" Lea asked in a gentle voice. Lea didn't turn around, but she was aware that Kamika and Mei had stopped talking in the hall behind her. She realized that they must have heard her. Lea kept her attention on the ghost woman.

The ghost nodded and beckoned Lea again. Then she turned back to the door. In a moment the woman had vanished through the door.

Lea turned to find Kamika and Mei staring at her. Mei looked confused, but Kamika gave Lea a look of wary understanding.

Kamika rushed down the hall toward Lea. "What is it? What did you see?"

Lea pointed at the door that the ghost had entered. It was labeled with the names Nicole and Monique. "Something is wrong inside this room. We need to get inside."

Mei walked up and joined them. She looked at the door. "How do you know?"

Lea met Kamika's eyes, asking her silently for support.

Kamika said, "You saw a ghost. The ghost wants you to go inside this room."

Lea nodded, hoping Mei would cooperate. "Yes. An older woman was standing here, pointing at the door. She nodded yes and beckoned me to come when I asked her if someone needed help. Then she vanished through the door into the room." Lea looked at Mei, pleading with her to understand. "We need to get into this room now!"

Mei hesitated. "Are you sure?"

"Yes. And we need to hurry."

Mei knocked on the door. No one answered. Mei banged on the door again. "I don't think anyone is in there."

"Someone is in there, and she needs help. Try putting your ear to the door. See if you can hear anything." Desperation was beginning to creep into Lea's voice. She forced herself to stay calm. She closed her eyes and tried to sense any emotion coming from the room. She could feel fear and a smothering sensation. "Please, Mei, someone needs help."

Mei put her ear to the door. "I hear a sort of gasping noise."

"Oh no. I think someone can't breathe. She's choking or something. We have to open the door!" Lea grabbed the doorknob and tried to turn it.

Mei fumbled for the keys in her pocket. "Hang on," she called out. "We're coming in!" She quickly shoved the key in the lock and twisted, pushing the door open. Mei rushed into the room.

Lea and Kamika followed. Lea's hand found the light switch as she entered.

Mei knelt by the lower bunk. A girl lay in the bed, unmoving except for gasping, labored breaths. Mei shook the girl, but her eyes didn't open. "It's Nicole. She's unconscious. Call 9-1-1, now!"

Lea complied, dialing 9-1-1 quickly on her cell phone.

Kamika joined Mei by the bed. She reached out to touch the girl's forehead. "She's clammy to the touch, and she's definitely having trouble breathing. Does her face seem swollen to you, Mei?"

Mei studied the unconscious girl grimly. "Maybe she's having an allergic reaction. Or maybe it's an asthma attack. I don't know."

Kamika looked around the room and spotted a medicine cabinet on the wall above the sink in the corner of the room. She crossed the room and opened the cabinet. "I don't see any prescriptions or inhalers."

"Look in the closets, on the dressers," Mei said.

Kamika pulled open each closet door in turn and examined the dressers hidden inside. "No nothing."

Lea relayed information to the dispatcher on the line about where they were and what was happening before handing the phone to Kamika. "An ambulance is coming. I'll go down to the lobby and show them where to go." Lea left the room. In the hall, she paused. A chill passed over her, and goose bumps appeared on her arms. She scanned the hallway until her eyes fell on the semi-transparent form of a woman hovering nearby. "Thank you. Help is coming. We'll get her to a doctor." Lea said.

The woman nodded and disappeared.

Chapter 18

A T THE SOUND OF THE AMBULANCE arriving, lots of doors had opened on the hall. Many of the girls Lea and Kamika had spoken to a few moments before stood in clusters in the hallway, talking. Lea hurried down the stairwell to the lobby. A few minutes later, she led paramedics back up the stairs to the second floor.

Mei and Kamika came out of the tiny dorm room to give the paramedics room to work.

Mei clasped her hands together tightly under her chin for a moment and closed her eyes. When she opened them, she said, "I need to call Nicole's emergency contact and her roommate, Monique. The contact information is down in my room. Excuse me." She ran down the hall and vanished out the door to the stairwell.

Lea, Kamika, and the residents of the hallway stood back out of the way as the paramedics transported the sick girl down the hall toward the stairs on a stretcher.

When the paramedics had gone, Kamika looked questioningly at Lea. "Is the ghost still here?"

"No, she's gone." Lea blew out a sigh of relief. "Thank goodness we were here this morning."

"No kidding." Kamika surveyed the crowd of girls still milling in the halls. "Let's finish asking if anyone recognizes this prankster."

"Okay," Lea said, tapping on her phone to find the image. Looking up, Lea found a crowd of girls led by Natalia, the advisory president, standing in front of her and Kamika. "Hi, Natalia."

"Can you tell us what happened? That was Nicole on the stretcher. Did the dorm's ghost vandal hurt Nicole?" asked Natalia in an anxious voice, brushing back the red-streaked hair that wanted to fall over one eye.

Lea could see the worry in the faces of the girls in front of her. "No, we don't think so. She seemed to be having trouble breathing. Do you know if she has asthma?"

Natalia shook her head and turned to the girls behind her. "Does anyone know if Nicole has asthma?" she asked in her booming voice.

Several girls shook their heads while a few said no.

"I wonder if the smell last night made her sick. It was pretty awful," said the girl named Marley that Lea had met earlier.

"It didn't make anyone else sick, did it?" Lea asked.

"A few of the girls gagged and felt ill," Natalia said.

"Did Nicole look sick from the smell? Did anyone see her last night?" Kamika asked.

The group of girls shook their heads in denial.

"I don't know," said Natalia. "Maybe her roommate, Monique, knows."

"You'll have to ask Monique. She wasn't there when we found Nicole," Lea said.

"She's probably in class," called a girl from the back of the group.

Lea considered the worried and tired-looking girls in front of her. "Y'all haven't had enough sleep lately. That can run down your immune system. Maybe Nicole caught a virus." Lea held up her phone. "Did all of you see the picture of the girl who's responsible for all the trouble? Does anyone know who she is? We need to catch her so everyone can get some sleep."

Three girls moved forward to see the picture, but none of them recognized the girl.

Lea and Kamika walked from group to group asking girls if they could identify the culprit. Then they finished knocking on doors on the second floor. No one recognized the girl in the purple hoodie.

Next, they walked from door to door on the third floor. No one admitted recognizing the girl, but half the residents weren't there.

"Well, we tried," Kamika said as they walked back down the stairs.

"We missed a lot of rooms where no one answered the door," Lea said, trudging along behind her.

They walked back down to the first floor to find Mei. She was in her room.

"Come on in," Mei said, opening her door for Lea and Kamika. "I called Nicole's parents and texted her roommate, Monique. Now I'm filling out forms online for the housing department." She shuddered. "I'm so tired. After the stink bomb evacuation last night, I had trouble sleeping. I kept watching the video feed from the security cameras. If I had been awake, I'd have seen that girl come in and leave the stink bomb. I feel like it's my fault that I wasn't awake to stop her."

Lea patted Mei on the shoulder. "Don't blame yourself. You have to sleep. You can't monitor the cameras twenty-four hours a day. In any case, now we have video of this girl and more leads to check. We'll identify her soon."

Tears slid down Mei's cheek. "My head knows that, but I still feel guilty. And now Nicole is sick. She was barely breathing. What if the stink bomb made her sick? What if she dies? This person has really crossed a line!" She sucked in a deep, steadying breath. "Did you finish asking girls on the second and third floors if they recognize the girl in the picture?"

"Sit down before you fall down," Kamika said, leading Mei to the rocking chair in her sitting area. "No one recognized the girl. Maybe you'll have more luck tonight at the all-dorm meeting. The video of her walking might stir someone's memory."

"I hope so." Mei's shoulders drooped. "What is Mr. Montgomery doing?"

"He's tracing the source of the chemicals used to make the stink bomb. If no one recognizes the girl from the video, we may be able to find her based on where she got the chemicals."

"That's good," Mei said, propping her chin on her fist.

Lea noticed that the dark shadows under Mei's eyes seemed to have deepened and nudged Kamika. "We should go so Mei can finish her work and get some rest."

Kamika cast Mei a concerned glance. "Why don't you take a nap? You need one. You'll feel better if you can get a little more sleep."

Lea stepped back toward the door. "Yes. Take a nap. We're going to update Montgomery on what happened here. I'm sure you'll hear from him later today." She opened the door to the hall and held it open for Kamika to exit first. "Bye," she called into the room as she closed the door.

"Now what?" Kamika asked as they walked into the lobby.

Lea's phone rang. "Hold on. Maybe that's Montgomery." Lea looked at her phone. "No, not Montgomery. It's Parker Poulsen." She answered the phone. "Hello?"

Kamika stood and watched as Lea talked on the phone. The instant Lea ended the call, she asked, "What's up? Is it about his friend, Cam?"

Lea shoved her phone back in her pocket. "Not entirely. He did email Cam and tried to call him, but he hasn't heard back yet. However, he was talking to a teaching assistant named Erika, who works for one of the United States history professors, one who specializes in the Civil War. Erika had a bad experience with Dr. Richardson too. Erika agreed to tell him all about what happened to her later today. She didn't have time to give him the whole story yet. They are meeting on the Drag," then, remembering Kamika, she explained the student term for her friend, "you know, Guadalupe Street on the edge of campus, at a coffee shop later today."

Kamika grinned. "And he called to ask you to come with him. Will you go with Parker to meet this person? If so, can I come too?"

"Yes. He's setting up a meeting. He'll let me know when and where." Lea suddenly felt as though she was being watched. She turned around to see Cressida looking daggers at her. She turned her back firmly on Cressida.

Kamika stood with her arms crossed facing Cressida, raised one eyebrow, and tossed her curls contemptuously. "Leave us alone, Cressida. Dr. Richardson is getting what he deserves for his crimes. And I do mean *crimes*, plural. Lea wasn't his only victim. The other victims will be coming forward soon!"

An angry scowl flashed across Cressida's face as she stomped past Lea and Kamika out the front door of the dorm into the quad. The muttered words "all liars" drifted back to Lea as Cressida went out the door.

Kamika clenched her teeth. "Ooh, that girl is gonna drive me crazy! Let's get out of here. We can call Montgomery from the café outside and let him know what happened. I want something to drink. I feel like we've been talking all morning and my mouth is all dried out. And we still need to talk to the café employees."

"Fine," Lea said, watching the door swing shut behind Cressida. "But if Cressida is in the café, we're going somewhere else and coming back later."

"Agreed." Kamika turned toward the door. "Come on."

✥

After updating Montgomery, they sat at a table under the shade of an umbrella on the café patio enjoying cool drinks.

Lea gulped a mouthful of Dr Pepper. She knew she probably didn't need the caffeine so soon after having so much coffee, but she wasn't worried about it. She wanted the sugar.

Kamika, on the other hand, sipped unsweetened iced tea. She asked Lea, "Hey, we don't need to resolve the ghost issue in this building, do we? Most of the time when we run into a ghost, we have to find a way to get it to leave."

Lea stared at the heart-shaped, decorative metalwork in the bars over the window in front of her. "If that was Olive looking out for the safety of the girls, I don't think we need to mess with her. Besides, no one hired us to neutralize the place or remove any ghosts."

Kamika grunted in satisfaction and glanced back into the interior part of the café, situated in what had once been the Dellonmarsh Dining Hall. "If the vandal got into the dorm through this café, maybe she works here. Maybe the employees will recognize her picture."

"You're reading my mind, Kamika." Lea pulled out her phone from her pocket and tapped to find the image of the girl who had left the stink bomb. "Shall we?"

"We shall," Kamika said, rising from her chair, bringing her iced tea with her.

Together, they asked the café employees to look at the image, from the register clerks to the cooks. No one recognized the girl.

Lastly, they found the manager, who introduced herself as Queenie Nawalanda in an accent that sounded Jamaican.

"This girl broke into the dorm upstairs last night. We think she accessed the dorm via the café here. Do you have any idea who she is? Or how she might have gotten into the café?" Lea asked, holding out her phone for the manager to see.

Queenie stared hard at the image, wrinkling her forehead in concentration. "I would say it should not be possible for this girl to do that. However, twice I have found one of the exterior doors not properly locked. Once was this morning. And the security camera was off. I noticed the light was not blinking this morning as it should. I turned it back on."

"Was the other time last week?" Kamika asked.

"No. It was several weeks ago. Why do you ask? Has the dorm had other problems?" She looked up from the image.

"Yes. There have been a number of incidents in the past two months. Someone used ketchup to write in a stairwell several weeks ago. Someone put angry notes under doors. Someone spilled shampoo on beds. Someone set off a small explosion, which caused water to splash everywhere in one of the bathrooms." Lea pointed to the image. "Do you know who she could be?"

Queenie examined the picture. "I cannot be sure. I don't think that she works here. The assistant manager, Kevin Fong, usually closes and locks up the café in the evenings. Perhaps he will recognize her. He does not come in until later in the day."

"What time?" Lea asked.

"He starts when I leave at two-thirty p.m." Queenie returned the phone to Lea.

"We'll be back later to talk to him," Lea said, accepting her phone.

"Thank you, ma'am," Kamika said.

Lea refilled her Dr Pepper as they walked out of the café and returned to a table on the patio. "Well, Montgomery was right. The vandal is getting into the dorm via the café."

"I'll bet she had help," Kamika said. "Maybe one of the second-shift employees left the door unlocked for her and turned off the security camera." She finished the last of her iced tea and got up to toss her cup in the trash.

Lea watched a squirrel hunting for dropped food under a table. The café was peaceful now, but the lunch rush would start soon. Under the nearby spreading oak trees, students made their way to class. Everything seemed normal. And yet the building next to her was awash in anxiety and exhaustion. She looked up at the dorm room windows above her and detected a presence. A watchful, protective presence that seemed to be warning her of something. Olive, maybe? As Lea stood to join Kamika, her phone began to ring. She looked at the screen.

"Who is it?" Kamika asked. "Parker? Or Montgomery?"

"Parker." Lea tapped the screen to answer the phone. "Hello?"

As she stood on the patio of the café with the phone to her ear, Lea was struck in the head. The impact jolted her head forward. She heard herself let out a startled shriek. Kamika jumped back several feet. Three brightly colored objects whizzed by them, barely missing Kamika. The objects exploded on the concrete.

Whatever had hit Lea soaked her hair and clothing. Lea shook her head to try and clear the liquid from her eyes. Her cell phone damp and forgotten in one hand, Lea wiped her eyes with her free hand. "What the hell was that?" she asked, turning to Kamika.

Kamika looked up at the dorm building and then down at the ground. "I'm not sure. Wait a second." Her eyes quickly scanned the ground around them. "Look! I see little pieces of something yellow. And this piece is green." She bent to pick up a large piece. "It was a balloon."

"Someone hit me with a water balloon?" Lea said. She could hear her voice rising in angry disbelief as she spoke. She bit her lip and choked back an angry scream.

Kamika yanked a stack of napkins from a container on a nearby table and handed them to Lea. "It was a balloon all right. But it wasn't only water. Here, wipe your face."

Lea wiped her hands and face and looked at the napkin. It had turned pale blue.

CHAPTER 19

"**T**HIS BETTER NOT BE SOME KIND of chemical!" Lea frantically wiped the liquid off her face and neck.

"You'd know by now if it was dangerous. I don't smell anything. It's probably water with food coloring in it." Kamika grabbed more napkins and began helping to sop the liquid off Lea's hair and shoulders.

"I hope so. Damn it! My phone is all wet too." Lea began using the napkins to wipe her phone when she realized that the call was still connected. "Oh no! Parker!" She put the phone to her ear. "Parker, are you still there?"

She heard Parker's Louisiana drawl, now tinged with concern, come through the phone. "I'm here. Are you all right? What happened?"

"I'm okay. Someone just bombed me with water balloons from the building above me."

She heard him gasp, taking in what she had said.

"Do you think it was intentional? Were they targeting you, or was it a random prank?"

"Someone in the building is a supporter of Dr. Richardson. She has taken every opportunity to get in my face and call me a liar. If I had to guess, it was probably her." Lea stepped back to get another, better view of the windows above. All of them were closed. She couldn't see any movement. "We saw her a little while ago, and she left the building right before we did. If she waited to see where we went, she could have gone back into the building and dropped the balloons on us."

"I see. Is Kamika with you? Is she okay?"

Lea glanced at Kamika, who was watching her talk. "Yes. Kamika's here. She's fine."

"I'm glad you're both okay. Listen. Erika agreed to meet us at Java Heaven on Guadalupe Street at four-thirty this afternoon. Is that okay with you? Can you be there?"

"Yes. I think so. I have to talk to my boss. He may want to come along."

"Okay. Call me if there's a problem. Otherwise, I'll see you at four-thirty at Java Heaven.

"See you then. Bye." Lea turned to Kamika. "We're going to meet Erika, another victim of Dr. Richardson's, at four-thirty at a coffee shop on the Drag."

"Parker asked about me?" She tilted her head in inquiry.

"He asked if you were okay."

"Ooh, he was worried about me. How sweet!" Kamika surveyed Lea's dark aquamarine-colored shirt and jeans critically. "It's a good thing you're wearing dark colors. The food coloring stains won't show on that outfit. But you look pretty wet. Do you want to get a change of clothes?"

Lea felt her jeans and shirt with her hands. "My jeans are mostly dry. And this shirt is lightweight cotton, so I think it'll dry fast enough. I don't need to change. My head is still soaked, though. Let's call Montgomery and let him know what's going on."

An expression of disagreement crossed Kamika's face. "I'll call Montgomery. If you squeeze some more water out of your ponytail, it won't keep dripping down your shirt. I really think dry clothes are in order." Kamika took out her phone and began to dial.

Lea listened to Kamika tell Montgomery about the sick girl, Nicole, who had gone to the hospital, and then update him on how no one had recognized the picture of the vandal so far. While Lea used more napkins to squeeze water out of her dark hair, Kamika told Montgomery about the water balloon incident, the appointment to meet Parker and Erika, and the need to return to the café later to show more employees the picture of the vandal.

As Lea collected used napkins to throw away, she again noticed the sensation that some presence was watching her, looking out for her. The note of warning she'd noticed before the balloon attack had vanished. *I need to pay better attention to Olive's warnings.* Lea tossed the napkins in a nearby bin and returned to join Kamika.

Kamika put her phone back in the pocket of her green, one-piece, linen outfit. "Montgomery says to take a break and dry off. He recommends we take a long lunch then come back here when the next shift starts at two-thirty. He's talking his way into getting permission to scan a chemistry storage room, or three. He says he'll call us if he gets permission to do it today. However, he thinks tomorrow is more likely. His request has to go up the chain of command."

"Knowing Montgomery, he'll talk them into it. He always does. He could persuade anybody to let him do anything, almost." Lea shook her damp hair back. "Come on. Let's walk over to the Drag and find a place to eat lunch off campus. I need to get away from here for a while."

As they walked, Kamika slid Lea a sideways glance under her long dark lashes and then said in a persuasive voice, "I saw some fashionable clothing stores on Guadalupe Street. I could help you choose a new look if you wanted to get some dry clothes."

Lea slapped Kamika's arm playfully. "I know you think I have no fashion sense. I have a sense of fashion. It's classic style. You like all the latest fads. That's not for me."

"Classic?" Kamika snorted and rolled her eyes. "For your look to be classic, it would have to be always appropriate, acceptable, and presentable. Like a pencil skirt or a little black dress. Your style isn't classic. It's nonexistent. Or, sometimes, it's ancient."

Lea laughed out loud. "I haven't experimented with ancient clothing in a while. Mostly, I've been trying hairstyles."

"The Roman tunic you tried was okay. And the Roman servant hairdo worked. Most of the makeup and perfumes you've tried were at least interesting. The elaborate Chinese hairstyle was great. I'm not so fond of the Suebian knot you've been trying out. It makes your head look lop-sided. But in between experimenting with the daily life habits of long-dead cultures, you could try a more modern look. I could help." Kamika shot Lea a hopeful look.

Lea sighed heavily but capitulated. "Fine. You can help me choose one outfit. Nothing haute couture! I want to be able to wear it next month without it being out of style already. And I'm not going to galas. I need to be able to wear it every day. Also, I am hungry after all. Let's eat lunch. If we have time to kill before going to see the rest of the café employees, then we can go shopping."

"Yay!" Kamika did a little dance as she walked.

✣

At two-twenty p.m., Lea and Kamika walked out of a trendy boutique on Guadalupe Street.

Kamika clutched the top of a white plastic bag covering a dress, still on a hanger. "I want to see Patrick's face when he sees you in this dress. It's perfect for you." She giggled gleefully and danced a little as she walked.

"You are way too happy about this. It's just a dress." Lea eyed the white bag, picturing the cherry red dress inside. It was casual, a simple baby-doll style that hugged the chest then fell straight down, ending at mid-thigh. The sleeves were three-quarter length. She could wear it to dinner or a movie. With leggings under it, she could wear it to work. The color wasn't one she typically chose—she usually preferred blues and greens—but she had to admit that Kamika was right. The color went well with her hair and eyes. Kamika knew color.

"You should let me help you shop more often. Look at this new blouse you're wearing. The tailored shape flatters you. Besides that, it's dry, unlike that t-shirt."

Lea glanced down at the teal blouse. She had to agree that it fit her well. "Fine. You win. I need help shopping for clothes. However, we need to get back to work. Let's go leave this dress bag in the van. The next shift of employees will be arriving at the café soon."

✣

Lea held her phone out for the employee running the cash register. He took the phone and stared down at the image on the screen before raising his eyes back to Lea's face.

"Nope. Sorry. Don't know her. I have to work. Excuse me." He handed the phone back to Lea.

Kamika tapped Lea's shoulder. "Let's try the busser clearing tables." She pointed across the café.

They showed the photo again, but the young woman clearing tables denied knowing the girl in the image.

Lea and Kamika sat down at a table. They'd spoken to everyone but the assistant manager in the Dellonmarsh Café with no luck.

Kamika angled her head, trying to see beyond the kitchen area to the back office. "Do you think the assistant manager really isn't here yet? Or do you think he's avoiding us?"

Lea drummed her fingers impatiently on the tabletop. "No idea. Let's wait a bit and see if he shows up. What's his name again, Kevin something?"

Kamika squinted, concentrating. "The lady this morning said his name was Kevin Fong. And look, maybe this is him."

Lea looked around behind her at the door Kamika was facing. A man in a button-down shirt and khaki pants had arrived, rushing through the door as if in a hurry. He had a name tag pinned to his pocket. Lea checked the time on her phone. "He's twenty minutes late. No wonder he's in a hurry." Lea started to slide out of her seat.

Kamika grabbed her hand and pulled her back down. "Wait. He's flustered about being late. Give him a few minutes to settle into his work, check in with his employees. He might not be willing to talk to us yet."

Lea sat back into her chair. "Fine. One of the other employees will probably let him know we're here. Maybe he'll come to us when he's ready." Lea tapped her foot, feeling full of nervous energy. *Why can't we find out this girl's name?*

Kamika leaned back and relaxed. "Come on, Lea. Relax. We're going to solve this soon. Think about something else. Tell me if you're graduating this fall. What's the plan for that?"

Lea forced herself to stop fidgeting. "I reviewed everything, and Dr. Tremayne is right. We did so much work to get ready for the integrity committee review that I'm way ahead of schedule. I'm meeting with her Thursday morning this week to discuss everything and tie up a few loose ends."

"Soooo?" Kamika drew out the word. "Then what? Job hunting?"

"As much as I hate the idea of interviewing, yes. I need to update my resume and jump into the job market. Once I got over the shock of realizing I could graduate early, I started to get excited. Finishing this program and working as a historian, doing research at a museum or university, has been my dream for a long time." Lea watched Kamika's face, hoping she would understand and not be upset.

A fleeting look of sadness crossed Kamika's face, then she smiled. "I'm so happy for you! You worked so hard to finish your degree and fight Dr. Richardson after he stole your work. You deserve the best job in the world. I'll miss working with you."

A few minutes later, Kamika and Lea decided they'd given the assistant manager enough time to get his day started. They rose from their table to ask if they could speak to him. As Lea approached the counter to ask to see Mr. Fong, the man himself appeared, walking toward her.

Kamika whispered, "From the look on his face, he was expecting us."

"Mr. Fong? My name is Lea and this is my colleague, Kamika. Do you have a minute?" Lea said, extending her hand to the approaching man.

The man glanced at her hand for a moment before shaking it. "The chef told me that you have a picture of someone you're hoping to identify. Something about vandalism in the dorm upstairs." He said the words with his mouth wrinkled in distaste. "I doubt I can help you."

Lea tapped on her phone to find the picture. "We are pretty sure this girl accessed the dorm via the café. She placed a stink bomb in the third-floor hall last night causing the building to have to be evacuated. The stink bomb may have contributed to a girl getting sick and having to go to the hospital." Lea held out the phone.

The man looked at the image for a fraction of a second and didn't raise his hand to take the phone from her. Instead, he put his hands in his pockets. "No. She doesn't look familiar." He started to turn to leave.

"Wait," Lea said. "Please look carefully. I have video of her walking too."

The man turned with obvious reluctance. He put his hands on his hips. "I've got work to do. Make this quick, please."

Lea played the video of the girl on the stairs.

The man watched the video with apparent indifference. "I don't see why this is such a big deal. So she played a prank."

Lea watched as the man shifted uncomfortably in front of her. "It's more than that. A lamp and chair were destroyed. The piano was vandalized. Girls have received threatening notes and had shampoo dumped on their beds. The whole dorm has been awakened repeatedly in the middle of the night with loud noises, an explosion of water in the bathroom, and now this stink bomb. It's an ongoing campaign of harassment that started shortly after the semester began."

The man's eyes widened with surprise before he quickly lowered them to the floor. "I don't know anything about that."

Lea asked again, "So you don't know who this is or how she could have gotten into the café? The morning manager, Queenie, said she had found the door to the café unlocked once or twice recently and found the security camera turned off. She said you were responsible for locking up at night." Lea paused, belatedly realizing that she sounded too strident, too accusatory.

The man's face reddened with anger. "I don't know what you're talking about. I lock this place up tight every night. And if you're suggesting that I turned off the camera, you're wrong! Now I have work to do. Goodbye." He turned on his heel and marched back behind the counter, vanishing into the kitchen area.

Lea stared after him. "Well, I really peeved him. Now he's not going to tell us anything."

Kamika frowned and raised one skeptical eyebrow. "I don't trust him. He knows something. He's lying."

CHAPTER 20

"**M**ONTGOMERY CAN HANDLE MR. FONG," LEA said. "He's definitely withholding something. I think he knows who this girl is." She turned toward the exit. "Come on. Let's go."

Kamika followed her to the door but paused. "You go out on the patio first. I don't want to be in the line of fire if it starts raining water balloons again."

Lea hesitated at the door and looked back over her shoulder at Kamika. "You really think she'd do it again?"

Kamika crossed her arms on her chest. "If she knows you're here, yes."

Lea looked around the restaurant. "We can exit by the other door, toward the parking lot instead of into the quad." She pointed across the room.

Kamika gave Lea a relieved nod. "Good idea. Cressida probably doesn't have access to rooms above both doors. And as much as I like shopping, I'd hate to have to get you dry clothes twice in one day."

As they crossed the restaurant, a young woman approached them. "I need a word with you," she hissed out of the corner of her mouth as she walked past them. The woman pushed the door open and exited the café without looking back at Lea and Kamika.

Lea glanced at Kamika, startled, but quickly hurried after the woman. Outside she found the woman wiping the umbrella-covered patio tables with a damp cloth.

"Don't come too close," the woman whispered. "Sit at a nearby table. I don't want Mr. Fong to see me talking to you."

Lea and Kamika chose a nearby table and sat down.

"What's going on?" Lea asked the woman while keeping her eyes on Kamika.

The woman didn't turn to look at them but kept wiping tables. "I've seen Kevin with a tall young woman before. She came in around closing a couple of times. I saw how mad he got when you showed him the picture, and it clicked in my memory. He knows that girl."

"Do you know who she is?" Lea asked.

"No." The woman sprayed cleaning fluid on another table and kept working. "I'm sorry, but I don't know her name. She might be a student here at the university. I've seen her walking toward the dorm across the street."

"Kinsolving Hall?" Lea asked in a soft voice.

"Yes."

"Do you know if she was here last night?" Lea whispered.

"I don't know. I wasn't working last night." The woman had finished cleaning and stood surveying the area with her back to Lea and Kamika. "That's all I know. I hope that helps." She walked back to the door and reentered the café.

Lea and Kamika rose from their table and quickly left the café.

"Let's call Montgomery," Kamika said as they walked toward the parking lot under the shade of an enormous oak tree.

Lea looked at the Dellonmarsh dorm behind them. "After you talk to Montgomery, let's go see if Mei has an update on Nicole's condition. Also, I want to tell her about the water balloon incident."

"That works for me." Kamika took out her phone.

Lea waited under an oak tree while Kamika talked to Montgomery.

Kamika finished her call and tucked her phone into her jumpsuit pocket. "Montgomery will investigate Mr. Fong and any relatives he might have on campus who live or work in Kinsolving. He'll speak to whoever is in charge of hiring for the café. If there's dirt to find, he'll find it. He says he'll question Mr. Fong himself once he gets the background information. Also, tomorrow we should be able to run scans on the chemistry storage rooms."

Lea nodded and started walking back through the quad toward the wide swath of steps at the front of the dorm. "Sounds good to me. He knows we're meeting Parker this afternoon, doesn't he?"

"Yes. If he's done crossing all the t's and dotting all the i's, getting permission to scan the chemistry storage rooms, he'll join us." Kamika began climbing the steps to the dorm.

As they approached the door, a girl came out, allowing them access to the lobby. They walked to Mei's door and knocked.

Mei opened her door and looked at them in dismay. "How did you get inside without a key card?" She stood back and let them enter the room and gestured for them to take a seat.

Kamika shrugged and grinned as she sat down on the pastel loveseat. "The same way people get in dorms all over campus. Someone was coming out as we reached the door."

Mei heaved an annoyed sigh as she sank her lanky body into a wingback chair. "With all the trouble we've had in this dorm, I've posted signs in all the halls and in the bathrooms telling the residents not to let strangers into the dorm. We've emphasized it at hall meetings. And still, anybody can waltz in here."

Lea, who had joined Kamika on the loveseat, gave her a sympathetic nod. "Next time, we'll call you and ask you to let us in. We wanted to let you know that we have a lead on the girl who left the stink bomb. We don't have her name yet, but she's been seen in the café. One of the employees saw her going to Kinsolving. Also, someone in the dorm decided to drop water balloons on me while I was on the café patio."

Mei's eyes widened. "Oh no. Do you think it was Cressida?"

"She would be my first suspect," Lea said.

Mei gritted her teeth. "I will talk to her. How on earth did she . . . Oh, she must have pried a window open. The windows are painted shut. Opening them is a rules violation." Mei put a hand on the side of her face in disbelief. "It's one thing after another around here lately!"

"We'd appreciate it if you had a word with her," Lea said. "By the way, have you heard any news on Nicole?"

Mei's mouth fell into a worried frown. "Nothing yet. I'm hoping her family will be in touch with her roommate or with the university. If I hear anything, I'll let you know." She studied Lea curiously. "You really saw a ghost? That's how you knew Nicole was in trouble?"

Lea smiled self-consciously. "It's a gift. Or a curse. Mostly a gift. Usually, I'm able to help in some way. Now you know that a benevolent ghost really is watching out for the girls here."

"I suppose." Mei leaned toward Lea and asked in a voice tinged with mild alarm, "Does that mean those girls may have really seen a ghost outside my door the other day?"

Kamika reached over and patted Mei's arm. "Yeah. That probably happened."

"Why was she outside my door?" Mei asked with a note of fear in her voice.

Lea wavered a moment, trying to formulate an answer. "We can't know for sure. The ghost may be concerned about what's been happening here. Why she was trying to come to you, I don't know. Maybe she chose you because you are the authority figure."

Mei bit her lip and her worried eyebrows came together. "So she wasn't trying to help me personally?"

Lea took a moment to study Mei and realized that the young woman was fighting down panic that threatened to overwhelm her. "Mei, do you need help personally? Is something wrong?"

Mei blinked hard and took a deep breath. "Everything is wrong this semester. I'm afraid I'm going to be fired as head resident if I can't get things under control here. Nicole is sick, and I don't know why. What if the terrible smell last night made her ill? What if she didn't evacuate with everyone else, and I missed that? What if she was too sick to evacuate?"

"Did you check to see that everyone got out of the dorm?" Lea asked, trying to keep her voice gentle.

"Each floor resident assistant was responsible for verifying everyone from their floor got out. All the RAs handed me checklists after they accounted for their residents. But what if they missed Nicole in the confusion? She might have died. As long as this crazy girl is still loose, anything could happen. More girls could get hurt. Someone might die. That would be my fault! It's my job to see that rules are followed and everyone is safe." Mei gripped her hands together tightly in her lap as misery twisted her face.

Lea left her seat and bent down in front of Mei to give the young woman a hug. "You're doing everything you can! Montgomery will solve this, I promise."

Mei sniffled slightly and dashed a tear off her cheek as Lea released her. "Thank you. I'm not usually so emotional. I'm sorry."

Kamika found a box of tissues on the nearby table and handed one to Mei. "You haven't slept well in ages. Everyone loses emotional control when they're sleep deprived. This will end and you will recover."

Mei's phone beeped. "Oh, excuse me. I need to check that. I'm waiting to hear back from Nicole's roommate, Monique." She grabbed her phone. "It's Monique. She says that Nicole's mother is going to come by the dorm to pick up some clothes and things for Nicole. She says Nicole has pneumonia and will be going home to recover." Relief flooded over Mei's face.

Lea felt a rush of relief as well. "It wasn't the stupid stink bomb."

Mei was still looking at her phone. "Monique says that Nicole had been coughing for the last few days. She's been exhausted, not getting enough sleep, and getting rousted out of bed last night while sick made things worse." Mei fixed her mouth in a grim line momentarily. "Her immune system was probably run down. All these stupid pranks are to blame."

"Maybe," Kamika said, "but that's not your fault. Besides, I'll bet a lot of students get sick their first semester away from home. It's stressful moving out and being in charge of your own schedule. Stress can wear you down too."

Mei nodded doubtfully. "I guess, but this has been more than your average amount of stress. By the way, I told my boss in housing that the dorm was being accessed from the basement. He said that a crew will check all the doors between the dorm and the offices and café in the basement. They will replace locks if they can't find any damage in case she somehow got a key."

"That's great!" Lea said, sitting back down on the loveseat. "When are they coming?"

"Tomorrow at the latest," Mei said.

"This vandal won't be able to get inside and do any more damage." Kamika was standing, looking around Mei's small room thoughtfully. "Come on, Lea. I have an idea. Let's take this picture across the street to that other dorm and see if anyone there recognizes the girl."

Mei rose resolutely from her wingback chair. "Good luck! That place is huge; over seven hundred residents live there. You could ask a hundred people and not find anyone who knows our vandal."

∷

An hour later, Kamika was ready to admit defeat. "We could stand here in this lobby all day and still not find anyone who recognizes this girl. Too many people come through here, and they are all looking at their phones. No one looks at other people anymore."

Lea could see that Kamika was as frustrated as she herself felt. "It was a worth a try. We asked all the cafeteria employees and all the people in the little convenience store. If they don't recognize her, maybe she doesn't live here after all."

Kamika shrugged. "She could still live here. Those employees see thousands of students a day. Why should this one girl stand out?"

"True. Let's get out of here. We need to get to the coffee shop to meet Parker at four-thirty."

Kamika's face lit up. "That's right! Let's go." She was headed for the door almost before Lea could respond.

Lea laughed and followed Kamika out the door. Quickly, they made their way through the throngs of students along Guadalupe Street toward the coffee shop.

Kamika pointed ahead of them. "There it is, Java Heaven. Mmmm, that coffee smells great."

Lea stopped walking suddenly and gasped. Her eyes were riveted to a person walking toward them on the opposite side of the street. "Is that? No. Yes."

"What's wrong?" Kamika turned, a wide-eyed look of confused alarm on her face.

"There! On the other side of the street! It's the girl in the picture!" Lea pointed south.

Kamika scanned the sidewalk full of people. "Are you sure? Where? I don't see her!"

"Come on!" Lea took off running down the street to the nearest crosswalk.

CHAPTER 21

KAMIKA CAUGHT UP TO LEA AT a street corner, waiting for the crosswalk signal. Lea was pacing back and forth and pushing the crosswalk button every time she came near it.

"Damn it! She's getting away." Lea stood on her toes looking down the street, trying to see over the crowds of people.

"Can you see her?" Kamika squinted down the street. "I can't. Are you sure it was her?"

"It was her. She was wearing that purple hoodie jacket, but she had the hood down. Her hair was dark on top, fading to lighter, then bleached to blond at the ends. Distinctive. No wonder she covered it."

Kamika gave Lea a doubtful glance. "Anyone could have a similar hoodie."

"The hoodie was the icing on the cake. I recognized the way she moves, the way she walks. I've seen enough video of her walking to recognize her body shape and motion. It was her!" Lea kicked the light pole next to her in frustration. "Stupid light won't change."

"Take a deep breath. We've lost her by now. She could have gone anywhere. I'm glad you didn't try to race across Guadalupe Street. This traffic is crazy right now."

Lea blew out an exasperated sigh. "Traffic is always heavy here." She stood on her toes again, looking for the girl. "Ugh. She's gone."

"We need to meet Parker." Kamika threw an arm around Lea's shoulder and turned her back toward the coffee shop. "We'll get her. Relax. We're close. Let's go."

"I know, but we've been trying to identify this girl all day. Then she walks right past us, and we can't get to her because of traffic. I'm frustrated."

"And what would you have done if you had caught her? Made a citizen's arrest? We can't prove she's the vandal. We don't even know her name. If you chased her, she'd be warned to cover her tracks. It's a good thing we didn't catch her."

Lea stared at Kamika blankly, beginning to feel vaguely sick to her stomach. "Damn. I would have looked stupid accosting her on the street. I guess I wasn't thinking."

Kamika gave her friend a comforting squeeze on the shoulder. "You're letting this vandal get under your skin because you're frustrated about the situation with Dr. Richardson. You got your name dragged through the mud by the university newspaper. That's what's eating at you. The sooner we present other victims of Dr. Richardson's to the paper, the sooner your name will be cleared. Parker is waiting to help us. Erika is too. You aren't alone in this."

"Thanks, Kamika. I am tied in knots. I suppose the stress is getting to me a little."

"A little? Ha! You're like a spring under too much pressure. Hon, you need a massage to work the knots out of your shoulders. Look. We're here. I can see Parker waving to us from that table in back. Let's go in and meet someone else who's on your side." Kamika pulled open the door to Java Heaven, releasing an even stronger aroma of coffee. "Inhale that smell. That alone should make you feel instantly better."

Lea grinned reluctantly and walked in the door, nodding to Parker as she did.

Parker leaped to his feet as they approached, in old-fashioned, southern-gentleman style. "I'm glad you could come, Lea, Kamika." His smile widened to a grin as his eyes met Kamika's. He turned quickly back to the biracial young woman with a freckled complexion seated across the table from him. "This is Erika. Erika, have you met Lea?" His soft Louisiana drawl held a hint of enthusiasm.

Erika shook her head, causing her low ponytail made up of multiple strands of dark braided hair to shake. She extended her hand to Lea. "I've seen you around, but somehow we haven't met."

Lea shook her hand. "I've seen you too. Thanks for coming to talk to me."

Parker gestured to Kamika. "And this is Lea's friend and coworker, Kamika."

Kamika reached forward and shook Erika's hand.

Everyone sat down around the small table near a side wall of the coffee shop. Lea looked around. The shop was narrow but deep. An assortment of tables, couches, and loveseats lined the wall going to the back of the shop. The line to order was short, but most people were getting their coffees and leaving. Their discussion would be private if no one sat nearby.

Parker tapped his cup of iced coffee. "We already ordered. Do y'all want something?"

Lea still felt too wound up. As much as she loved coffee, she couldn't think about ordering a drink right then. She gave a tiny shake of her head.

Kamika pursed her lips thoughtfully before answering. "I need some water. So does Lea, whether she knows it or not." She glanced at Lea, assessing her.

Lea started to disagree but changed her mind. "No. Wait, yes. We've been talking to people since lunch. Water would be best."

Parker rose. "Two glasses of water coming up." His long legs covered the short distance to the bar. In a moment, he returned with a glass of ice water in each hand.

Lea and Kamika thanked him.

Lea sipped her water and turned to Erika. "So you had a problem with Dr. Richardson too?"

"I did. I kept telling myself that there had to be another explanation, that I must be wrong. He's doesn't seem like the sort of person who would take advantage of people. He seems so charming and sweet and attentive to other people."

"He'd make a great actor or con artist. The best scammers are people who look trustworthy," Lea said.

"Then he'd be one of the best. He can look you straight in the eye and lie convincingly. He can make you believe that you're the one who made the mistake. He sure pulled that on me." Erika's mouth drooped and her eyelashes hid her eyes.

"Did he steal your work?"

"No, some things vanished: receipts for a fundraiser he was in charge of organizing."

Lea put down her water cup. "What happened?"

"I was helping with the fundraiser for the families that the history department adopted for Christmas. Dr.

Richardson asked me to bring him a file folder full of receipts for the expenses. I was in charge of collecting receipts. I swear that I put it on his desk, like he asked. But he claimed that he never received it and that I lost it."

Kamika's forehead wrinkled as she thought. "Why is that a problem? They were receipts, not bills that still needed paying, not cash or checks."

"Without the receipts showing how much he spent to set up the event, I can't prove that he didn't take too much to reimburse himself. And I really think he embezzled some of the funds." An angry flush filled Erika's cheeks. "But, of course, when I asked my boss about it, he ignored me because I had no proof and because he thinks Richardson is a great guy to organize the event year after year. My boss trusts Richardson and thinks I'm either overreacting or trying to cover for losing the receipts myself."

Kamika leaned forward on the table. "No one believed you?" Her eyes flashed in sympathetic anger.

"No one believed me or wanted to even hear me out. I'm only a lowly grad student trying to get a master's degree." Erika blinked rapidly and took a swallow of her coffee, hiding her hazel eyes. She cleared her throat. "This year, when I offered to help organize the event, Richardson turned me down, suggesting to my boss that I'm not reliable because of the issue with the receipts. He knows that I'm onto his game."

Kamika's green eyes narrowed. "So he's a con artist, an embezzler, and a thief of other people's work. This guy is scum."

Lea looked at the ceiling, thinking. "He puts himself in charge of parties and events in the department. Everyone thinks he's generous with his time because no one else wants to take on the responsibility, but he's actually doing it for his own profit. He's charming, so people like him and trust him. Students ask him to be their advisor because he's a great teacher and attentive to students, giving him access to steal their work. And his ability to charm people means that a lot of people never see the truth. That's how con men operate. They make themselves seem trustworthy and caring, but it's all a con to get what they want."

Parker fingered his cup of iced coffee, making marks in the condensation on the exterior. "If he's this rotten, his coworkers would have noticed, wouldn't they? He's worked here for years. How could he get away with this act for so long?"

Erika leaned forward on the table with her hand under her chin. "Most of the faculty are so busy with their own lives that they take his charm at face value. Richardson takes the time to do things that they don't want to do, like organizing events. That charm of his is practically bulletproof. He could get away with almost anything. Consider how long it takes to catch really charming pedophiles or con men, people who gain trust for nefarious purposes. Some aren't caught for decades until a victim finally speaks up. Victims are silent because they think no one will believe them because everyone likes and trusts the abuser or con man. Or, like in my case, no one believed me. I'm a nobody teaching assistant. He's a tenured professor. They took his word over mine."

Parker frowned. "Richardson stole Cam's work because he knew he could get away with it. Richardson was banking on his charm and the fact that he's well liked to keep Cam silent. And then, when Cam complained, he refused to accept Cam's thesis and failed him to force him out of the university. He muddied Cam's reputation to protect his own. Then, Erika, you got suspicious of him stealing money, so he made you look unreliable. He probably thought he could get away with it again with Lea. He stole her work, and now some supporter of his is slinging mud at Lea in the newspaper, trying to ruin her reputation. He may have even instigated that attack by asking someone to write in his defense." He glanced sympathetically at Lea.

Lea felt their eyes on her, full of sympathy and support, and was almost overwhelmed. She blinked back tears. "Well, I won't let him beat me! I'm lucky to have Dr. Tremayne's support. And you and Erika. Thanks." Lea smiled gratefully at them both. Then her smile fell. "Unfortunately, we don't have the evidence to prove that Dr. Richardson was stealing from the fundraising events. He's good at covering his tracks. We can't take that accusation to the news without proof. He could sue us for defamation."

"We need Cam to step forward and tell his story," Parker said. "I still haven't heard from him."

"Montgomery will find him. As a private investigator, he has access to databases that we don't," Kamika said in a confident voice as she met Parker's eyes.

"The sooner the better," said Parker. He checked the time on his phone. "It's five-fifteen already. Erika, you said you have to go at five-twenty."

Erika reached for her backpack, resting next to her chair. "Thanks for reminding me." She turned to Lea. "I'm sorry. I wish I had evidence to give you to use against that jerk Richardson."

"Don't worry about it. I'm glad he didn't destroy you academically too. Besides, we may still be able to do something with your information. I'm not sure how, but my boss may have an idea."

"Let me know," Erika said, rising from her chair.

They said their goodbyes, with Kamika and Parker shaking hands for a moment longer than was necessary.

Lea and Kamika left the coffee shop behind Erika and Parker.

Kamika walked with a happy bounce in her step and grinned. "That Parker is a real cutie, and so smart. I'm looking forward to going to dinner with him on Friday!"

Lea's phone pinged to indicate a text message and she glanced at it. "It's Montgomery. He says to join him at the Dellonmarsh Café. He has news for us."

Kamika pumped her fist. "See? News! Things are looking up. What's the news? Did he catch the vandal?"

"I don't know. He doesn't say. Let's go find out."

CHAPTER 22

Lea and Kamika found Montgomery sitting inside the café wolfing down a hamburger.

"Hello, ladies," Montgomery said after swallowing a large bite. "I'm starving. I missed lunch. Sit down and tell me how the meeting with your friend Parker went."

Kamika slid into the bench across from him and Lea followed her.

Lea glanced around the café. "We'll tell you all about it. But first, tell me. Did you have a chance to talk to the assistant manager of the café, Kevin Fong?"

Montgomery wiped his mouth with a napkin. "No. I did not. Mr. Fong left suddenly this afternoon. He claimed he was feeling ill."

Kamika narrowed her eyes. "He ran after we talked to him. He's gone to find our suspect and talk to her."

Montgomery met her comment with unsurprised agreement. "That was my assessment of the situation as well. Now, tell me, did the person you met have anything we can use to show a pattern of misbehavior for Dr. Richardson?"

Lea slumped back in her chair with disappointment on her face. "Nothing we can verify or publish without opening ourselves up to a defamation case." She quickly outlined what Erika had told them about Dr. Richardson's behavior over the receipts from the fundraiser.

Montgomery sat back and listened to her story. "Then Dr. Richardson is probably an embezzler too." He squinted thoughtfully. "That's something I can dig into also."

"How?" Kamika asked.

"I'll contact the major donors for the events he's organized and get an estimate for the total amounts donated. Then I'll contact the recipient organizations for whom the funds were raised and verify how much they received. Also, nonprofit organizations file tax records that I can access. If he's an embezzler, he may have his hand in all sorts of cookie jars."

"But you won't have the expenses for the events. The receipts are missing. How can you prove he took extra money for himself?" Lea asked.

Montgomery grinned widely. "Because I'm betting Dr. Richardson was greedy and took way more than would ever be needed to be reimbursed for expenses. For instance, if a small auction for a school raised at least $25,000 according to the donors, but only $5,000 made it to the school, Richardson would have a hard time explaining spending $20,000 in expenses. If we can demonstrate a disparity between the amount raised and the amount given to the charity, the police will investigate and search Richardson's financial records. This man is confident that no one knows what he's doing. If large amounts of money appear in his accounts after fundraisers he was organizing, then he'll have a hard time explaining what that money was for."

"He'd have to be stupid to put the money directly into his own accounts. Do you really think he'd be that brazen?" Lea asked.

Montgomery nodded confidently. "Overconfidence is what gets criminals caught all the time. This man is a con artist. He thought no one would ever suspect him, and no one would ever audit the fundraisers."

Kamika nudged Lea. "Erika will be thrilled to know that."

Montgomery grinned. "I have another piece of news. I found Parker Poulsen's friend, Cam."

"You found Cam!" Lea looked from Kamika to Montgomery. "That's great. What did he say? Will he talk about what happened to him?"

"He is willing to give a statement. He seemed wary at first, like he couldn't quite believe this would change anything. He didn't sound hopeful, but I talked him into fighting Richardson. After all, he's already hit rock bottom from this situation. He can only gain from helping us expose Richardson for the scoundrel he is." Montgomery gathered the detritus from his late lunch and crushed it all into a ball. "I told Cam that I would help him clear his name too."

Lea nodded, but her stomach was still clenched with anxiety. "How soon will we be able to present this all to the public, to try and clear my name and Cam's?"

Montgomery reached forward and patted her hand. "Patience, Lea. I'm sorry I can't make this all go faster. Cam's working on his statement. I'll warn the chair of the history department about the possible skimming of funds from fundraiser events. The department chair may even ask me to do a discreet forensic accounting investigation. If I find enough information to support either a police or IRS investigation, we can let the university handle announcing that. But it all takes time. We'll clear you, Lea. Unfortunately, you may have more mud slung at you in the meantime."

Lea bit her lip nervously but nodded that she understood.

Kamika gestured toward the dorm above them. "What's the word on the dorm investigation? Did you find the source of the chemicals?"

Montgomery rose from the table and threw away his trash. "We are scanning chemical storage areas and possibly one lab classroom in Welch Hall tomorrow. Hopefully that will give us a new lead. Tonight, I'll initiate a background check and research the family of Kevin Fong. As for now, it's after five o'clock. Let's get you ladies back to the office so you can go home."

::::

Wednesday morning, Lea entered the office breakroom to find Kamika sitting at the table looking deflated with a frown plastered on her face. Even her dark maroon blouse and black slacks seemed less vibrant. She was staring into space, not seeming to have noticed Lea's presence. Looking at her friend more closely, Lea noticed Kamika's eyes were a little red rimmed. And in spite of the makeup Kamika had used to conceal the circles under her eyes, Lea still noticed the dark areas. Something was very wrong. "Kamika, are you okay? Is Jasper the kitten keeping you from sleeping?"

Kamika looked at Lea with disappointed eyes. "No. It's not Jasper. I may have to shut down my blog and business. This stupid troll is making Kamika's IDEA too hellish to handle. Last night when I got home, I found hundreds of obscene comments awaiting moderation on my blog. That troll that I blocked created a new user identity to make nasty comments on all of my posts. Luckily, I decided to set things so I have to approve all new users' comments, or that nastiness would have been all over my blog. Now I have to sort the good comments from the bad. It took forever to review."

Lea sat down at the table opposite Kamika. "Why don't you remove the comments altogether? Wouldn't that be easier?"

"But then I'd lose the sense of community and the question-and-answer interactions with my readers. Lots of my readers share ideas and ask questions in the comments section. The comments are a huge part of the blog!" A tear slid from Kamika's eye. "What is wrong with some people? Why do they have to ruin things for everyone?"

"I don't know what drives someone like that, someone who takes pleasure in causing pain." Lea could feel the pain and disappointment emanating from her friend. She got up from the table. "Can I get you some tea? One of those herbal ones you like?"

"Thanks. Lemon tea would be nice." Kamika used her fingertip to delicately wipe the dampness away from her eye without disturbing her mascara.

Lea quickly heated a mug of water in the microwave and dropped a tea bag in it to steep. "Here you go. Sip this. Don't give up on your blog because of one sociopath. I know you're tired. Did this keep you up all night?" She handed the tea to Kamika.

Kamika nodded miserably as she accepted the mug. "Yes. I couldn't sleep. Some of those comments were vicious." She hunched forward over the table. "I was scared too."

"Oh, Kamika. I'm so sorry." Lea poured herself a large mug of coffee, grabbed several packets of sugar, and sat down at the table again. "Are the comments uniformly mean and filthy or do they have a pattern to them? Are they getting worse or more threatening?"

Kamika stirred her tea. "At first they only accused me of being paid to write my blog by big international conglomerates. All the messages call me nasty names while making accusations about lying for the sake of money. It's so weird. I just accepted my first advertisements for a paint company. I like their paint. I've used it. I never thought allowing advertising would lead to this. Do you think it's because I accepted money?"

Lea stirred several packets of sugar into her coffee. "Did the comments start coming after you started allowing ads? I thought the comments started earlier than that, via the contact form."

"Yes. You're right. This person started emailing me even before the first ad came out. I almost forgot." Kamika rubbed her eyes.

"So this started before the advertising. Don't blame yourself for trying to monetize the blog. Making money from doing what you love is everyone's dream. You didn't do anything wrong. You haven't written blogs in favor of products that you've never used, just for money, have you?"

Kamika gave Lea an affronted look. "Of course not! That wouldn't be right!"

"People have done that and gotten in trouble for not marking their writing as paid advertisements. This troll is accusing you of something that others have done but that you haven't. Maybe you should write about that. Not in a blog post, but maybe in your 'About' page, where you describe who you are and what the blog is about."

"Make it clear that I'm not advertising in my posts and that I'm writing about how I do things? I sort of did that already. I can emphasize it more." Kamika fingered her mug of tea. "Do you think that will stop this person?"

"No. I think Montgomery will have to identify this jerk and send a notice directly to him advising him that any continued threats will be turned over to the police. If he continues to attack you online, you could threaten legal action for cyberstalking or harassment or defamation."

Kamika winced. "Go to court? Involve lawyers? No way!"

"I know how you feel. I didn't want to go through the formal complaint process with Dr. Richardson, but I had no choice. We can't sit back and let these bullies walk all over us. Besides, some of these cyberbullies are cowards, hiding behind the anonymity of the internet. The threat of legal action might be sufficient to stop this one," Lea said in a placating tone.

"I hope so." Kamika shot Lea a miserable look. "I hate this. Montgomery has enough to do without me adding my troubles to the pile."

"Don't worry about that. You know how he is. He's not happy unless he's juggling a dozen different things. This will probably only take him five minutes." Lea gave Kamika an encouraging smile as Montgomery entered the room. "Speak of the devil. Here he is."

Kamika laughed softly.

"What now?" asked Montgomery, looking from Lea to Kamika before settling on Kamika's anxious face. "What's wrong?"

"She has an internet troll attacking her blog business, Kamika's Interior Design for Emotional

Atmosphere—Kamika's IDEA, for short. It got really bad yesterday," Lea said. "She may need help with a cease-and-desist letter."

Kamika explained about her blog, the advertising, and the person who'd been bullying her online.

Montgomery settled his bulk into one of the chairs at the table. "I'm happy to help. Show me your blog." Montgomery pulled out his tablet computer and handed it to Kamika. "Log in and let me see what you're dealing with."

Kamika tapped on the screen for a moment, accessing her blog, and handed the tablet back to Montgomery. "Here are comments I've blocked. Based on the language and user name, I think it's all from one person. At first the comments were accusing me of lying. But here, look at this one." Kamika read from the screen, "'I will stop your lies and close your mouth permanently.' Or this one. 'I know where you live. Gas can and match. That's all I need.' After that, the troll noticed from my bio that I'm multiracial and started spouting racial slurs."

Montgomery began to read, a frown deepening the lines on his face. After a moment of scrolling and skimming, he looked up at Kamika. "Kamika, this is some of the ugliest bilge I've seen in a while. I'll see what I can do to identify the perpetrator. A threat of legal action will be more powerful if we send it to the person's legal name."

"Thanks, Montgomery," Kamika said. "I know you're busy with the dorm case and Lea's problem with Dr. Richardson, and probably six other cases right now. This can wait."

Montgomery's face hardened into a stern look. "No. It can't wait. From what I can see, this situation is escalating. We need to nip it in the bud now. I'll deal with it today." He pushed himself up out of his chair. "Ladies, we leave for the university in forty-five minutes to scan a few rooms for evidence of theft of chemicals. I'll locate and send a notice to this cretin before we leave." He walked swiftly out of the room, leaving Lea and Kamika at the table.

Lea took a large swallow of her sweet coffee. "See? He's indefatigable. He lives for this kind of stuff."

"I know. He's got more energy than six people put together. How else does he run two businesses at once, keep up with Dr. Tremayne, and do speaking engagements displaying his inventions for law enforcement?" Kamika paused. "I hope this idiot really does cease and desist. I'd hate to give up my blog."

"Dr. Richardson and your troll both thought we were easy targets, but I think they're both going down," Lea said. "I won't let it get to me if you won't give in either."

"Deal," Kamika said, mustering a real smile. She held out her mug of tea and Lea clinked her own mug against it. "We fight!"

Lea and Kamika finished their drinks, washed their mugs out, and met Montgomery in his office.

"Kamika, I've identified the responsible party and sent *her* a notice to cease *her* harassment and threats, or else face legal action," Montgomery said as they entered his office.

CHAPTER 23

"IT'S A WOMAN?" KAMIKA SAID IN a surprised tone. "I would have sworn all that vile language was coming from a man."

"I traced the user ID and email used on the contact form to a woman in New England, specifically in Vermont. I have certified letters arriving tomorrow at her home and at her place of employment. She has to sign for the letters. I'll be notified when they're delivered. She was easy to find for someone who likes to make terroristic threats over the internet. She may not know that she's opened herself up to criminal charges with the threats to burn your house down and beat you to a pulp. I have the whole situation documented and ready to deliver to the authorities. In fact, I recommend that you take this to police." Montgomery smiled like a hunter with his prey in his sights.

Lea leaned against the door frame with her arms crossed over her orange University of Texas t-shirt. "She didn't bother to cover her tracks at all?"

"Nope. Another stupid person." Montgomery shook his head.

Kamika stood with a troubled expression on her face. "Why is she attacking me? Did you find out anything about her?"

Montgomery's eyes took in Kamika's worried face. "As near as I can tell, she thinks she's the world's greatest consumer advocate, fighting to expose advertising masquerading as blog posts or friendly advice. Based on her own blog and tweets, she thinks the internet is a world of lies and conspiracies meant to lead people into the hands of big corporations. She thinks your blog is actually written by a corporate employee being paid to look like an innocent interior design advice blogger."

Kamika's green eyes widened. "I've got my biographical information and picture on the blog. She can look me up!"

"She thinks it's all fake, a cover created by a corporation." Montgomery pushed away from his desk and rose from his chair. "She doesn't want to know the truth. It interferes with her mental image of herself as a hero exposing lies."

"Should I talk to her? Prove that I'm me?" Kamika asked.

Montgomery shook his head. "A certain percentage of people don't want to believe the truth about anything: from the moon landing to the September 11 attacks to mass shootings. You can't reason with these people. Logic isn't part of their makeup. Leave it to me. Some of them do respond when faced with criminal charges for making threats. I can take it to the police on your behalf, as your lawyer." He collected his tablet from his desk. "Are you ready to scan some rooms today?"

"Yes. Thank you for your help. I feel so much better right now," Kamika said, walking over and giving Montgomery a grateful hug.

Montgomery patted her on the shoulder. "I'm happy to help. You ladies are part of my team, and I take care of my people. Now, let's go deal with this vandal." He led the way out of his office to the van.

Forty-five minutes later, they all arrived at the University of Texas at Austin and walked from a parking garage to Welch Hall, lugging bags full of scanning equipment with them. They were met by the chairman of the chemistry department, Dr. Roger Dubois.

Dubois spoke with a slight French accent but dressed like a modern cowboy in pressed jeans, a pearl-snap shirt, tooled leather belt, and custom boots. He was slight of stature with narrow hips and shoulders. "We have ascertained that certain supplies have been taken from one chemical storage area. The storage room is connected to a laboratory used for undergraduate classes. A class is currently in session. Will you be able to do your work quietly so as not to disturb the students? The chemical storeroom is accessible from the hall and from the laboratory. Please do not open the door to the lab."

Montgomery frowned. "It would be best if we could scan the lab too, but if it's in use, we could always come back after the class."

Dr. Dubois shook his head. "*Non.* Classes run all day in four-hour sessions, ending at ten p.m. In between sessions, the teaching assistants must prepare the room for the next lab."

Montgomery paused thoughtfully. "If it's always in use, chances are our thief didn't access the chemicals from there. Someone would have seen her. Our best bet for finding evidence may be by the hall entrance and in the storage area itself. Perhaps we won't need to scan the lab at all."

"That would be good," said the professor. He led them down a long hallway and up a set of stairs to the second floor, his boot heels clunking loudly on the floor as he walked.

Lea glanced at the notices and signs on corkboards in the hallway as they walked. Tutoring information, society meeting flyers, and department notices were posted.

"Tell me, Professor," Montgomery said as they walked, "what chemicals were missing?"

"As you suggested, we checked supplies of sodium metal and diammonium sulfide. Both were missing in measurable amounts. However, we were also missing a very large amount of a substance that might not be related to your case."

Montgomery shifted his bag of equipment on his shoulder. "What substance is that?"

Dr. Dubois stopped walking and leaned closer to Montgomery. "A large amount of phenolphthalein, two liters of indicator solution. We are investigating, checking all of the research labs to see if there might be a reasonable explanation for such a large amount to be taken. Please say nothing to anyone about this." His eyebrows rose expressively.

Montgomery asked quietly, "What would happen if someone ingested this stuff?"

Dr. Dubois frowned, "Ingested it? Well, it used to be the active ingredient in certain laxatives. It works very quickly, violently quickly. Provided the person didn't ingest too much, they would find themselves in the bathroom with diarrhea. Consequently, it can cause dehydration through the loss of body fluids."

"Damn! I hope that has nothing to do with this prankster I'm after. But what if it does? She could sicken the entire dorm if she put that stuff in something!" Montgomery sounded appalled. "If that were mixed into a punch or popsicles and a lot of people ingested it . . ." His voice trailed off.

Dr. Dubois looked aghast. "Yes, that would be a nightmare scenario. Anyone who ingested too much could become violently ill. Someone might even die, though that is less likely."

Lea could feel anxiety building in her stomach. She met Montgomery's eyes. "Should we warn Mei to avoid free drinks or anything that shows up at the dorm that might contain the phenolphthalein?"

Montgomery dug his phone from his pocket. "That would be prudent. Give me a moment." Montgomery scrolled through his phone and placed a call. He spoke for a few moments before ending the call. When he turned back to Lea, a relieved look filled his face. "No unusual food or drink items of any kind have shown up at the dorm. Mei will confiscate anything that turns up and warn the girls to avoid eating anything suspicious."

Kamika waved her hand. "I'm no chemist. If this stuff is a nasty laxative, why do you have it here?"

Dr. Dubois looked at Kamika with surprise. "Oh, well, phenolphthalein is used as a pH indicator. Our beginning chemistry students use it to do simple acid-base titrations."

Kamika squinted thoughtfully. "Acids, bases, and pH. Okay, got it."

Dr. Dubois led them to a door on the right side of a hall that smelled strongly of acetone. "This is the room that's missing chemicals." He pulled a key card from his pocket, slid it across a reader, and opened the door.

"How many people have a key card for this door?" asked Montgomery.

"Over two dozen," Dr. Dubois said, putting the card back in his pocket. "I've checked and found no unusual activity by anyone. Whoever took the chemicals either came in at an expected time, when the room would usually be accessed for lab preparation, or came in with a graduate student who has access for a legitimate research project."

"Is there any chance I could get a list of names of those who have access?" Montgomery asked.

Dr. Dubois's heavy eyebrows came together. "I don't know that I can let you have that information. However, if you bring me the name of a suspect, I could check to see if that name is on the list."

Montgomery nodded, hiding a flash of disappointment in his eyes. "Fair enough. Thank you, Dr. Dubois." He put his equipment bag on the floor and turned to Lea and Kamika. "Okay, ladies, let's get this scanning done."

Lea and Kamika put down their bags and unpacked the scanning equipment.

Dr. Dubois watched for a moment, checked his watch, and sighed. "Most reluctantly, I must leave you. I have an appointment. Please advise me of your findings when you are done."

"I'll send you a complete report," Montgomery replied. "Have a good day."

Dr. Dubois inclined his head in a goodbye and left with the sound of his boot heels echoing behind him.

Lea pointed at her scanners. "Sound scan first?"

"Yes. I'll start on the interior of the storeroom. Lea, you scan the exterior door and nearby hallway. Kamika, can you handle the incoming data from both scanners?" Montgomery handed Kamika two computer tablets, each linked wirelessly to a scanner.

Kamika accepted the tablets. "Absolutely. Let me get the programs up and running." She tapped rapidly on the screens, opening programs to accept incoming data, while Lea and Montgomery prepared their sound scanners.

Montgomery entered the storage room and began his scan.

Lea carefully moved her scanner in long strips up and down the exterior of the door to the storeroom.

"Good coverage, overlap looks good," Kamika said, watching the data appear.

Lea finished the door and moved to scan the walls on either side of the door. She finished and turned off her sound scanner. Walking over to join Kamika, Lea said, "If you give me one tablet, I'll work on the analysis while you handle Montgomery's incoming data."

Kamika handed Lea one computer tablet and turned her attention to the other.

Lea quickly initiated the analysis program, watching the screen as the information processed. She adjusted the program parameters to focus on sounds absorbed recently, the newer layers of data. The building was old. She didn't need to see the analysis of several decades of noises absorbed by the walls. That would take forever to process.

As her analysis was finishing, Lea heard Montgomery turn off his scanner.

A moment later, he appeared coming out of the storage room. "Did the scan look complete?" he asked Kamika.

"Perfect. You didn't miss anything," Kamika said, handing him the tablet. "I've started the analysis, limiting it to more recent layers of sound."

"Good, good." He accepted the tablet.

At that moment, a bell rang. A rumble of noise within the labs followed as students scrambled to collect their belongings and leave the rooms. Soon the hall was filled to bursting with a swarm of students flooding down the hall toward the stairwells. Lea, Kamika, and Montgomery grabbed their equipment and moved against the wall to avoid being crushed by the crowd. Within a few moments, the crowd thinned out and vanished.

Lea glanced down at her tablet and found the analysis was complete. "I've got something!" Excitement filled her voice, and she forced herself not to yell. "We have names for the people involved!"

CHAPTER 24

KAMIKA AND MONTGOMERY BOTH MOVED NEXT to Lea to see her tablet.

Lea pointed to the screen "Two voices, one male and one female based on the vocal registers. The female said, 'make . . . worthwhile,' and the male voice said, 'sodium' and 'dangerous.' They weren't talking very loudly, so I've only got bits and pieces of the conversation. But the male voice said the name 'Mallory' and the female voice said 'Barry' or 'Perry.'"

Lea watched as a few students trickled through the halls, glancing curiously at her. "Let's go into the storage room to discuss this. We have a lot of ears around right now."

"Agreed," Montgomery said, ushering them into the storage room and closing the door behind them. Montgomery held up his tablet. "I got part of the conversation too. A male voice and a female voice." He read from his screen. "The female voice called the male 'Barry' or 'Perry.' The analysis gives it a sixty percent chance of being a p sound versus the b sound. The female said 'Perry, $500 for sodium and ammonium.' The male voice again said, 'sodium is dangerous.' Then he said her name again: 'Mallory.' And she said, '$500 more for the rest.'"

Lea looked up from her tablet. "Do you think 'the rest' means the phenolphthalein?"

"Most likely." Montgomery tapped the screen, examining the data for any other useful results.

Kamika leaned against the closed door to the storage room. "Do you think Dr. Dubois will give us the rest of the name for our Perry or Barry person?"

"We can ask," Montgomery said.

At that moment, the door behind Kamika swung open and she fell backward, landing on her rear. A word Lea didn't understand, probably a curse in Swedish, came out of Kamika's mouth as she hit the floor.

Two young men, apparently graduate students in their mid-twenties, stood above Kamika, looking down at her, mouths agape with surprise.

One of the young men, who had dark brown skin and black hair, knelt down next to Kamika. "Sorry! Are you okay? Can I help you up?" he said with a distinct Indian accent. He held out a hand to help her.

Kamika brushed her corkscrew curls out of her face and smiled up at the young man. "I'm fine, only embarrassed. I may have bruised something, but I'll live." She accepted his hand, allowing him to pull her to her feet.

The other young man, who had thin, light brown hair and wore jeans and a t-shirt, looked at Lea and Montgomery suspiciously. His dark eyes wandered from one to the other, taking in Lea's dark hair in its lopsided twist and Montgomery's bulk. "Who are you? Why are you in the storage room?" Spotting their bags, he asked, "What's all this? What are you doing?" His voice rose as he spoke.

Montgomery held out both hands, palms down in a placating gesture. "Calm down. Dr. Dubois, the chairman of the chemistry department, asked us to check on some things in here for him."

"What things?" asked the suspicious young man, glowering at them.

"That's between him and us." Montgomery looked at the young men. "Are you teaching assistants coming to get supplies to prepare the labs for the next classes?"

"Yes," said the Indian student. "We will be quick and get out of your way." He turned to his companion. "Come on, Perry, let's get our things and go."

Lea, Kamika, and Montgomery all looked at the young man with the thin brown hair, whose name apparently was Perry.

"Your name is Perry?" Montgomery said. "I'm Montgomery. Would you mind answering a few questions for me?"

Perry narrowed his eyes and set his mouth in a belligerent sneer. "I'm busy right now. I have to get the class set up." He brushed by Montgomery into the storage room.

Montgomery put on an innocent and polite face. "Of course, I understand. Get your work done. We didn't mean to interrupt. We're almost finished here."

The other student shot a look of questioning surprise at the back of Perry's head. "I'm Arjun. It was nice to meet you." He smiled at Kamika, apparently trying to make up for his coworker's rude behavior, then began to collect items that had been prepared in advance and laid out on a countertop.

Montgomery knelt and began to pack up his equipment bag deliberately and with great care.

Lea and Kamika followed his example, moving slowly.

"Perry," Montgomery said in a conversational tone, pausing in his position by his bag, "which class are you preparing for?"

Perry frowned at him but answered, "Chem 204."

"Mostly freshmen and sophomores?"

"Yes." Perry turned his back again.

"Have you had any issues with students cheating or stealing materials?" Montgomery asked in a casual tone.

Perry stiffened. He cleared his throat and clenched his jaw. "No," he said through his teeth.

"Funny you should ask that," said the other young man, Arjun, with a look of surprise. "I'm about to set up a trap for a student who I think has been cheating. The professor and I are changing a titration experiment so the resulting measurements will be off by twenty-five percent. I think a student has been altering her results to be perfect rather than reporting actual findings. This will catch her."

Lea asked, "Does this cheating student, by chance, have blue hair?"

Arjun's jaw dropped. "How did you know?"

Lea stood up with her packed bag on her shoulder. "I talked to a freshman this week who was upset about a classmate cheating in lab. She said the blue-haired girl had the same results that she herself had on the lab, but got better grades. The blue-haired student was turning in a premade lab result sheet, not the one she filled out during the lab."

Arjun nodded. "That is probably the person who sent me a note informing me about the cheating and asking that I watch. Dr. Reams and I devised this lab to catch her."

Lea smiled at Arjun. "I'm glad you're taking action. The girl I spoke to was extremely upset about the situation."

"Well, we can't have that sort of academic dishonesty. It's wrong," said Arjun.

Perry snorted derisively. "Stupid girl."

Arjun turned back to Montgomery and asked, "What did you say about stealing? Has equipment gone missing from the labs?"

Montgomery, now standing with his own bag on his shoulder, said, "No. Not equipment. Supplies from this storage room have been taken." He met Arjun's eyes and held them. "Have you seen anyone take any of the chemicals or materials? Have you seen anyone in here who didn't belong?"

Arjun's eyes slid to Perry and back to Montgomery. "I haven't seen anyone I didn't recognize in here, except for you all, of course." Arjun bit his lip and glanced at Perry again with an anxious look on his face. "I hope Dr. Dubois doesn't think the TAs have been taking materials. I would happily assist in any investigation. Is that why you're here? You're investigating?"

"Yes," Montgomery said. "If I have any more questions, I'll let you know. We're only at the start of our investigation right now."

"Oh, okay," Arjun smiled. "Well, you know where to find me. I'm on this hall all day today."

Perry snatched up one last stoppered glass container of liquid and walked to the door. "We really have to go, or we'll be late preparing the lab. Excuse me." He left the storage room.

Arjun checked the time. "He's right. Please excuse me." He departed with containers of liquid in each hand and a jar of something in powdered form in the crook of his arm.

Lea waited until the door closed behind the two teaching assistants. "Why didn't you ask Perry about the missing sodium?"

"We know where he is, and he thinks we're just starting to investigate. I don't want to spook him into hiding from us. I don't have the authority to hold him or force him to answer questions. His boss does have the ability to call him in for questioning. I'm going to have Dr. Dubois call all the TAs to his office for a meeting to discuss security, then we'll pull Perry out for questioning." Montgomery smiled at Lea and Kamika. "We have a name. Mallory. We're closing in on her. Kevin Fong in the Dellonmarsh Café knows who she is. That teaching assistant, Perry, knows who she is. One of them will give her up. I'm going to meet Dr. Dubois and update him on what we've found. Could you deposit the equipment bags in the van and go to the dorm? They're having their meeting this evening. Maybe the picture with the name Mallory will be recognized by one of the residents. Fill Mei in on what we found. I'll catch up with you shortly."

Lea held out her hand to take Montgomery's bag. "Sure."

꒯

"Let's talk over here," Mei said as she walked Lea and Kamika to the large common living room in the Dellonmarsh dorm. They passed by several rectangular study tables. Around one table, six girls sat studying, so focused on their tablets and notes that they didn't even look up.

In the living room, Lea was glad to see a man bent over the piano, a bag of tools near his feet. "I see the piano is being fixed."

Mei nodded with a grimace on her face. "The repairman is having a terrible time getting that slime off the keys. He says it's slow going. I could strangle whoever did that. He's been working for a couple hours now."

They sat down in a grouping of chairs in one corner of the room. Mei took a wingback chair while Lea and Kamika choose an overstuffed sofa across from her.

"So," Mei said, looking from Lea to Kamika, "what's the news?"

Lea glanced at Kamika, who nodded for her to answer. "We got a first name to go with the picture of the vandal. Mallory."

Mei's eyes lit briefly before narrowing. "Only a first name? No last name?"

Lea shook her head apologetically. "No, not yet. But we are close. We know where this girl got the chemicals that she used to cause the explosions and make the stink bombs. I know Montgomery warned you not to eat any gift foods. Did he tell you why?"

Mei leaned forward and whispered, "Phenolphthalein was taken too. He said it's a violent laxative. Ick!" She shuddered slightly. "I've sent a group message to the entire dorm on each floor's group chat warning all the girls to be wary of any free food that comes to the dorm."

"Good," Lea said, relieved. "I'd hate to see anyone ingest that stuff."

Kamika said, "I know you have a meeting this evening, but did you send the picture of the suspect to all the girls already? On the group chat?"

"I did, but no one responded about knowing her. A lot of the girls only check the group messages when they feel like it. Also, some girls are in classes and haven't had a chance to look at messages. I doubt everyone has seen the picture. I'm going to show the video we have of her tonight. The video plus the name Mallory might jog someone's memory." Mei pulled out her phone and tapped on the screen, accessing her messages. "No. No new messages."

Kamika's green eyes widened in alarm. "Wait. If the girls don't check their messages, that means some girls may not know to avoid gifts of food right now!"

Mei nodded. "That's why we have to have the meeting. We can't be sure everyone gets all the messages otherwise. The resident advisors will be taking attendance at each floor's meeting tonight. Anyone who doesn't attend will get a personal visit to show them the picture and warn them to avoid food from unknown sources."

"How's the girl who went to the hospital? Nicole?" Lea asked.

A soft smile curved Mei's lips. "I spoke to her. She says thank you for saving her life. She could have drowned from the fluid in her lungs if we hadn't found her. She's taking antibiotics and starting to improve but still coughing terribly."

Lea smiled. "That's good news. Tell her she should thank Olive too."

"I don't want to scare her. Maybe when she gets back. I want to be able to see how she takes the news that a ghost saved her," Mei said.

A voice called from across the room, "Mei, come quickly!"

Mei jerked her head around to see who was calling her.

Natalia, the president of the residence hall advisory committee, stood at the entrance of the room.

"What is it?" Mei asked, surging to her feet.

Natalia gestured with her thumb behind her back toward the lobby. "FedEx delivered a box to the dorm. It's addressed 'to the residents of Dellonmarsh.' What should we do with it? Do you think it's dangerous?"

"Hell, yes, it's probably dangerous!" Kamika said, jumping up from her seat and following Mei, with Lea close behind her.

CHAPTER 25

M EI SKIDDED TO A STOP IN the lobby so fast that Kamika ran into her back. Lea sidestepped them both and found herself staring at two girls, Matty and Corinna, bent over a large box. The box was open. Another girl, Evie, was entering the lobby.

"Stand back!" Mei yelled. "That might be dangerous."

Matty and Corinna looked at Mei as if she had lost her mind. Matty pointed at the box. "It's full of sports drinks!"

Mei, Kamika, and Lea walked over to peek into the box.

"Grape sports drinks," Kamika said, looking at Lea. "What do you want to bet it's full of phenolphthalein?"

Mei picked up one of the bottles and examined the lid. "It's still sealed. How did that girl poison it?"

"Poison?" said Corinna. "What poison?"

Lea selected a bottle. "I see how. See this sticker that was added near the top?" The sticker read, "A gift for a Dellonmarsh lady."

"Yes," Mei studied the sticker. "What about it?"

"She hid a tiny hole from a needle under the sticker."
Lea peeled the sticker off and located a tiny hole in the

bottle. A small amount of fluid began to leak out, so she stuck the sticker back over the hole.

Mei shot Lea an impressed look. "Wow. You figured that out quickly. So this girl used a needle to add phenolphthalein to the bottles and covered the holes with stickers." She dropped the bottle she was holding back in to the box. "We need to call the police."

Corinna and Matty watched with interest as Mei pulled out her phone and dialed.

Evie, who had been watching from across the lobby, walked over and asked Lea, "Is this from the dorm vandal? How do you know?"

Lea replied, "It's a long story. We've discovered where the she got the chemicals for the stink bomb and the explosions in the bathroom. She apparently also took a supply of phenolphthalein, which is used in chemistry as a pH indicator but works as a nasty laxative if you ingest it."

"A laxative!" Corinna yelped. She wrinkled her nose. "Yuck!"

Matty gestured to the bottles. "That bitch in the picture you showed us tried to feed the whole dorm laxatives? That's . . . that's . . ."

"Criminal?" Kamika supplied.

"Yeah," Matty agreed. "She should be arrested. Why hasn't she been arrested?"

"We still haven't identified her conclusively. But we're closing in on her," Lea said. "We know her first name, how she got into the dorm, and how she got the chemicals."

Corinna's eyes widened. "Oooh, what's her name?"

Kamika said, "We're pretty sure it's Mallory."

Corinna and Matty looked at each other and then shrugged.

"I don't know anyone named Mallory," Corinna said.

"Me either," Matty said. She frowned in disappointment.

"Neither do I," Evie said.

Kamika looked at Lea. "We should text Montgomery and update him. I'll do it." She extracted her phone from her pocket and tapped on the screen for a moment. "Done."

Montgomery and a university police officer arrived at the same time.

After explanations of the problem, the officer donned gloves and inspected the drinks. Finally, he took the box of drinks into evidence. The officer said, "If this stuff has been dosed with a laxative, your prankster just moved up to a whole new class of criminal. Trespassing and criminal mischief and vandalism are nothing compared to trying to sicken an entire dorm. If she was stupid enough to involve a professional delivery company, we can track her."

Montgomery advised Lea and Kamika to go to lunch while he went with the officer to give a statement regarding his investigation into the vandal's activities and identity. He turned over the surveillance video of the girl and his finding regarding the thefts from the chemistry building.

Lea and Kamika walked to the Dellonmarsh Café and ordered lunch. Lea selected a hamburger and a Dr Pepper while Kamika chose a grilled chicken salad and water.

As they sat down in a booth to eat, a nearby newspaper display stand caught Lea's attention. "Look at that! Does that headline say, 'History Department Investigation'?" She jumped up out of the booth to retrieve a copy and began to skim the article.

"What does it say?" asked Kamika. "Does it mention Dr. Richardson?"

"Yes. Hang on, give me a minute. It's what Montgomery contacted the department about after we talked to Erika. An anonymous source leaked to the reporter that the history department is investigating allegations of irregularities in record keeping for charitable fundraisers sponsored by the department. And here's a quote from Richardson. He says it's a witch hunt by people jealous of his position in the department, that the only irregularities involved an irresponsible graduate student losing some receipts. That liar! He's going to try to blame it all on Erika!" Lea slammed the paper down in anger and took a sip of her soda to calm herself.

"He's a slimy con artist. What do you expect? Hand me the paper. I want to read it."

Lea slid the paper across the table to Kamika.

Kamika read the article slowly as she ate. "This article is more evenhanded than I expected. There's no bias toward assuming Dr. Richardson is innocent. They rehash the situation with your stolen research too."

Lea grunted an acknowledgment.

Kamika's eyebrows came together. "What's this? Did you see this line?"

"What line?" Lea leaned across the table to see where Kamika was pointing.

"It says that additional allegations of research theft by Dr. Richardson have been reported to the newspaper," Kamika said.

"New allegations? Do you think Parker's friend Cam contacted them with his story? He said he would."

"Probably they're writing it up for publication. It may even be in the online version already. Check on your phone. In the meantime, I'll tell Montgomery that the investigation into the fundraising has been leaked. He may already know, since he knows everything, but I'll text him anyway." Kamika put down the newspaper and took out her phone.

"Send him a link to the online version of the article," Lea said. She began scrolling through her phone. "The online site doesn't have anything from Cam that I can find. Maybe it's still being written."

They finished their meal and gathered their trash as an employee approached them.

"Hi, did you find Mr. Fong's friend?" the woman asked as she began to clean the table.

Lea recognized her as the one who had told them to try looking for the suspect at Kinsolving. "Not yet. Her name is Mallory, we think, but we don't have a last name. Is Mr. Fong here?"

The woman paused in her cleaning. "No. He called in sick. He's the type who vanishes when trouble appears. Angry customers? He's nowhere to be found until we've dealt with the matter and everything is resolved. When everything's over but the handshakes, he reappears." She shook her head in disgust and went back to cleaning.

Lea noticed that Kamika was staring at nothing. "What's up? You look like you have something on your mind."

"I do. Let's call Parker. Maybe he heard from Cam. Also, we should let Erika know that she has our support."

Lea raised her eyebrows. "Those are all great reasons to call him. You could call him because you want to talk to him too. Finalize your date plans, maybe?"

Kamika giggled. "That too, but really all the other reasons first."

"So call him. We have time. We can take a walk in the quad under the trees." Lea pointed to the rectangle of space surrounded by dorms on four sides. A student or two sat on benches eating.

"Okay, let's go."

Lea and Kamika left the café and walked slowly around the quad under enormous, spreading oak trees. Kamika called and spoke to Parker for several minutes. Lea could hear most of the conversation, but after the call ended, Kamika clarified a few points.

"As you may have heard, Cam called Parker and they talked for a long time. Cam contacted the *Texan* staff and offered to give a statement about his situation with Dr. Richardson. Someone is writing the article now, and it should come out any time."

Lea nodded. "And has he heard from Erika?"

Kamika shook her head. "No. But he's going to call her."

"And your date?"

Kamika grinned and her eyes sparkled. "Still on for dinner Friday night: cozy Italian food, candlelight. It sounds wonderful. I'm looking forward to it. Enough about me; tell me about Patrick. Have you heard from him?"

Lea laughed. "I talk to him every day. And I'm holding his dog, Wally, hostage until he comes back to see me."

"Oh yeah. I forgot about the dog. If you wear that new red dress you bought next time you see him, he'll never want to travel for work again." Kamika waggled her eyebrows suggestively at Lea. "I have one word for you two: cohabitation."

Lea shook her head. "You know where I stand on that. I'm not moving in with someone unless I'm married to him. I've seen that blow up too many times for people. Living with someone is a huge commitment, but most people see it as a half commitment, not a whole commitment. They see it as easily undone. From my view, cohabitation is for people who either are afraid to commit or don't know how to commit completely. Either way, it's not for me. I don't want a halfway commitment."

"Lea, you are from a different century," Kamika said.

"That's fine with me," Lea said.

"Wear the red dress, and I'll bet he proposes."

Lea rolled her eyes dramatically. "What's next?"

"We kill time until we hear from Montgomery. He's the man with the plan."

Lea's phone pinged to indicate a text. "Speak of the devil," she said, glancing at her phone. "It's Montgomery. The police want statements about what we've witnessed in the dorm. We have to go to the UTPD station."

"Where is it?" Kamika asked. "Do we need to drive?"

"No, it's on campus here. We jump on the bus that runs around the edge of campus. Let me map it to be sure." Lea tapped on her screen, finding a map. "Taking the bus would definitely be faster than walking. The good news is that the bus stops right in front of Dellonmarsh. Let's catch a bus."

"Lead on," Kamika said, gesturing for Lea to go first on the sidewalk that led out of the quad.

As they left the quad, Lea noticed a news van pulling into the parking lot near the Dellonmarsh Café. She pointed at it. "The news found out about the possibly poisoned bottles of sports drink."

Kamika looked toward the van. "It's a big deal. What if the girls had opened the bottles and drunk that stuff?"

"The police are probably going to have to have a news conference about it. I'll bet that's why we're being called in to give statements. They need to make sure they've dotted the i's and crossed the t's on this one. The public is watching." Lea looked down the street. "Here comes our bus. Come on."

They sprinted the last few yards to the bus stop and caught the bus.

∺

Several hours later, Lea and Kamika left the police station and were picked up by Montgomery.

"Sorry that took so long, ladies." He maneuvered the van back toward I-35 to head north. "However, we're done here for the day. I had to wriggle out of doing an interview and standing with the police at the news conference about the poisoned drinks. Also, Dr. Dubois has asked all the teaching assistants to see him one by one tomorrow, so Perry shouldn't be suspicious when he's questioned. Mei is holding the dorm meeting tonight to make sure every girl in the dorm has seen the suspect's picture. She'll let me know if anyone recognizes Mallory."

Lea was disappointed. "Perry's the second person that could identify this criminal, but we still don't know this girl's full name. First, Kevin Fong from the Dellonmarsh Café won't talk and vanishes. Then we find Perry, and he won't talk either."

Montgomery shrugged. "Sometimes that's how a case goes. Not everyone wants to talk to me. Not everyone tells the truth. All in all, though, we did a good day's work. We got ahead of this perpetrator and prevented her sickening a lot of people."

Kamika clapped Lea on the shoulder. "Yeah. We did good work today." She turned back to Montgomery. "Now, how are we doing with that con artist Dr. Richardson? Someone leaked the fundraising story to the paper. Will that hurt the investigation?"

"It gives him more time to cover his tracks, but we've seen how he does that continually anyway. The minute anyone asked him a question about paperwork for the events, he would have realized that he was under scrutiny. Dr. Richardson followed a pattern with his research thefts. He probably has a game plan or pattern that he follows for embezzling schemes. If he's scammed multiple people, someone may have noticed irregularities. The news article may inspire them to step forward with information."

A wave of relief washed through Lea. "That's true. Cam is coming forward to help me. Someone else may come forward to support Erika." Lea's phone pinged again with a text. "It's Parker's friend Erika. She says she has someone who wants to talk to us about Dr. Richardson!"

CHAPTER 26

LEA CALLED ERIKA AND TALKED TO her for several minutes as Montgomery drove them north on I-35 through evening traffic. When she finished the call, she summarized it for Montgomery. "Good news. Erika's working with Dr. Heathe, a professor who specializes is pre-Columbian American history. Dr. Heathe and Erika were talking about the article that appeared today, and Erika was mad that Dr. Richardson was trying to place the blame on her. Anyway, Dr. Heathe said she knew how Erika felt because Richardson tried something similar with her."

"How similar?" Montgomery asked, keeping his eyes on traffic.

"Almost identical to the vanishing-receipt trick he pulled with Erika," Lea said. "But with one major difference. Dr. Heathe scanned all the receipts into a file and was carefully tracking expenses on a spreadsheet. When Dr. Richardson accused her of having lost the original receipt envelope, which conveniently disappeared from Dr. Richardson's desk, Dr. Heathe produced the scans. She hasn't trusted Dr. Richardson since then."

"Why didn't she say anything?" Kamika asked from the back seat of the van.

"She had no proof that Richardson did anything other than try to blame her for losing the receipts. Dr. Heathe thought Richardson had simply lost the receipts himself. She didn't realize it was a trick that could be used to skim money from the fundraiser. Also, Dr. Heathe was made a full, tenured professor this past summer. Before that, she was in no position to ask any questions about a tenured professor whom everyone else seemed to really like and trust. She thought Richardson wasn't as great a guy as everyone said, but she didn't think he was a criminal."

"What's she going to do?" Kamika asked. "Go to the police?"

Lea shook her head. "No. She doesn't have evidence of theft or fraud. She can present evidence of a pattern of behavior though. She's going to report it to the department chair."

Montgomery grinned at Lea. "That's another brick in the wall of evidence against Dr. Richardson. One accusation against a well-liked, charming guy can be brushed aside. Multiple accusations creating a pattern give people pause and make them take a second look. Slinging mud at his accusers won't get him very far now, Lea."

Kamika tapped Lea's shoulder. "That Cressida girl should get off your back soon. All this stuff coming out about Dr. Richardson should make her think twice about accusing you of lying."

"Cressida and Dr. Richardson's family are in for a shock," Lea said. "Cressida didn't believe the accusations at all. She thought she knew what kind of man he was. It will be even worse for his family. What do you do when you realize someone you love has done something terribly wrong?"

Montgomery gave Lea a sad look of commiseration in the mirror. "That's life sometimes, I'm afraid. Sometimes people we love fail us. Speaking from experience, when you get burned like that, learning to trust again takes time. I think it will be hardest on Richardson's kids. It's hard to trust humanity, to believe people are basically good when a parent fails you like that. His wife knows he's flawed, like every other person, even if she didn't see the depth of the flaws. Kids may still have parents on a pedestal. It takes wisdom to see and accept flaws in people we love and admire. Probably therapy would help the kids."

Kamika sat up straight, as if a thought had occurred to her. "I remember hearing about television news people years ago who worked with reporters who were sexual harassers, and none of them saw it. They couldn't wrap their brains around the accusations at first. It took time."

"Exactly," Montgomery said. "It will take time. Lea, aren't you off tomorrow morning, working on your thesis?"

"Yes. I should be free after lunch. I'll be on the UT campus meeting with Dr. Tremayne. Also, she said she'd update me about the investigation into the theft of my work, if she can. According to the university's rules, the committee convened to investigate my complaint is required to present a report of its findings soon. She filed the complaint on my behalf, so she'll get a copy of the report."

⁂

Thursday morning, Lea went to Garrison Hall and knocked on Dr. Tremayne's office door frame. The door to the tiny room was open, giving her a view of Dr. Tremayne sitting at her desk.

Dr. Tremayne looked up from her laptop, tucked her short dark hair behind one ear, and smiled at Lea. "Come in. Take a chair. I have news for you!"

Lea opened her backpack and removed a package. "This is from Kamika. It's the bright yellow cloth to cover that wall and brighten up the space."

Dr. Tremayne accepted the package. "Wonderful! Please thank Kamika for me."

"I will." Lea sat in one of the two chairs across the desk from Dr. Tremayne and gestured to the wall behind her. "How does the office feel since we improved the atmosphere?"

"Great. It's not so claustrophobic anymore." Dr. Tremayne cleared her throat and picked up a packet of papers. "The research integrity committee issued its preliminary report on the situation with Dr. Richardson. Here's a copy. Take a look at it. The research integrity officer asked your other advisor's widow to look for evidence of your work in his home office. Dr. Zarolt's widow sorted all his papers and found several early outlines and a draft of your thesis. The committee, with evidence of the work you did in hand, concluded that Dr. Richardson did publish your work as his own work without crediting you at all. This is a distinct violation of procedures regarding research publication for the department."

Lea picked up the report. "Oh, thank God. What happens next?"

"We have to comment on the report before it's finalized. So does Dr. Richardson. Given the findings, I can't imagine anything Richardson says, short of a full apology and accepting responsibility, will matter. Then, the legal affairs people will review the report before it goes to the

Provost, who will issue the final determination. Finally, all of the academic journals where the article appeared will be notified to issue a correction listing you as the main author on the article."

"That's a relief! We found another student who says Dr. Richardson did the same thing to him several years ago. His thesis was rejected by Dr. Richardson, and he had to leave the program after the research integrity officer found no grounds for a full investigation."

Dr. Tremayne looked shocked. "Really? That's terrible!"

A wave of sadness passed over Lea. "It gets worse. The student slumped into a depression and couldn't get into another university's program. He's telling his story to the newspaper now, hoping to help me and get himself back on track by clearing his name."

Dr. Tremayne drummed her fingers on her desk thoughtfully. "If he couldn't get into another program, Dr. Richardson may have told other programs not to accept him. Richardson's been around a long time and knows a lot of people at other history programs around the country. He could have blacklisted that student."

"Blacklisted? If that happened, do you think we could undo it now that the truth is coming out?" Lea asked, leaning forward on the desk in front of her.

"I could make some calls to find out. I'll need the student's name."

Lea opened her phone and checked her messages from Parker. "His full name is Cameron Stewart."

Dr. Tremayne jotted down the name on a yellow tablet of paper that she kept on her desk. "I'll see what I can find out."

"What about here? Could the university review the situation?"

"I'm not sure about the rules on that," Dr. Tremayne said. "Once they close a case, I don't know what it takes to reopen it, especially with no proof. I'll have to research it."

Lea nodded, a little disappointed. "Even if we can't get him back here, I hope we can get his reputation cleared so that he can enter another program. I hate to see his entire career ended by what Dr. Richardson did."

Dr. Tremayne smiled at Lea. "We'll do what we can. In the meantime, let's review the report from the committee. I've printed copies for each of us. We need to go through it to make sure it's accurate." She handed Lea a copy of the document, and they spent the next hour reviewing it before moving on and discussing a few areas in Lea's thesis that needed improvement.

Lea said, "I'll work on these sections we discussed. Do you think I'm on track? If the committee clears me completely, will I be able to defend my thesis in the spring as planned?"

"Yes, Lea, you've done beautiful work. You knew your topic and started your research earlier than most students. You don't have much left to do. You could easily finish in December and not wait until spring."

Lea collected her papers. "I have a lot to think about. My next steps, mainly. When I started the program, I wanted to get a job as a historian. But I couldn't find any open internships or part-time positions in a museum that paid as well as Montgomery did at Bad Vibes Removal Services. So I took the job with Montgomery to help pay for my master's classes. I love working with Kamika, but it's time to start looking for another position. I had scheduled searching for a new position for the spring. My whole timetable needs to shift."

Dr. Tremayne gave Lea a reassuring smile. "Ah, I understand. Change is hard, but it's what you've been working so hard to accomplish, isn't it?"

"Yes, it is. I do want to be a historian."

Dr. Tremayne closed her laptop. "Good." She glanced at the time. "Well, it's time for me to go. Call me if you have any questions about those sections that we discussed."

Lea rose from her chair. "Thank you, I will. Good-bye." Lea picked up her things and left the office. As she walked down the hall, she decided to call Montgomery and see if she was needed.

Twenty minutes later, Lea joined Montgomery and Kamika at a taco joint on the edge of campus.

"How was your morning?" Lea asked Kamika.

Kamika frowned at Lea's hair, back in the Suebian knot, but didn't comment on it. "We talked to Mei. No one in the dorm meeting last night recognized the girl in the video. Then we talked with that rat Perry in Dr. Dubois's office." Kamika grimaced. "He was a real jerk. A UTPD detective showed up too."

"What did Perry say?" asked Lea.

"He denied knowing anything about the stolen materials at first," Montgomery said with a chuckle. "Perry said our scans were falsified and that he didn't know anyone named Mallory."

"What did Dr. Dubois say?" Lea asked indignantly. "He must know we didn't invent that scan."

Montgomery nodded, taking a bite of his taco. "Dr. Dubois supported us. Then the detective told Perry he was digging an even deeper hole for himself, read him his Miranda rights, and said that he'd better help us or he could face charges for aiding and abetting in criminal activities, like the attempted poisoning of over one hundred students. He told Perry that he could get a reduced sentence, like probation instead of jail time, for aiding the police."

Kamika nodded. "That did it. Perry spilled his guts. Then Dr. Dubois suspended Perry from his position, and the detective took Perry to the police station to make a formal statement."

Lea looked from Kamika to Montgomery. "He spilled everything? Does that mean we have Mallory's last name?"

Montgomery took a gulp of his iced tea. "Name, address, phone number. Mallory Janet Carroll. The police are getting a warrant to search her place and a warrant for her arrest as we speak. And I verified that her address is the same as Mr. Kevin Fong. He is her uncle by marriage."

Lea sighed and leaned back in her chair. "Hooray! That's great."

Montgomery's phone rang. He glanced at the screen and frowned. "Excuse me, ladies, while I answer this." He walked away from the table and outside the restaurant.

Lea and Kamika went back to eating their tacos.

Lea was about to tell Kamika about her morning with Dr. Tremayne when Montgomery reappeared at the table.

"Lea, Kamika, hurry up and finish eating. We need to go." Montgomery's mouth was in a flat line and a wrinkle had appeared between his eyes.

"I'm ready," Lea said, hurriedly gathering up her trash as Kamika did the same. "What's up?"

The worried look in Montgomery's eye deepened. "Mallory Carroll has been missing since the day before yesterday. The police found evidence of fire accelerants in her room. She may be planning something worse than sickening an entire dorm."

CHAPTER 27

L EA GASPED.

"What can we do?" Kamika asked.

Montgomery led them out the restaurant door. "The police will cover all the usual methods for finding her, monitoring her financial data and phone usage. While they do that, we're going to scan her room to see if we can find evidence of where she might be before she does something even more dangerous."

"Do we have permission to scan her room?" asked Lea.

Montgomery shot her a look of determination. "She's been living with her uncle, Kevin Fong. I have the address. By the time I'm done talking to him, he'll give us permission."

Lea nodded, not surprised by his answer. Montgomery was famed for his verbal powers of persuasion. She glanced at Kamika, who giggled nervously as they followed Montgomery back to his van.

Twenty minutes later, they arrived on a residential street north of the campus. The homes, all similar-looking 1950s tract housing, were small and old but well-cared for, in spite of the crumbling curbs and sidewalks that the city needed to repair. Kevin Fong's house had a white picket fence around the yard with a posted Beware of Dog sign on the gate at the front walk.

Kamika pointed at the sign. "How are we going to get past that?"

Montgomery glanced at the sign and then studied the yard. "I don't see a dog. Maybe it's in the house. You two wait here. I'll talk to him alone first. Once I have permission to scan her room, I'll call you inside." He pushed on the latch holding the gate closed and entered the yard. Montgomery was halfway up the front walk to the door when furious barking ensued. Suddenly he was surrounded by four dark brown dachshunds.

Kamika stifled a yelp. "Are you okay?"

Montgomery leaned down and petted the head of a dog that was standing on its hind legs trying to jump on his leg. The dog's tail was wagging like a whip cord. "I'm fine. They're friendly." He gently knocked the dog off his leg and proceeded to the front door, which opened before he reached it.

Kevin Fong stood at the door, apparently alerted by the yapping pack of dogs. "Who are you? What do you want? If you're selling something, I'm not buying it." He looked beyond Montgomery and spotted Lea and Kamika. "Oh, you people," he said flatly as he recognized them. A resigned look came across his face.

Montgomery introduced himself and asked to speak to Mr. Fong inside the house.

Kevin Fong reluctantly let him enter.

Kamika nodded with satisfaction. "If he can get into the house, he can get permission to scan the room." She peered over the fence at the small dogs now gathered around the gate sniffing at her and Lea through the slatted fence. Their tails were a wagging blur. "Aren't you little cuties?" She petted one pointed nose that poked out.

Lea laughed as one dog licked her hand through the fence. "They make a great alarm system but don't do much to defend the property."

Kamika squatted down on the sidewalk and continued petting the dogs. She cocked her head up at Lea. "Maybe that's all he needs, an alarm system. If someone got bitten delivering a package, that would be bad." She stood up and studied the house. "This place could use decorating help, some color in the yard, maybe flowers or a crape myrtle."

Lea turned an eye to the property. "It's okay. All the bushes are trimmed off the house. The yard is mowed and edged. The house paint isn't peeling or anything."

Kamika raised a critical eyebrow. "Yes, it's neat. But it could really shine with a few touches here and there."

Lea laughed and shook her head. "You can offer him decorating tips some other time. His exterior decorating isn't important. Right now, we need to scan Mallory's room."

Kamika put her hands on her hips. "Decorating is always important." She gestured toward the house. "This is the face he shows the world. And it's bland!"

After running her eyes over the house again, Lea shrugged nonchalantly. "It's haunted too, but I don't suppose that bothers him either."

Kamika froze, and then she took a step backward. "Haunted? Are you kidding me?"

"At the corner of the house, an old woman is digging in the dirt, planting something. She must have loved gardening during her lifetime." Lea nodded to the left to indicate which corner of the house.

"Does she look friendly?" Kamika asked warily.

"She doesn't even notice us. She's very old, very wrinkled, and wearing clothes in a 1940s-farmer's-wife style. Maybe she lived here when the house was first built, or lived with a son or daughter in her old age."

Kamika took a deep breath and exhaled slowly. "I prefer the ghosts that leave us alone."

The front door opened and Montgomery appeared in the doorway. "Get the equipment bags, ladies. We have work to do."

Kamika nodded with satisfaction. "See. He always gets his way."

Lea and Kamika grabbed the equipment from the van and entered the gate, being careful not to release any of the dachshunds. They entered the house and followed Montgomery and Mr. Fong down a short wooden-floored hall to a room at the back of the house.

Lea noticed that the room, a plain guest room with a few textbooks and teenage girl's shoes and clothes scattered around it, smelled vaguely of gasoline.

"If you really think this might help find her, I'm willing to try anything," Mr. Fong was saying to Montgomery. "We need to find her before she does something that can't be undone. My brother and his wife will be here soon. I want to be able to tell them that we've tried every avenue to find Mallory."

"She's your brother's daughter?" asked Montgomery.

"Yes," Mr. Fong replied. "Well, not biologically. My brother married her mother when she was two. He's raised her and loves her as his own."

"Do you have a photo of her?" Montgomery asked, glancing around the room.

"Yes. I took of picture of her with her parents a few weeks ago. It's still on my phone." He removed his phone from his pocket and thumbed the screen. "Here it is." He held up a photo of a tall Caucasian girl standing between her brunette mother and a man with Asian features who resembled Mr. Fong. The girl wore a purple hoodie and had hair that was dark at the roots but faded to bleached blond at the ends.

"I need a copy of that picture," Montgomery said.

Mr. Fong forwarded the picture to Montgomery and then stared at the photo. "Her parents are very protective of her. Too protective, I think. I told them that they should send her to school, but they insisted on homeschooling her because they didn't want her to be teased over her height. She's always been very tall, five feet eleven inches now, but five feet five at age eleven. They didn't send her to public school until her junior year of high school. And then she was so much younger than the other students, she had a hard time making friends." Fong paused to take a ragged breath.

"How young is she?" Lea asked.

"She's only fifteen years old. She was fourteen when she graduated from high school last spring. She really wanted to come to college here at UT. She applied but wasn't accepted." A worried look filled Mr. Fong's eyes. "She doesn't know how to handle people who . . . who . . . well, who are dishonest or who cheat. She doesn't understand how to deal with differing levels of intelligence. A few weeks ago, she saw a girl she knew in high school at UT. She's angry that a girl that she considers to be dishonest got into the school when she didn't. The knowledge seems to have pushed her over the edge."

Kamika looked up from unpacking her equipment bag, surprised. "If she graduated from high school that young, she must be really smart. Why wasn't she accepted to the university?"

Mr. Fong suppressed a sigh. "She's a bright girl, but she graduated young by doing the homeschool curriculum year round. She finished grade levels quicker. She isn't a genius or anything. She graduated in the top twelve percent of her class with very good grades. But that wasn't good enough for automatic admission to the university. She was advised to go to another college for a year or two, and then reapply as a transfer student if she really wanted to attend UT."

"Is that what she's doing?" Lea asked.

Mr. Fong nodded. "She's enrolled in Austin Community College."

"And why is she living with you?" Montgomery asked.

"She wanted to be here. In Austin. She could have gone to community college near her home in Dallas, but she insisted on coming here. She knows a lot of UT students take basic classes at ACC because it's cheaper and because the credits transfer easily." Mr. Fong paused. "I guess she wanted her goal in sight. So I agreed to let her stay with me while she's going to school. She's too young to be on her own." He ran a hand distractedly through his dark hair. "We have to find her!"

A perplexed look crossed Kamika's face. "If she lives with you and doesn't attend the university, why did someone tell us that they thought she lived in a dorm on campus? What's it called? Kinsolving?"

Mr. Fong raised his eyebrows. "Oh, my wife's niece, Fleur, lives in Kinsolving. She is a freshman. Mallory likes to visit her."

"What do you know about Mallory sneaking into the Dellonmarsh at night via the café?" asked Montgomery.

Mr. Fong put one arm across his chest and put his other hand over his mouth. "She was supposed to be spending the night with Fleur. I think she borrowed my keys to the café and made copies. I heard that the door was found unlocked one morning. She must have forgotten to relock it." Tears came into his eyes. "I had no idea that she was harassing those students. I did know that she was angry. She was visiting Fleur when she saw a girl that she knew in high school, someone she considers a cheater. Seeing her at UT made Mallory so mad that she stomped around the house in an angry funk for days. Maybe that girl lives in Dellonmarsh."

Montgomery stood studying the room. "We need to find that girl. She may be Mallory's target. Where did Mallory go to high school?"

"Turner High School," Mr. Fong said.

"We'll find out if any students in Dellonmarsh went to that high school. Give me a moment to text the head resident there." Montgomery took out his phone and sent a message. Then he looked at Mr. Fong with sympathy in his eyes. "The good news is that Mallory hasn't directly hurt anyone, yet. She's young enough that you may be able to keep this in juvenile court. She's already going to be in trouble for paying a teaching assistant to steal chemicals for her and for attempting to feed laxatives to the entire dorm. But we need to stop her before she does something worse, especially something involving the gasoline I smell in here." He looked at Lea and Kamika. "Are we ready to scan for sound patterns?"

Lea nodded, holding the sound scanner. "I'm ready."

"Me too," Kamika said, holding the tablet in her hand.

"Then let's see what we can find. Lea, you scan the left side of the room. I'll scan the right side." Montgomery picked up his scanner and they went to work, slowly passing the scanner in even lines up and down the walls.

While Lea and Montgomery scanned the walls, Kamika monitored the incoming data. When the scanning was finished, Montgomery and Lea joined Kamika to watch as the data analysis processed.

"I see a few words here and there," Kamika said, "but nothing that looks helpful yet."

"Wait, here's something coming in," Lea said. Then she inhaled sharply as the meaning of the words on the screen hit her. "Oh, damn!"

Montgomery looked up from the tablet and met Mr. Fong's eyes. "This looks bad. Very bad."

CHAPTER 28

"WHAT IS IT?" ASKED MR. FONG.

Montgomery cleared his throat. "We've found a conversation that got loud. Maybe a phone conversation because what I see is one voice, not two. She said the words 'brand her' and 'cheater' and 'show the world.' We also have the words 'newsworthy' and 'kill.' That's all we can get. Those are the words she said emphatically, loudly, while she was talking. The rest of the conversation wasn't loud enough to leave a pattern."

Mr. Fong went pale and sat down on the edge of the bed in the room. "She wouldn't kill anyone. It must mean something else."

"I'd love to believe that, Mr. Fong." Montgomery handed the tablet back to Kamika and looked grimly at Mr. Fong. "Do you have any idea who she might have been talking to on the phone? Someone knows what she's planning. If we can identify that person, maybe we can find out where she is and stop her."

Mr. Fong rubbed his hands over his face and cast despondent eyes at the ceiling. "I don't know who her friends are. She doesn't really have any." His eyes widened, and he jumped up from the bed. "Except my wife's niece, Fleur. If anyone knows anything, it's Fleur."

Montgomery stood with his hands on his hips. "Right. We need to move. Lea and Kamika, go to Dellonmarsh and keep your eyes open for Mallory. Find Mei. See if she identified a student who went to a Turner High School in the Dallas area who lives in the dorm. Let Mei know that Mallory Carroll has an accelerant that smells like gasoline. Let her know Mallory might be dangerous. Tell her to inform the residents to be on the alert. I'm going to update the police, and then Mr. Fong and I are going to find Fleur and see what she can tell us." He looked at Fong. "Is that okay with you?"

Fong nodded. "Yes. Let's go now."

Lea and Kamika took Montgomery's van while Montgomery went with Mr. Fong in his car. After parking in the garage off Guadalupe Street, the women ran through crowds of students to the dorm on Dean Keeton Street. It was only two-thirty in the afternoon, and lots of students were still attending classes for the day.

Kamika was huffing and clutching her side as they climbed the stone steps to the door on the back of the building. Sweat was trickling down Lea's temple as she found her phone in her pocket and called Mei, who answered quickly.

"Mei, it's Lea. Kamika and I are at the door to Dellonmarsh on the Dean Keeton side of the building. We need to talk to you. Can you let us inside?"

In a moment, Mei pushed open the door and ushered them into the lobby.

Taking in their hot and breathless appearances, Mei asked in a worried voice, "What's going on? What happened?"

Lea explained about Mallory Carroll and the need to find a girl linked to Turner High School in the Dallas area.

"I got Montgomery's text. I haven't found who it could be yet. Each room has a sign outside the door with the residents' names and a map showing their hometowns within their home states. Most of them are from Texas. We'll have to access their records or ask them each directly to find out what high schools they attended. I don't have access to their records, and it will take too long to go door to door, besides being pointless, since a lot of residents are still in class. A third of the girls probably come from around Dallas/Fort Worth." Mei clasped her hands nervously in front of her.

Kamika grabbed Mei's shoulder. "Can't we use the dorm group chat? Ask who went to Turner High School?"

Mei's face brightened. "Yes! I'll do that." She took her phone from her pocket and starting typing rapidly. "There. I've asked for anyone who attended Turner High School or who knows if their roommate or neighbor attended to contact me immediately."

Seconds later, Mei's phone buzzed. She read the message. "It's Belinda. She says she thinks Gwen Carter went there."

Kamika cast Lea a wry look. "Well, that makes sense. Mallory's doing this because she's mad at a cheater who got admitted to the university, and we've been told Gwen has issues with academic honesty."

Mei asked, "This Mallory is mad because Gwen got admitted to the university? Why?"

"Because Mallory wasn't admitted. She's furious that cheating got Gwen to the top of the class and allowed her to be automatically admitted. Mallory wouldn't cheat and was only in the top twelve percent of her class. She wasn't admitted."

Lea wrinkled her nose in puzzlement. "Didn't Gwen recognize the picture of Mallory? Did you ask her at the dorm meeting?"

Mei shook her head. "She didn't speak up. Who knows, she may not have even spoken to Mallory in high school. Maybe Mallory knew who Gwen was, but Gwen didn't know Mallory. That happens at large high schools." Mei gestured for them to follow her. "Come on. I can finally see the light at the end of the tunnel for this whole mess. Maybe once we catch Mallory, Gwen will be less moody. She's been angry and suspicious of everyone since someone, probably this Mallory person, dumped shampoo on her bed."

Lea followed, glancing around the lobby as a few girls walked through. "Where are we going? We need to warn Gwen that she could be in danger."

Mei trotted toward the hall to the stairs. "We're going to Gwen's room. She lives on the third floor. Let's knock on her door. If she isn't there, I'll send her a message."

Kamika called after them, clutching the cramp in her side. "You two go ahead and run up three flights of stairs. I'm done running. My side is killing me. I'm going to let Montgomery know that we think Gwen Carter is the target. He can let the police know. If she's in class somewhere, they can find her and protect her. I'll wait down here in the lobby."

"Good idea!" Lea said before she followed Mei up the stairs.

A few minutes later, Lea and Mei found Kamika sitting on a chair in the lobby.

"Well?" asked Kamika.

Mei shook her head. "She's not in her room. She must be in class."

"Montgomery or the police will find her. We can wait here and catch her when she comes back to her room," Lea said, dropping down onto a chair near Kamika.

Mei sighed. "I need to report all this to my supervisor. Do you mind waiting here? I'll be back in a minute. And I'm going to message Gwen directly."

"Go ahead. We'll watch for Gwen." Lea said.

Mei crossed the lobby and vanished into her first-floor suite.

Lea and Kamika faced opposite directions from positions across the lobby from each other, each watching different entry doors to the lobby. Lots of girls came and went, but Gwen wasn't among them.

Two hours later, Gwen still hadn't appeared. Mei, Lea, and Kamika sat in chairs around the dorm watching the entry doors.

Lea turned to Kamika and called out across the dorm. "Kamika, isn't Gwen's chemistry lab in the evening, six to ten p.m. on Thursday? That's why she wasn't there when her room was vandalized."

Kamika crossed the lobby. "I think you're right." She checked the time. "It's after four-thirty now. Gwen may not come back here for hours. She might get dinner and go right to her lab."

Lea watched as more residents passed through the lobby. "That means she'll be walking back to the dorm tonight in the dark after ten p.m. She'll be an easy target."

At that moment, Mei called out to them, gesturing for them to join her. Lea and Kamika walked over to Mei, who led them into her room and closed the door. "I got word from my boss that the police are guarding Gwen. I've been assured that they will escort her to class and then back to the dorm tonight"

Lea blew out her breath in relief. "Thank goodness."

"Sit down," Mei said, gesturing to her pale-blue wing-back chair, rocking chair, and pastel-print loveseat.

Lea and Kamika sat down on the loveseat while Mei took the chair.

"I've been thinking," Lea said, "and something puzzles me. We know that Mallory broke in at night. She probably wrote the ketchup message in the stairwell. She caused explosive banging noises in the bathrooms with sodium metal. We have video of her setting up a stink bomb. We know she sent the laxative-tainted drinks. Given that Gwen's room was one of the ones targeted, she probably vandalized the rooms, spilling shampoo on the beds."

"Yes," Mei said. "That makes sense."

Lea asked in a perplexed voice, "So how did she know things to write in notes to put under doors? She doesn't live here. Some of the notes were specific, mentioning incidents that happened in the dorm, like Evie being reprimanded for being too loud. And why didn't Gwen get a note under her door? And why vandalize the piano and the study nook. Gwen didn't play piano as far as we know."

"I don't know," Mei said. "Maybe damaging those was part of a general attack on the dorm as a whole because Gwen lives here, part of a campaign of harassment. Someone could have told her what to put in the letters. Or if she accessed our group chat somehow, she would know a lot of things about happenings in the dorm."

Lea stared thoughtfully out the window toward the quad. "I guess."

Kamika leaned on the arm of the loveseat with her hand under her chin. "Maybe Mallory decided that everyone here is a cheater. Or maybe she didn't think it through and chose the piano because it was easy to get to."

Lea tapped her foot impatiently on the floor. "It's a possibility, but getting upstairs to damage the third-floor study nook wasn't easy. Besides, damaging the piano and study nook mainly hurt Izzie." She paused, and pieces of the puzzle snapped into place in her brain. "But what if Mallory isn't behind *all* of it? What if someone else did the notes and the piano? And the study nook damage! Those all happened during the day. Wouldn't it be more likely that a resident was behind those events?"

"Why would a resident do that?" asked Mei.

"For the same reason we've been hearing from all the girls. To throw someone off and hurt their grades. Izzie was really upset by the damage to the piano. It threw off her practice schedule. And she loved to study in the study nook and received a mean note. Suppose she's in an English class or math class with someone who wants to get a better grade than she does. The notes under the doors could be that same kind of thing. Or suppose someone thinks Izzie is the one who spilled the shampoo and made all the night noises. What if a resident is trying to get revenge but settled on the wrong person as the guilty party?" Lea wriggled in her seat, full of anxious energy.

Kamika and Mei stared at her for a moment.

Mei jumped up. "Let me get the notes." She opened her laptop and found a file. "I have photos of each note." She read them quickly. "You're right. These are all very specifically aimed at the resident who received them and intentionally hurtful."

"Who do we know who will do anything to get the best grade, even cheat in lab? Someone who is angry and suspicious of everyone right now?" Lea asked, raising both eyebrows at them.

"Are you saying Gwen might be behind the notes? And the piano and study nook damage?" Mei asked.

Lea leaned forward. "You said yourself that Gwen's been mad and suspicious of everyone. What if she thought someone in the dorm was trying to psych her out and damage her grades with the noises and shampoo on her bed, so she retaliated? She'd already argued with Izzie over her piano playing in the living room. Look at the timeline. A few days after arguing with Izzie, Gwen found shampoo spilled on her bed. She might conclude Izzie or another student in class with her was behind it. Since she can't be sure who it was, she sends multiple mean notes. Then, as Mallory continues her noise attacks, Gwen decides it's someone on her floor, maybe Izzie, so she damages the study nook and piano that Izzie likes to use."

"We have no proof," Mei said, "only speculation. Besides, why go looking for more suspects when we have one guilty party already identified?"

"Because Mallory didn't have the inside information needed to write the notes."

Mei rubbed both hands over her eyes. "That doesn't mean Gwen did those other things. It could have been anyone."

"True," Lea said, biting her lip. Her hair, in its Suebian knot, was coming undone after all the running she had done. She took out the rubber band holding it in place and let her dark, heavy hair fall down around her shoulders. Suddenly, an overwhelming sense of urgency filled her mind, making her skin tingle.

Mei changed the subject. "I saw that Dr. Mortimer Richardson is being investigated over missing funds from some of the department fundraisers he organized."

Kamika sat up straighter. "You bet he is. That man is as crooked as they come. Stealing Lea's work was only the tip of the iceberg."

Mei listened with interest as Kamika outlined what she knew about the incidents involving Dr. Richardson. "Cam's story should be coming out in the papers shortly. And when Montgomery finishes his investigation into the fundraisers, I'd be surprised if he doesn't find evidence of embezzlement."

"The Richardson family and Cressida will be even more heartbroken." Mei took out her phone and made a note. "I'll need to check on Cressida."

Lea glanced at the time on her phone as the feeling of anxiety in the pit of her stomach increased. She tried to shrug it off but decided she needed to move. She needed to leave Mei's room, though she didn't know why. Maybe the why would present itself if she left the room. "Come on, Kamika. It's almost five o'clock. Let's check in with Montgomery. He must be up to something since we haven't heard from him. There's nothing else we can do here." She got up from the loveseat.

"I'll walk you out. I need to get an early dinner and get some studying done." Mei extracted her lanky body from her chair and led the way out her door.

Lea, Kamika, and Mei crossed the lobby together and walked out the doors into the quad. As Lea scanned the area around them, searching for a reason for her worry, her feeling that something was horribly wrong grew stronger. While walking down the wide stairs leading to the grassy area of the quad, Lea suddenly stopped. She felt as if she'd been tapped on the shoulder and told to look straight ahead. What she saw made her grab Kamika's arm.

"What is it?" Kamika asked, looking at Lea in surprise.

"Do you see what I see?" Lea nodded in front of them.

Kamika and Mei looked out into the quad.

"What?" Mei asked.

Lea spoke softly, trying to remain calm. "There. In the middle of the quad. By the statue of Diana the Huntress. The tall girl. She was walking in a weird pattern. It looked like she was spilling something out of a water bottle, but she's stopped now. She's wearing a purple hoodie."

As they watched, the girl bent down, holding some kind of device in her hand. In an instant, flames erupted around her.

CHAPTER 29

THE TALL GIRL SCREAMED AND JUMPED back from the flames. The sleeve of her jacket was on fire. She waved her arm wildly, trying to put it out, but only managed to fan the flames.

"Kamika, call 9-1-1!" Lea yelled as she sprinted toward the girl. As she ran, Lea could hear the sounds of other students screaming, "Fire!" She reached Mallory, hitting her full force and knocking her to the ground. The flames had spread up her sleeve and around her back.

Two other students appeared from somewhere and helped Lea roll Mallory and beat out the flames.

Behind her, Lea heard the sound of a fire extinguisher being used. She turned to see Mei and another student putting out the fire in the grass. Mallory let out a whimper, and Lea returned her attention to the girl, now lying on the ground with charred pieces of purple cloth covering the ground around her.

"Are you Mallory?" Lea asked as she helped the girl carefully remove the remnants of her smoldering jacket and drop the smoking material to the ground. Lea could see that the girl's left forearm was badly burned, the skin reddened and blistering in the less-damaged areas but charred and blackened in spots. The short-sleeved shirt that she had been wearing under the jacket was mostly intact.

The girl looked at her, shock and pain lining her face. "How do you know my name?" she gasped, biting back a moan.

"Stay calm. Help is coming. We've been looking for you. Your uncle is very worried about you, and your parents are on the way."

"Uncle Kevin called my parents? Oh, my arm hurts! I want to go home. I want my mom." Mallory burst into tears.

The sound of sirens filled the air. A fire truck drove into the quad, followed by a police car. In seconds, several firemen and police officers exited the vehicles.

Lea raised her hand and yelled, "Come over here! She's been burned!"

Lea backed away as the paramedics took over and began examining Mallory. She looked around for Kamika and Mei and spotted them standing together a few yards away. Mei was still holding the heavy fire extinguisher, which was pulling her narrow body into an s-curve as she counter-balanced its weight. Lea walked over to join them as she heard someone yell her name. She turned to see Montgomery, Mr. Fong, and a dark-haired girl running across the quad.

Mr. Fong and the girl ran right by Lea to join the paramedics by Mallory.

Montgomery jogged, moving rapidly in spite of his bulky size, to Lea, Kamika, and Mei. He pointed at the girl with Mr. Fong. "Fleur thought Mallory might be here, so we came to try to find her. I see we were too late. What happened?"

Lea explained. As she finished, paramedics wheeled a stretcher bearing Mallory Carroll toward a waiting ambulance. Mr. Fong and Fleur walked behind it. As the crowd of people in the quad moved out of the stretcher's path, Lea caught a glimpse of the burned area on the ground. She could make out words, seared in black letters two feet tall, "GWEN CARTER IS A CHEATER."

Montgomery, seeing the words, said, "Fleur told us that Mallory was going to make a sign saying Gwen was a cheater. She didn't know about the gasoline. Fleur said Mallory asked her not to tell Mr. Fong what she was doing, that her parents would be upset if they found out. Mallory wasn't planning to kill anyone. She wanted to let everyone know Gwen was a cheater, and she wanted it to make the news. The laxative-laden drinks got news attention but didn't send the message she wanted. No one connected that to cheating. She decided to do this instead." He shook his head and looked at Lea, frowning. "Are you okay? You're holding your hand against you like it hurts."

Lea looked down at her left hand, which she was cradling unconsciously in her right hand. A blister had formed on her thumb and index finger. "I must have burned myself when I grabbed Mallory to put the fire out. She was on fire."

Montgomery took her hand and examined it carefully. "This doesn't look bad, but I'm sure it hurts. You should get it checked."

"I hadn't noticed it until now. The adrenaline rush must have covered the pain," Lea said, realizing that the pain in her hand had become intense. "I need to put some burn cream on it, maybe something with a painkiller in it." She winced. "Ouch!"

A police officer standing nearby heard her and said, "Are you injured, miss?"

Lea replied, "It's nothing serious."

The officer raised both eyebrows and called out to a fireman who came over to examine Lea's fingers. Lea declined the opportunity to ride in an ambulance to the hospital, saying she could treat the minor burn herself. Her hand hurt, but she had burned her fingers accidently before while getting a hot pan out of the oven. She knew the pain would subside.

The fireman who was examining her hand winked at her and nodded his understanding. "I would do the same thing, miss."

As the fireman left her, Lea turned to see Cressida and a handful of other Dellonmarsh residents, including Evie and Natalia, standing nearby, watching the activity. Lea met Cressida's eyes, and Cressida dropped her eyes to the ground. Lea was surprised but wary as Cressida suddenly walked toward her with a purposeful stride.

Cressida stopped in front of Lea and stared a moment. "I . . . I talked to Paisley Richardson." She gulped air and swallowed. "Paisley said you were right. She said that every day they learn a little more about the awful things her dad was doing. At first, she thought it was all lies made up by jealous people, but she heard her mom and dad fighting over money. Her mom accused her dad of taking it from the fundraisers he ran. Dr. Richardson had told Mrs. Richardson that the money was from a bonus or a dividend off an investment, but when she tried to trace it, she couldn't. She knew he had lied. Paisley thinks her dad lied about a lot of things." She shifted her eyes to her shoes again as a tear rolled down one cheek.

"I am really sorry for the Richardsons. I'm sure they're in a lot of pain right now. It's hard when someone you love and trust fails you like that." Lea patted Cressida's arm. "You're a good friend to Paisley. She's going to need your support."

Cressida nodded and wiped her face. "I'm sorry about the water balloons. I shouldn't have dropped them on you. I didn't know . . ." Her voice trailed off. "Umm, I have to go."

Lea nodded and turned to find a police officer waiting to speak to her.

∺

Several hours later, Lea, Kamika, and Montgomery were ushered to a booth in a country-kitchen-style diner. Giving statements about the fire to the police had taken hours, and they were all starved. Mei, who had been collected to give a statement as well, went back to the dorm to explain to the girls what had happened after finishing with the police.

Lea, Kamika, and Montgomery ordered drinks and began to study their menus.

Lea sat with her hand bandaged. She'd smeared a thick layer of burn cream on her thumb and index finger before wrapping them in gauze. As she read the menu, trying to decide between chicken-fried steak and chicken-fried chicken, she heard a familiar voice and looked up to see Dr. Tremayne arriving.

Montgomery stood and quickly kissed Dr. Tremayne, stooping to reach her since she was considerably shorter than he was, before sliding over and making room for her on his side of the booth.

Dr. Tremayne raised her eyebrows, which vanished under her thick bangs, and nodded toward Lea's bandaged hand. "I heard there was a fire, but I thought the one who set it was the only one injured. How bad is it?"

Lea raised her hand. "I'll live. It hurts, but it will heal."

"How did it happen?" Dr. Tremayne asked.

Kamika jumped into the conversation. "Don't ask her. I'll tell you. Lea ran over and knocked down the little idiot fire-starter, who had set herself on fire. Lea put the flames out and kept the girl from burning to death."

Lea shook her dark hair over her face, embarrassed. "I wasn't the only one. Several students helped me." She mumbled under her breath, "Not a big deal."

Kamika squared her shoulders. "Not a big deal? You saved her life!"

Dr. Tremayne smiled kindly at Lea, and, noting her embarrassment, she turned to Montgomery. "I guess you caught the Dellonmarsh prankster then."

"Yes, but we were too late to stop her from injuring herself." Montgomery explained how they tracked down Mallory Carroll. "Her burns weren't bad enough to send her to the burn unit in San Antonio, so she'll recover. But she is going to have some scars on her arm. The police have placed her under arrest at the hospital. However, evidence suggests that she wasn't the only person responsible for the troubles in the dorm."

Lea gave Montgomery a startled look. "That's what I thought! I couldn't understand how Mallory could have known the things written in the rude notes that some of the girls received. And someone seemed to be targeting Izzie, the girl who played the piano and used the third-floor study nook, which were both damaged."

Montgomery smiled widely at Lea. "Very nice, Lea. You noticed that too? While you were at Dellonmarsh this afternoon, Mr. Fong and I couldn't immediately find Fleur. While Mr. Fong searched for her, you identified Gwen as Mallory's target. So I went and had a long chat with Gwen Carter."

Kamika leaned forward. "You talked to Gwen? What did she say?"

"She didn't admit to anything, but she did say that if anyone tried to psych her out by playing tricks, she would get them back double. Gwen suggested that Izzie was responsible for the noises in the dorm. She thought Izzie was trying to keep her from studying by playing the piano in the common room. Gwen was surprised when I told her that Izzie wasn't the prankster and that the prankster didn't live in the dorm. She had been ignoring the dorm chat group and hadn't seen the picture of Mallory. She also skipped the dorm meeting. When I showed Gwen the picture of Mallory, Gwen didn't even recognize the girl. I told her that they were in the same high school. Gwen shrugged and said it was a big school and that she couldn't know everyone."

Kamika gasped. "Wait a minute. Gwen thought Izzie was guilty? Did Gwen damage the piano?"

"I suspect she did, and the study nook as well, but I can't prove it yet. She thought someone was playing tricks on her as a kind of psychological warfare, but she didn't know who it was. I think she started seeking revenge by targeting people in classes with her who lived in Dellonmarsh. I checked. Everyone who received one of those notes is in a class with Gwen. I took the liberty of collecting a water bottle she tossed in the trash. I have her fingerprints to try to match to the mean notes."

Kamika frowned. "She started by striking at people she thought might have spilled shampoo on her bed by sending them all rude notes. Then, after the noise attacks and explosion kept her awake at night, she settled on targeting Izzie and damaged the piano and study nook?"

"That fits the sequence of events," Montgomery said.

"You couldn't get Gwen to confess?" Lea asked.

"I ran out of time. I might have gotten Gwen to say more, but Mr. Fong called me to say he'd found Fleur and that he thought Mallory was at Dellonmarsh. I had to leave Gwen to join him there." Montgomery looked around the table. "Is everyone ready to order food? I'm starved." Montgomery waited for them all to assent before raising his hand to signal for the waiter.

Dr. Tremayne dropped her menu on the table and said, "After we order, I have news regarding the situation with Dr. Richardson. We may be able to undo the damage he did to Cam's career. And Lea, it's a good thing you're finishing your thesis early. Since you're finishing this fall, I can help straighten out Cam's problem during the spring semester by stepping in as his advisor."

Montgomery gave Lea a perplexed look. "This year? I thought you weren't graduating until next spring."

A voice behind Lea said, "I told you to tell him sooner rather than later." And a shiver went down Lea's spine.

CHAPTER 30

LEA TURNED AND JUMPED OUT OF her seat with a huge smile on her face. "Patrick, you're back. I didn't expect you until tomorrow evening." She walked into his arms for a hug and a quick kiss. "How did you know we were here?"

Patrick's dark eyes twinkled. "Montgomery told me, of course! I called to report on the Dallas office situation, and he asked me to come back today so that we can have a planning session tomorrow."

Montgomery stood to shake Patrick's hand as Dr. Tremayne gave him a nod and a smile.

"Hi, handsome," Kamika said with a wink as she slid over to make room for him in the booth. "You're in time to rub ointment on your girlfriend's burned hand. She's been putting fires out bare-handed this evening."

"She's been *what*?" asked Patrick, turning a stunned face to Lea, who held up her hand so that he could see the bandage.

Montgomery and Kamika explained the fiery ending of their case.

A waiter arrived to take their orders—chicken-fried steak for Patrick and Montgomery, chicken-fried chicken for Lea and Dr. Tremayne, and a grilled chicken salad for Kamika.

As the waiter left, Dr. Tremayne said, "Now, as I was saying before, I have a way to undo the damage Dr. Richardson did to that young man Cam's career. I've reviewed his file. He completed all his master's classes and completed his thesis, which was well done. Mortimer Richardson stole his work and then rejected the thesis as incomplete. I've spoken with the department chairman, and, given Lea's situation with Dr. Richardson, he reviewed Cam's file as well. He decided to offer Cam the opportunity to return in the spring, meet with new advisors about his thesis, complete his defense, and graduate, as if he had taken a medical hiatus or some other emergency break. I've agreed to be one of the advisors since Lea plans to finish her work this fall, leaving me room to take on another student."

"I can do it," Lea said. "I'll have to put in a few extra hours on that and a few less at work," she paused and glanced at Montgomery, "but I'll get it done."

"Good," said Dr. Tremayne. "I'll be contacting Cam tomorrow to make the verbal offer before the department chair emails him a letter from the history department formalizing everything."

Montgomery said, "Congratulations, Lea. I suppose you'll be looking for work related to your degree now?"

"That was the plan, yes." Lea put an arm around Kamika's shoulder. "Even if we don't work together, we'll still see each other."

The conversation turned to other subjects, including Kamika's kitten's antics, as the food was served. Then they all parted ways for the evening.

⁘

Friday morning, Lea, Kamika, Patrick, and Montgomery gathered in the kitchen breakroom at Bad Vibes Removal Services for coffee and doughnuts.

"Who brought the doughnuts?" Kamika asked, her fingers poised over a white, powdered-sugar-coated one.

"Your favorite dispatcher, Miguel," Montgomery said, laughing at Kamika's shocked expression. Miguel was infamous for his pessimistic attitude, which frequently clashed with Kamika's upbeat outlook.

"Well, even that sourpuss has his virtues. Who knew?" Kamika said before biting into the doughnut. "I really shouldn't be eating extra sweets today. I have my date with Parker tonight and he's taking me for a big dinner."

"Now, ladies and gentleman, if you would join me in the conference room, I have a number of business matters to cover this morning. No one likes long meetings, so the sooner we start, the sooner we'll finish." Montgomery picked up the box of doughnuts and his coffee and led the way to the conference room.

Once everyone was seated around the table, with the doughnuts in the center, Montgomery opened his tablet computer and found his notes. He cleared his throat. "First of all, regarding the case in Dellonmarsh Residence Hall, Ms. Gwen Carter's fingerprints matched the unknown sets found on three of the notes that were pushed under residents' doors. Mei, the head resident in the dorm, has been advised, and she will begin disciplinary measures for that infraction. I understand that the professor in charge of her chemistry lab will also be having words with her regarding cheating. I foresee academic probation in Gwen Carter's future, if not expulsion."

"Good," Lea said, clapping.

Montgomery continued, "Next, Mallory Carroll's family has requested she have a psychiatric evaluation in an effort to prevent her from being charged as an adult for her crimes. Mallory will likely be charged with arson, attempted poisoning, theft of chemicals from the university, and breaking and entering into the dorm. I'm not sure what the charge will be for causing an evacuation with a stink bomb, probably criminal mischief, which is nothing compared to the other charges she's facing. I've been informed that the hospital had to place her on suicide watch. She tried to strangle herself with her bedsheet last night."

Kamika shook her head sadly. "She wasn't very well prepared to handle life. And she's so young, she wasn't thinking about the long-term consequences of her actions."

"I agree," Montgomery said.

Lea asked, "Can we link Gwen Carter to the slime on the piano or the damage to the study nook?"

Montgomery shook his head no. "Although Gwen is the most likely suspect, we can't prove she did those things. Mallory, by the way, admitted to spilling shampoo on beds. She did Gwen's room, then searched each floor for unlocked doors because she was angry. She asked her parents to apologize to the girls that she harmed other than Gwen Carter." Then Montgomery turned to Patrick. "Could you report on the opening of the Dallas branch of Montgomery Investigations?"

Patrick explained how the training of the detectives had progressed. He concluded by saying, "The office is already getting inquiries about using the equipment to reset businesses and spaces, which, as you know, is a

Bad Vibes service, not an investigation service. Given the number of inquiries, I wanted to ask if you were planning on opening any additional branches of Bad Vibes Removal Services."

Montgomery grinned. "And that is why I called this meeting. I don't want to lose my best employees because I didn't respect their skills and didn't pay them appropriately." He turned to Lea and Kamika. "Kamika, you have the business sense, financial skills, and design talent to run an interior design business of your own. Your recommendations have improved the entire redesign process for the company, from the materials we use to the techniques used in the designs. I know you were considering expanding your website-based business, but I have an offer for you. How would you like to be responsible for training and managing all interior designers for Bad Vibes Removal Services as well as overseeing the selection and purchase of our redesign materials? I have decided to open a new branch office in Dallas, so I will need a manager to oversee our nationwide interior redesign department and employees at multiple future locations."

Kamika sat, stunned. "Manager of the interior redesign department? For Bad Vibes Removal Services *nationwide*?"

"You can think about that for a moment. Let me go on." Montgomery turned to Lea. "I'm going to need a staff historian too: someone to oversee all the historical building requests that we've been getting from all over the state and all over the *country*, someone to train staff in the best techniques for reading old buildings, someone who might also be available to help me with the occasional investigation. Lea, I need a lead historian and a manager to oversee employees doing historical readings around the state and an investigation associate willing to come help as needed. Really, I'm offering you two jobs, one full time and the other part time."

Lea glanced at Patrick, who was smiling at her, and at Kamika, who looked like she was about to burst with joy. "Wow."

"Wait," Montgomery said, putting up a hand to stop her from speaking. He looked at Lea and Kamika both. "Pay for both of you would be salaries for management positions, so this means raises as well as promotions." He grinned at them. "I have written job descriptions and benefits packages in documents, which I emailed to you. Please review the offers and let me know your answers next week. By the way, you have the rest of the day off. Enjoy your long weekend. I have some matters to wrap up regarding Dr. Richardson, who will be arrested for embezzlement later today, according to my sources, so I need to get back to work." He collected his tablet and pushed away from the table. "Meeting adjourned." Montgomery rose from his chair and trotted briskly out of the conference room.

⁜

Saturday afternoon, Lea and Kamika met for lunch at their favorite café in Georgetown, Texas, a few steps off the old town square.

Kamika sat at the table with a radiant smile on her face, nibbling a scone.

Lea sat down across from her and began to giggle.

"What?" Kamika asked, giving Lea a suspicious look.

"You have an aura of happiness coming off you, practically in waves. It's adorable. I guess your date with Parker went well." Lea said before sipping her well-sugared iced tea.

"My date was wonderful. We talked and talked about all sorts of things. I felt like that girl in that musical after the dance." Kamika danced in her chair, raising her arms above her head.

"Which musical?"

"The one where the girl learns how to talk properly and they pass her off as a duchess. You know, *My Fair Lady*. 'I Could Have Danced All Night.'" Kamika waved her hands excitedly as she talked. "I wonder if he can dance. He moves that long, lean body so gracefully, I'll bet he's an excellent dancer. Oh, I'll have to find out."

"You're floating on clouds right now. I'm glad you hit it off."

"I can't wait to see him again. We're going to lunch tomorrow." Kamika sighed happily.

"A second date! You haven't had one of those in a while. Congratulations!"

Kamika gave a satisfied nod and then looked at Lea intently. "Have you considered Montgomery's offer? I looked at mine, and I'm taking it. I'll be in charge of the entire interior redesign department. I get to handle planning of large client requests, like whole building redesigns. I get to select products and create preset design packages for the company. It's a dream job with pay to match." She paused, looking at Lea with concern. "But you wanted to teach. Do you still want to do that?"

Lea shrugged. "Montgomery did his homework. The pay is much better than I'd make teaching. He included a list of locations and organizations that had reached out to him from all over the state, asking for readings at historical locations. If I say yes, I'll almost certainly be dealing with more ghosts." She sighed thoughtfully. "Patrick and I talked about the job last night. It means travel, but I'll be able to see and study a lot of historical locations. I could still write and publish research articles about the different locations. If I decided to go back to academia later, for a doctorate, I'd be ready."

Kamika clapped happily. "Then you've decided to take the job?"

"I have. And another new position as well." Lea paused as a huge smile lit her face. She stuck her hand into the pocket and pulled something out. "I was hiding this from you because I wanted to surprise you. Look what Patrick gave me last night." Lea placed on the table a vintage, platinum, art deco ring on which sat a sparkling ruby encircled with tiny diamonds.

"Is that an engagement ring?" Kamika picked up the ring and squealed delightedly. "I knew that man was going to propose to you. Can I be in the wedding?"

"Can you be the maid of honor?" Lea asked.

"You bet! I'll be the best maid of honor ever!"

Lea held up one hand in a restraining motion. "But no wild bachelorette party. I'm happy with an old-fashioned wedding shower."

"Can we at least have a lingerie shower?" Kamika asked pleadingly.

"Okay, fine. But no male strippers or anything wild like that."

"Yes, ma'am." Kamika gave Lea a mock salute, but grinned wickedly.

HALLOWEEN VIBES:
Pumpkin Bread and Poltergeists

A BAD VIBES REMOVAL SERVICES
SHORT STORY

HALLOWEEN VIBES:
Pumpkin Bread and Poltergeists

MONTGOMERY KNOCKED ON LEA'S OFFICE DOORFRAME with his knuckles, the bulk of his more than six feet of height and almost three hundred pounds blocking the open entrance. "I have a personal favor to ask. I know you have a full schedule between work and wedding plans, but if you could squeeze in checking an eighty-year-old farmhouse for ghosts, off the books, I'd appreciate it."

"Off the books? Is the owner a friend?" Lea asked, turning away from her work to give her boss her full attention. She studied Montgomery's round face, which projected a look that many people took for good-natured, guileless vacuity. Lea knew better than to underestimate the man in front of her. As a private detective, lawyer, inventor, and owner of Bad Vibes Removal Services, Montgomery was persistent, highly intelligent, ambitious, and loyal to his friends, but at the moment he was radiating what felt to Lea like embarrassment and concern. She raised one questioning eyebrow and waited.

Montgomery took in her look and sighed. He came all the way into the office and closed the door behind him. "Whatever you're thinking, you're wrong. Sort of." Montgomery rubbed one hand over his bald pate, smoothing the blond circle of hair around the edges of his head. He threw Lea an apologetic look. "My ex-girlfriend . . . no, ex-wife, Linda, owns the house."

"Your ex-wife." Lea could feel her eyes widening. "You have an ex-wife? Okay." Lea hadn't known he'd ever been married, having always taken him to be a middle-aged, workaholic bachelor. She wanted to ask if he'd mentioned the previous marriage to his current girlfriend, Dr. Jenny Tremayne, a University of Texas professor who had recently served as Lea's thesis advisor, guiding Lea through the completion of her master's degree in history. Lea swallowed the question. It was none of her business what Montgomery had or hadn't told Dr. Tremayne. She closed her mouth and waited for him to tell her what she needed to know.

Montgomery shrugged. "It's a long story. It was a long time ago and only lasted three weeks before it was annulled. Linda's married with kids now. She didn't tell the kids that she was married before, so don't mention it while you're there. I'm doing this one off the books because she's having some financial troubles, recovering from a bankruptcy caused by the expense of the long illness and then death of her youngest child." He looked at Lea with empathy in his eyes. "She's had enough trouble to last a lifetime. She needs help, and we're in the position to provide it."

Lea nodded, tears welling under her eyelids. She blinked a few times to control her always-overly empathetic response and nodded. "You're the boss. I'll do what I can to help. What's the problem? Not the child who died, I hope?"

Montgomery met her eyes with a dark, serious look. "She thinks she has a poltergeist."

"A poltergeist?" Lea sat back in her chair in surprise. "Most supposed poltergeist activity has been found to be caused by a living child seeking attention or turned out to be visual hallucinations by the person reporting the problem."

"I know, I know. I suspect Linda's ten-year-old son of being the real culprit, not a poltergeist. The boy's activities and whole life were put on the back burner during his younger sister's losing battle with a brain tumor. This may be a cry for attention. I thought the quickest way to know for sure was to ask to check it out. If you don't find a ghost, we'll know the cause is something more mundane, and we can recommend that the child's parents take him to a psychologist."

Lea nodded her understanding. "Are you coming with me?"

Montgomery's faced blanched. "No. Hell, no!"

Lea stared at him in surprise.

"Sorry." He exhaled loudly, struggling momentarily for words. "Linda's mother, Raquel, lives with the family. She came in to help while the little girl was sick and has stayed. Raquel hates my guts. She's the one who tracked us down after we eloped and had the marriage annulled."

Lea's jaw dropped. "*She* had it annulled. How old were you?"

Montgomery pursed his lips into a flat line. "Seventeen."

"And Linda was . . . ?"

"Sixteen."

Lea studied Montgomery's embarrassed eyes. "Someday, I'd like to hear the whole story on this. For now, get me the address, and I'll let you know what I find."

A knock sounded on the door behind Montgomery. "Lea, are you in here?" called Kamika right before she poked her pretty mocha face into the office.

Kamika saw Montgomery and apologized. "Sorry, y'all. I didn't mean to interrupt a meeting. I'll come back."

Montgomery reached out and opened the door wider. "No, we're finished. Come in." He smiled at Kamika. "How would you like to accompany Lea on a job for me? Do you have time?"

"You know me," Kamika said with a toss of her curls and a wide smile, "I can always make time. What's up?"

Lea grinned at her friend and coworker. "I'm going to investigate the possibility of a poltergeist in an old house."

"More ghosts? Cool! I'm in!" Kamika said, giving Lea a thumbs-up. "As long as I don't see it, it won't bother me." She paused, struck by a thought. "Wait a minute. Are poltergeists the ones that bite and scratch and throw things?"

Lea nodded at her, laughing. "But you probably won't *see* anything."

Kamika rolled her eyes. "Oh, darn it. Fine. Let's go."

⁜

The van stopped in front of a farmhouse on a hill encircled by a white picket fence. A traditional red barn stood to one side with a riding lawn mower parked in front of it. Lea got the impression that the farm had once been larger, but fields had been sold off and newer houses were built around it as nearby cities grew and an area that had once been rural became suburban.

Lea surveyed the structure. The white frame house had windows all around to take advantage of breezes and a wraparound porch. The house had a slightly neglected look: weeds had sprung up on the walk, a board was broken in the fence around the yard, and the windows were dirty. However, someone appeared to have made recent efforts to push back the tide of entropy. The yard within the fence was newly mowed, and fresh mulch had been spread around a tree. Three fat pumpkins sat on the porch next to a fluttering flag that said "Welcome Fall."

Lea and Kamika got out of the van. Since they were only checking for ghosts, they wouldn't need their usual Bad Vibes Removal Services equipment for reading or neutralizing emotional atmosphere or sounds built up in the walls.

Kamika's eyes ran over the house. "The pumpkins and flag suggest that they're trying to move on, but this place could use a redesign with bright colors. That touch of orange isn't enough to cheer the place up."

As they walked toward the house, Lea noted that the sense of grief in the air became stronger. Under the grief, she could feel sadness, confusion, and loneliness. The property was heavy with emotional atmosphere. "I'm going to recommend a neutralization treatment to Montgomery. It might help a little as the grief runs its course."

Then the front door of the house swung open and a middle-aged woman in loose blue jeans and a t-shirt appeared. She was tall and looked like she'd lost too much weight. Her face was drawn tight across her cheekbones and chin, emphasizing the skull beneath the skin. Gray streaks erupted from her forehead, leading back into dark and lustrous hair. A strained look pulled her mouth into a flat line. Lea could feel a wave of grief emanating from the woman.

"I'm Linda," the woman said as she came down the porch toward them. "Are you Lea and Kamika?"

Lea and Kamika reached the gate in the picket fence at the same time as Linda.

Lea extended a hand over the fence and shook Linda's hand. "Yes. Montgomery sent us. I'm Lea. This is Kamika." She gestured to Kamika, who reached out to offer her hand as well.

Linda shook Kamika's hand and then opened the gate. "Come in. I'm glad you could come this morning. I didn't want Monty here while I talked to you. He's at school right now."

Kamika tilted her head, "Monty? Is that short for Montgomery?"

The woman blushed. "Yes. I told Monty that I'd always liked the name, and that was why we gave it to him. My husband knows the truth. Montgomery is a good man, but we were too young. He saved my life, though, for which I'll always be grateful." She chuckled. "I owe him so much that I named my firstborn child after him. I'd have named the second after him too, but she was a girl." She ran a nervous hand through her graying hair. "I don't suppose he told you the whole story." She paused and glanced at them.

Kamika and Lea both said, "No."

Linda nodded, satisfied. "He wouldn't. He keeps his secrets close. Anyway, that's a story for another time. Come inside the house. We can talk there. Montgomery says you have a knack for detecting ghosts." She looked curiously at Lea.

"Yes," Lea said, but she didn't elaborate.

"She's being modest," Kamika said, nudging Lea with her elbow. "If you have a ghost, she'll know it."

"Good," said Linda. "I hate to think something might be attacking my son in his sleep, leaving scratch marks, and moving things around the house." She looked down. "And I hate to think he might be doing it to himself."

Linda led them into a square living room that looked like it belonged in a bungalow by the beach instead of a farmhouse in central Texas. A collection of seashells filled a side table. Between family photos on the walls hung paintings of seashores and water birds. On the sand-colored sofa sat throw pillows decorated in a seashell and seagull print. A large sign above the fireplace proclaimed, "'I'd Rather Be at the Beach."

"Sit down," said Linda, gesturing to the sofa as she seated herself into one of a pair of rocking chairs facing the sofa.

"Can you tell us what's been happening? Why you think you might have a poltergeist?" Lea asked after she had settled into the sofa next to Kamika.

Linda clasped her hands together in her lap tightly. "I don't know what Montgomery told you, so I'll start by saying that my daughter died four months ago." Her voice cracked and tears filled her eyes. She grabbed a tissue from a box on a table at her elbow and wiped her eyes. "Her death was a long time coming, a hard-fought losing battle with a brain tumor. Most of my time was spent at hospitals and doctor appointments with her. Monty had to drop being on his traveling soccer team because we didn't have time to get him to cities all over the state. I know he hated having to quit, but he seemed to understand the necessity. Maybe I wasn't paying enough attention, maybe I just wanted to believe he understood and was okay with it."

"You did what you had to do," Kamika said. "Illness in the family is a problem that will affect all the members. Even if your son didn't like it, I'm sure he'll appreciate that fact eventually, as he gets older."

Linda tried to smile, failed, and wiped her eyes again. "Anyway, about a month ago, Monty came down from his room one morning and showed me a scratch on his arm. He said it hurt and that he didn't know how it happened. He also told me that he'd had nightmares."

"What did you do?" Lea asked, glancing at a family portrait on the wall showing a smiling, chubby-faced man; Linda; a frail-looking, red-haired girl; and a dark-haired boy with mischievous eyes. She saw a flash of a happy girl laughing and chattering as her mother combed her fine red hair—not a ghost, but an echo of a moment in time. The happy image was at odds with the waves of grief rolling off of Linda. Lea blinked, pulling herself back to the conversation.

"I put some cream on the scratch and told him he'd probably bumped something in his sleep. If he'd been having nightmares, he could have thrashed or rolled off the bed." Linda frowned, her eyebrows coming together, thinking.

"Then what happened?" asked Lea, sensing her confusion and worry.

"A few days later, Monty said he saw his soccer ball fly across his room and knock over his lamp, breaking the bulb. I thought he'd been playing ball in the house again and made him clean up the mess." She paused. "After that, it escalated. Things broke every few days, and then daily. My husband and mother blame Monty."

"But you don't?" Kamika asked.

"At first I did," Linda said, clutching the damp tissue in her hand. "But three days ago, I heard something moving upstairs in Monty's room while he was at school. I went upstairs to look. I thought a squirrel had come into the house. We've had squirrels in the attic. But when I got to Monty's room, I didn't find any squirrels. Monty's bookshelf had tipped over."

"Was it unstable? Could it have fallen by itself?" Lea asked.

Linda shook her head with fear in her eyes. "It was anchored to the wall. The entire anchor had been pulled free as if it had been yanked out of the wall."

Lea glanced at Kamika, who met her look with raised eyebrows. "Linda, do you mind if I walk around the house?" Lea asked.

"Is that how you check for ghosts? Can you see them?" Linda stood up from her rocking chair with an inquiring look on her face.

"That's part of it," Lea acknowledged as she rose from the sofa.

Kamika jumped up to join them. "Lea also sees history sometimes, and she has a great sense for the emotional atmosphere in a building."

"Well, can we walk and talk?" Linda asked gesturing toward a door. "That way leads to the kitchen."

"We'll follow you," Lea said. "We'll try to answer any questions you have as we go."

Linda opened the door, and they followed her into a large, updated country kitchen with shiny new appliances and modern cabinetry. A round dining table with a red-and-white-checkered tablecloth stood by a large window. A few dishes sat in the sink waiting to be washed. A broom and dustpan leaned in one corner.

Lea glanced around the room but saw nothing unusual. She found Kamika and Linda watching her, so she shrugged. "I like your kitchen." Pointing to a row of cookbooks, Lea said, "I see you like to bake."

"Yes," said Linda. She shot Lea perplexed look. "You will tell us if you see a ghost, won't you?"

Kamika giggled. "Oh, we'll know. She'll start talking to it."

Linda turned to Kamika. "Really. She can talk to them? Do they talk back?"

"Sometimes they do. Sometimes they don't seem to be able to talk," Kamika said.

Linda crossed her arms on her chest and hugged herself. "Have you ever seen a ghost move things around a house?"

"I've seen one knock pictures off a wall," Lea said. "Can we go on to the next room?"

Linda stared at her in surprise for a second. "Yes, of course." She led them to a laundry room with large sinks next to a modern washer and dryer set. "Was the ghost who knocked down pictures a poltergeist?"

"He was a murder victim, and angry. I wouldn't call him a poltergeist." Lea looked around the laundry room, then turned and walked out. "Upstairs next?"

"Yes, unless you want to see the bathroom first." Linda pointed to a door next to the laundry room.

Lea opened it and peeked inside before reclosing the door. "Let's see upstairs." Lea thought they would be there all day if they didn't get moving. They needed to finish before the boy came home from school.

Linda led them up a narrow stairwell. She glanced at Lea and Kamika behind her. "What's emotional atmosphere?"

Lea said, "Have you ever been in a room that felt tense, or angry, or creepy? Have you ever been in a peaceful church or visited a battlefield that seemed to have a sense of gravity, grief, or death lingering in the air? That emotion you sense in a particular place that seems to emanate from the place itself is that place's emotional atmosphere. It's created by all the emotion expended in that place, sort of radiating out of the people and marking the environment."

"Oh. I guess that makes sense." She paused at the top of the stairs. "Does my house have an atmosphere?"

Lea reached the top of the stairs and stopped in a hallway running the length of the house. She put one hand gently on Linda's shoulder. "Right now, your downstairs has a feeling of sadness and grief." Lea glanced down the hall. "It seems less sad up here. I'll let you know how the different rooms feel."

Linda nodded. "The first door to your right is my daughter's room. We . . . we haven't touched it since she . . . she passed. I'm not ready." Her voice broke, and she stifled a sob.

Kamika put one arm around Linda's shoulders and squeezed her, trying to comfort her.

Lea opened the door and stepped into a pink-walled, frilly, girl's room with eyelet curtains and a Hello Kitty bedspread on the single bed. A dollhouse sat on the floor in one corner with the furniture scattered on the floor in front of it. Stuffed animals spilled from an open toy box under the window. Lea was relieved to find the room free of ghosts. She would have hated to find the little girl's spirit still lingering there. To her amazement, she noticed that she was smiling as she looked around. This room was happy, almost bubbly. Lea rejoined Kamika and Linda in the hall.

"Well?" asked Linda.

"I didn't see any ghosts. Also, that room makes me smile. It feels warm, happy, cheerful, even joyful."

A wavering smile came to Linda's lips, sparking in her eyes for a brief second. "Her name was Joy, and it fit her perfectly. She was the sunniest child you ever saw. Even when she was sick, she could make everyone around her smile."

Lea pointed to the door across from Joy's room. "Whose room is this?"

"That's Monty's room." Linda walked forward and opened the door.

Lea walked into the room and found the air saturated with rage and grief. Broken toys sat on the desk in various stages of repair. The *Star Wars*-themed bedsheets were on the floor, twisted into a mess as if someone had tossed and turned violently in them. In the corner near the window stood an elderly woman. She was translucent. Her gray hair was pinned up on her head. Her 1930s-style dress was covered with an apron.

Lea stopped and stared at the woman, who nodded politely, even graciously at her. "Hello," Lea said.

Kamika and Linda stepped into the room.

Linda asked in an anxious voice, "Who is it? It's not my Joy, is it?"

Lea kept her eyes on the ghostly woman, but answered Linda. "No. It's not Joy. It's a woman. Wait a moment and let me try to talk to her." Lea asked the ghost, "What's your name?"

"Bessie."

"Hello, Bessie. Did you live in this house?"

"Yes. We built this house, Joe and I."

Lea tried to figure out a delicate way to ask the ghost why she was still there. "It's a nice house. Did you not want to leave? Is Joe here too?"

"Joe isn't here. He's waiting for me."

"Do you not want to join him? Can't you join him?" Lea wished there was a book of rules for the afterlife that she could consult. She knew some ghosts seemed to have a reason for staying.

"I can't. I'm stuck here."

A whiff of wistful sadness reached Lea. She asked, "Why?"

"I don't know."

Lea gestured to the broken toys. "Can you tell me what's been happening in here?"

"The child is angry. He blames himself and his parents for the loss of his sister. He injured himself." The woman moved toward the bed slowly with a limping gait.

"Did he break the toys?" Lea asked.

"I told him to break something when he felt like hurting himself. He needs to release his anger. If he bottles it up inside it will make him bitter, drive the hope out of him, like it did to me when I lost my child to polio. I tried to go on, but the darkness inside built year after year, eating away at me, until finally one day I gave up." She turned back to the toys. "I thought breaking things would help, but his anger seems to be getting worse. He thought he might need medicine, but I told him to avoid those patent medicine salesmen. That stuff will rot your gut and destroy your mind."

"I see." Lea studied the woman, noting what appeared to be blood on her hands. The blood was leaking from under her sleeves. Lea suddenly saw a flash of the woman, sitting in the corner by the window in a rocking chair, crying. The room was almost empty except for a small bed with a rolled up, old-fashioned mattress. Lea blinked and the scene was gone.

"Are you trying to stop him from hurting himself like you hurt yourself?" Lea pointed to the blood.

Bessie studied the blood on her hands. "Yes. I suggested he chop firewood first, but he said they don't use it. I broke a stack of dishes after my Amy died." The woman turned toward Linda, who still stood near the door with Kamika. "I told the boy it's not his fault. I told him it's not his parents' fault either. He still wants someone to blame. I told him to blame the sickness. But his rage only increases."

"Thank you for trying to help." Lea said. "Wait a minute while I explain to his mother."

Linda took a hesitant step forward toward Lea. "What's going on? Who's in here? Is it a poltergeist?"

"There's a woman named Bessie who committed suicide after her own child died of polio. She's been trying to stop Monty from blaming himself for Joy's death. She suggested he break things when he got angry instead of hurting himself. You need to get him to a doctor for evaluation. He is terribly angry, hurt, and depressed over the loss of his sister. Bessie says Monty's rage is getting worse. He needs help."

Tears filled Linda's eyes and a sob escaped her mouth. "I'll call the doctor right away."

Kamika put her arm around Linda again. "Also, call his school counseling office. They might be able to suggest resources."

Linda bit her lip and tried to get herself under control. "That's a good idea. Thanks."

Bessie's voice drifted to Lea, thin and whispering. "They must help him before the darkness consumes him. It's growing. You can see it."

Lea looked back to Bessie. The woman stood in front of the window, looking out and pointing. "See what?" Lea crossed the room and looked out the window into an abyss.

Bessie whispered in Lea's ear. "The darkness feeds off despair and multiplies it. I brought the darkness here. I'm stuck between it and the light, waiting. Dark voices come from there and whisper to the boy at night, in his dreams. I've taught him to avoid them, not to listen, while he is awake. But it's harder to keep them out of dreams. That takes work, resilience, and strength, which he doesn't have yet."

Lea stared into the abyss, feeling terror in her gut, knowing something awful resided inside that never-ending blanket of cold emptiness. She stepped back from the window hastily. "How do we get rid of that?"

"I don't know." A nearly transparent tear rolled down Bessie's face.

"Can you leave this room? Get away from it?" Lea asked in a horrified voice.

"No. It tries to come in, but I fight it back every day."

"How do you fight it?"

"I picture Amy and Joe waiting for me. But I know that I can't be with them. I gave up." Bessie's eyes shifted to Linda. "I should have been like her and made myself face the future. Then I would be with my Amy and Joe now."

"If you leave, will the darkness leave too?" Lea shivered as her knowledge of the darkness encroaching on the room threatened to overwhelm her.

"Maybe. But my only option for leaving is to enter the pit, and I won't do that. So I'm stuck fighting the darkness forever." Bessie's face was a bleak mask of despair.

Lea turned back to Kamika and Linda. "We have a problem. I don't know how to solve this yet. I need to think." She looked at Bessie. "We're going to leave you now, but we'll be back. Don't give in to the abyss. We can figure this out." Lea pushed Linda and Kamika out of the room and closed the door behind them.

"What did you see? Get rid of what? What darkness?" Linda asked in a confused and terrified voice.

Lea took a calming breath to get herself under control. "I think the woman in there is in some kind of limbo. Bessie is trying to help Monty fight the depression that she succumbed to herself, but I think her presence is adding to the problem. She's stuck by an abysmal pit of darkness so terrifying that it felt like staring into hell. She's fighting it by thinking of her husband and daughter waiting for her, but she thinks she can never join them. She has her own blood on her hands, literally and figuratively, and her despair might be influencing your son subconsciously. The darkness might leave if she entered it, but she refuses. She's fighting it."

Kamika gasped.

Linda looked taken aback. "So she's trying to help, but her very presence might be part of the problem?"

"Exactly," Lea said, her dark eyes watching Linda process the information.

Linda stared into space. "She wants to help, so she's not a bad person. She doesn't want to go into what looks like hell but doesn't believe she's allowed to join her husband and daughter. She's stuck." Her focus came back to Lea. "How does she know she isn't allowed with her husband and daughter? Has she asked? Tried to join them?"

"I don't know. Maybe the fact that she isn't with them is all she needed to know that she couldn't join them." Lea puzzled over the matter.

Kamika waved one hand and said, "What if she needs to make amends? Isn't trying to help Monty enough?"

"Wait!" Linda yelped, struck by a thought. She put her hand over her mouth for a second, then said, "What if it's simpler than that? What if she has to accept that she can be forgiven? What if she can't go to her family because *she believes she can't*, because she doesn't think she deserves to join them, because she thinks she is beyond forgiveness? She has no hope left in her, so she has rejected the possibility."

"You think she's separated from her family because of her rejection of forgiveness?" Lea asked.

"Yes." Linda's eyes grew large. "How do we convince her that she can be forgiven?"

Lea frowned and ran one hand through her heavy, jet-black hair, pushing loose strands out of her face. "*We* don't convince her. *Monty* does."

"Why Monty?" asked Linda.

Lea stared in consideration at the door to the room. "Maybe if he helps her, it will help him stop blaming himself for his sister's death. And maybe if she knows she helped him, she'll gain enough hope to know that she isn't beyond forgiveness."

Linda checked the time on her wrist and gave the door to Monty's room an anxious glance. "That's a lot of maybes. But I can see what you're thinking. Let's go downstairs. I need to think about this."

Linda led Kamika and Lea down the stairs and back to the kitchen. Once in the kitchen, she directed Lea and Kamika to sit while she bustled about, setting a kettle to boil and slicing a loaf of bread. After a few minutes, Linda joined the others at the kitchen table, bringing a tray containing a teapot, cups and saucers, milk, sugar, and the sliced bread. "Help yourself. The tea is English breakfast. The loaf is pumpkin spice bread with walnuts."

Lea selected a slice of the sweet bread. "Thank you."

Kamika poured the tea, sending Lea and Linda questioning glances and receiving nods before pouring tea for them as well. Then she passed around the milk and sugar.

As Linda took her tea with milk and sugar and two slices of the pumpkin bread, a door leading from the kitchen to the outside opened. An older woman with short, gray curls and a permanently frowning expression stepped into the room. She was carrying a shopping bag. She stopped short when her eyes found Lea and Kamika and looked at Linda with raised eyebrows.

"Mother, hi. This is Lea and this is Kamika. They're . . . friends. Ladies, meet my mother, Raquel," said Linda in a strained voice.

"I suppose they go with that van out front that says Bad Vibes Removal Services on it," replied the woman in a sarcastic voice.

Linda exhaled loudly and said in a firm voice, "Yes, they do. And they've been providing me with the answers I need."

"Telling you want you want to hear, you mean. Pair of charlatans, ought to be arrested." Raquel's dark eyes looked at Lea with hatred. She stepped over to the countertop and put down her bag, turning her back to them.

Linda stood up. "No, they told me what I didn't want to hear. That you were right. That Monty has been breaking things."

Her mother turned around. "I told you that already. You didn't need to hire some group of crooks to tell you that. They just want money."

Lea stood up and said in a placating tone, "First of all, we aren't here for money. We aren't charging anything for our services today. But we did find a serious problem upstairs that needs to be handled quickly."

Raquel looked at Lea suspiciously. "What problem?"

Linda put up a hand in a gesture telling Lea to stop. "I'll explain. Lea, have some tea and pumpkin bread." Linda turned back to her mother and explained about Bessie.

When she had finished her story, Raquel said, "The ghost of a suicidal woman opened the gate to hell in Monty's room? Oh, that's ridiculous. I think both you and Monty need your heads examined." The older woman stood with her arms crossed on her thin chest, radiating anger. She glanced at Lea and Kamika and spat her words with venom. "You should be ashamed of yourselves! You're con artists taking advantage of gullible people."

Linda stomped her foot. "They work for Orestes Montgomery. I asked him to send them. And if you think he would do me any harm, you had better reconsider. If you're going to be insulting, you can leave now. Come back tonight after we've resolved the problem."

Lea saw Kamika's eyes widen and knew her eyes probably matched Kamika's. No one ever called Montgomery by his first name. While she'd seen his name on company documents and knew his signature included the first initial O, it was strange to hear someone say the name Orestes.

Lea could feel the tension and anger in the room building. She wanted to excuse herself or vanish into the floorboards while the mother and daughter argued. She could sense Kamika's discomfort as well. Instead, she took a sip of tea and ate some more pumpkin bread.

Raquel seemed to be weighing her daughter's words. "I don't know what Montgomery might do. I haven't seen him in almost thirty years. People change."

Linda's eyes narrowed. "Do you think he would ever change to the point where he would rip people off and try to take advantage of them? Try to take advantage of me? Was that ever in his character? We're talking about someone who went out of his way to help me, no matter the cost to himself, because you wouldn't listen and didn't protect me. He stepped in to help when you failed me, just like he's doing now. And again, you have a choice, you can help or you can turn your back."

"I never turned my back on you!" Raquel said, outraged.

"You didn't believe me, which amounted to the same thing," said Linda with a sad smile. "I intend to help my son in any way I can. You can help or you can disbelieve, again."

Raquel's face crumbled. "I didn't know. I never meant to allow harm to come to you."

"You could have believed me when I told you about the abuse. You chose Uncle Ray over me. Now I'm telling you, again, something you don't want to hear or believe. And again, you have a choice to make." Linda turned deliberately away from her mother and sat down at the table with Lea and Kamika. She took a sip of her tea and a bite of her pumpkin bread. She cleared her throat and said to Lea, "Monty will be home at three o'clock. How do you want to do this?"

Lea could feel Raquel's eyes on them but decided to follow Linda's lead. "We need to talk to Monty first, to see what he says about Bessie and about breaking things. After we assure him that we understand and that we want to help him, we need to explain to him that Bessie needs his help." She glanced at Kamika, pausing, looking for words. "What is Monty like? Is he the kind of kid who wants to help people? Is he sympathetic to others' pain at all?"

Linda's eyebrows came together, considering. "He isn't what I'd call a sensitive child, like Joy was. She cried over injured animals. But he does like to be helpful sometimes, and he used to try to entertain Joy when she was unable to do much more than lie in bed."

"Good," Lea said. "Then he might be willing to help Bessie, which in turn could help him." Out of the corner of her eye she noticed Raquel approaching the table. Lea shifted her eyes sideways to watch warily before noting that the anger seemed to have left the older woman.

Raquel pulled out a chair and joined them at the table.

Linda acknowledged her mother's presence with a brief glance.

Kamika, who had tensed as Raquel moved toward them, relaxed her shoulders and sipped her tea. "After we've dealt with Bessie, you should take Monty to a therapist or psychologist who helps children deal with death. Then, if you call us back, we can neutralize some of the lingering negativity in the atmosphere and add design touches to improve the emotional atmosphere in the house. Color, sound, and scents in the right places will help create a more positive emotional atmosphere. I can leave you some material to review that explains the process."

Lea nodded agreement. "But first, we have to deal with Bessie and her abyss of darkness. Since Monty won't be home until three o'clock, Kamika and I could leave and come back later, around three-thirty."

Linda put down her now-empty teacup. "That sounds good to me."

Raquel clenched her hands together on the table. "And if Montgomery wants to come, tell him he's welcome," she said in a gruff voice.

A small smile played across Linda's lips for a moment. She put her hand over her mother's hands and patted them. "Thank you, Mother."

When they had all finished their tea and pumpkin bread, Linda escorted Lea and Kamika out of the house. "See you this afternoon. And if you see him, tell Montgomery that Mother won't cause a scene if he comes here," she said.

⁑

At three-twenty, Lea, Kamika, and Montgomery arrived back at Linda's house.

Montgomery surveyed the property. "I always liked this place, but I didn't foresee Linda living here given her history. This place belonged to her grandparents. They held family parties here that were, well . . . I won't go into it. But then, Linda's a fighter with more resilience than anyone else I know."

Linda appeared on the porch. She saw Montgomery and her face broke into a smile that melted away grief and age. She trotted down the steps and ran out to hug him.

Montgomery pulled her into a bear hug. "Hello, Linda. It's great to see you. I hear you have the gate to hell upstairs." He grinned at her as she stepped back from him.

"Ah, so that's what brought you: curiosity. Of course, I should have known." Linda expelled a hearty, crowing laugh, deep and loud. "I'm so glad you came."

They all turned toward the porch as the house door swung open, and Raquel appeared. Her lips were flattened into a thin line.

Montgomery's grin disappeared and a cautious look came into his eyes. "Good afternoon, Mrs. Gerald."

Raquel tilted her head sideways and peered at him. "You were all about science, obsessive about it. Where does this ghost nonsense fit in with that?"

"Let me get out my equipment, and I'll explain." Montgomery went around to the back of the van and removed the sound and emotional energy-scanning equipment bags.

Lea took one bag and Montgomery took the other. Then they all walked up the porch steps and into the house.

In a few minutes, as they all sat in the living room, Montgomery explained how, as a private detective, he had begun to search for new ways to solve crimes. First, he'd found that he could detect the patterns left by very loud sounds in wood and wall board. This had led him to detect the patterns created by extremes of emotion. He'd designed and built the software for analyzing and neutralizing the sound and emotional energy patterns.

Raquel nodded. "I understand that. That's the inventor in you. But where do ghosts come into this?"

Montgomery conceded with a shrug. "They don't. That's all Lea. She's a better emotional atmosphere detector than my equipment. And when a lingering spirit is the cause of the negative emotional atmosphere in a house, my equipment isn't going to be able to neutralize the problem. I'm lucky to have her working for me."

Somewhere upstairs, a door slammed. The sound of running feet on stairs drifted down. A moment later, a dark-haired boy with Linda's eyes bounded into the room. He looked to be ten or eleven years old and was athletically slim. He stopped, looking at Lea, Kamika, and Montgomery with surprise.

Linda waved him to her. "Come in, Monty. We need to talk to you."

Monty came toward her, a troubled look bringing his mouth downward into a frown. "What's going on?"

Montgomery rose from his seat on the sofa, his more than six feet of height and almost three hundred pounds towering over the slender boy. He extended his hand. "My name is Montgomery. Is that your name too?"

Monty put out his hand hesitantly and shook Montgomery's, looking up at him. "Yes. I've never met anyone with my name before."

"Neither have I." Montgomery smiled at him. "Your mother called me because you've been having some problems lately."

"Are you a doctor?" Monty asked, a veiled look coming over his face.

"No, I'm a detective. And these ladies," Montgomery gestured to Lea and Kamika, "work for me."

"A detective?" Monty turned to his mother and grandmother in confusion.

Linda took Monty's hand. "Yes. They helped me find out how your toys and the other things in your room got broken."

Monty looked at his sneakers.

"It's okay, baby. Everyone is here to help you." Linda put one hand under Monty's chin and raised his head so that she could look him in the eyes. "We know you broke those things. We also know that a woman name Bessie, who died in this house a long time ago, suggested it."

Monty looked at her with wide, scared eyes. "She has bloody hands," he whispered. "But she's nice."

"Bessie was trying to help you, and now Bessie needs your help, Monty." Linda explained to her stunned son about how Bessie was stuck, unable to join her family, possibly because she didn't believe she deserved to go to them.

"But she should get to see her family," Monty pronounced decidedly. "How can I help her?"

"You're going to thank her for helping you. And you and this lady who can also see Bessie," Linda pointed at Lea, "are going to talk to her about joining her family, leaving this house. The rest of us can't see Bessie, so it's hard for us to talk to her."

Monty looked at Lea with a mixture of curiosity and interest. "You saw her?"

Lea nodded and gave the boy a reassuring smile. "I know about the dark place by the window that she's fighting."

"The bad voices come from the dark place." Angry tears filled Monty's eyes. "They say it's my fault that Joy died. They say that Bessie will never see her family." His face went red and he clenched his fists into balls by his sides, shaking with anger.

"Those voices are lying," Lea said firmly. "Take a deep breath and try not to let them agitate you. Think of the voices like they're bullies. You've been taught how to deal with bullies, haven't you?"

Monty froze, momentarily surprised out of his rage. "Like bullies?" He paused thinking before a look of wonder crossed his face. "That's it. They're bullies picking on me and Bessie!" Then his mercurial emotions shifted again, and anger and doubt returned to his face. "But the voices are right. I didn't help Joy and she died."

Raquel gasped in anguish, then covered her mouth with her hand. "No, dear!"

Linda rushed to hug Monty as if she wanted to squeeze the negativity out of him. "No, no, no. You did all any big brother could do for her. Only, people haven't found the right medicines and treatments yet to cure all the bad diseases. Disease killed Joy. It wasn't anyone's fault, not mine, not Dad's, not Grandma's, and definitely not yours. Though it's hard on us because we miss her, we know that she isn't in pain anymore." Linda gulped back a sob, and her voice cracked. She cleared her throat, pulling herself together with obvious effort. "Joy's not still here, like Bessie. Bessie needs help. She's here because she's in pain over what she did. We need to help Bessie. If she can join her family, the darkness and the voices will leave you alone too."

The boy pushed away from his mother and looked at her in confusion. "Bessie says she isn't allowed to go to her family. She can't leave unless she goes into the blackness. I don't want her to do that. When she gets too close to the darkness, she says it hurts her. She called it 'agony.'"

Lea knelt in front of the slender boy. "Monty, we think that Bessie can choose to go to her family if she understands that she can be forgiven for what she did. If she doesn't think she should be forgiven and doesn't accept forgiveness, she can't go to her family. Do you think that she's sorry and deserves to be forgiven for what she did wrong?"

Monty nodded so quickly he almost banged into his mother. "She's sorry. She should be forgiven."

Lea gave the boy an encouraging smile. "I think so too. But we have to help her accept forgiveness. Can you help us tell her that she deserves forgiveness and should go join her family now?"

Monty nodded sagely and gave them all a look that was mature beyond his years. "You mean she was bad because she gave up and killed herself." He sighed heavily. "That was wrong. She told me that she shouldn't have done that when she told me not to scratch myself. The voices made me so mad at myself, but she told me to break things instead when they make me mad." He looked around the room. "Are we going to talk to Bessie now?"

"Yes," Montgomery said. "Let's go."

⁑

Linda led the way up the stairs and paused outside Monty's room. She looked at her small son. "Are you ready?"

Monty arranged his face into a resolute expression and squared his shoulders. "Okay."

Linda opened the door and allowed Monty and Lea to enter the room first. Linda, Raquel, and Montgomery crowded around the doorway, watching.

Monty walked toward his bed and paused, looking toward the window.

Lea followed him and saw Bessie standing by the window where she'd been earlier. "Hello, Bessie. Monty and I have come to talk to you."

Bessie turned and smiled at Monty. "I was waiting to say goodbye. I can't let the voices from the darkness hurt you anymore. It's not safe for you. I'm going to give myself up to my fate and close this breach." She turned to face the abyss and stepped toward it.

"No!" cried Monty in a horrified voice. "Don't!"

Linda stepped into the room, looking alarmed and rushed to put her arm around her son. "What's wrong?"

"Bessie says she's going to go into the darkness to protect me from it! She can't!" Monty looked to his mother, wide-eyed, for help.

Linda looked quickly at Lea.

Lea darted toward Bessie. "Wait, Bessie. We have another way to close out the voices and protect Monty." Lea felt fear tightening her throat as the abyss by the window, now yawning wider, seemed about to swallow the woman.

Bessie shook her head in despair. "There is no other way! I must give up." She turned toward the abyss, which seemed to be throbbing, preparing to engulf her.

"No!" Lea yelled.

Bessie hesitated. "What else can I do? I can't allow the child to be subjected to this evil any longer."

"Go to your family instead!" Lea said, holding her hands up imploringly, every ounce of her being praying that Bessie would listen. Her eyes felt transfixed by the darkness by the window. She could sense a hissing, somehow exultant whisper emanating from it.

Translucent tears dripped down Bessie's face. "I can't. I don't deserve to join them."

"No," Lea said. "Anyone who's ready to sacrifice herself to protect a child," she gestured toward Monty, "absolutely deserves to see her family again!"

Monty broke free from his mother's arms and ran toward Bessie. "You helped me not to hurt myself. You taught me to ignore the lying voices. Now you have to ignore them too! The voices say you can't go to your family. But they lie! You can! You did something wrong, but you can say you're sorry."

Lea dragged her eyes from the abyss and back to Bessie. "You have to forgive yourself and accept that you can be forgiven. Allow yourself to go to your family. *You* are the only thing stopping you from going into the light."

Bessie looked from Monty to Lea, comprehension dawning on her face. "Me? I'm separated from them because I chose to be?" A spark of hope came into her eyes.

Suddenly a blinding light appeared where the abyss had been, instantly annihilating it.

Bessie looked surprised. "Amy? Joe?" She walked forward into the light and vanished from sight.

Monty turned and looked at Lea. "She's gone! Is she with her family?"

Lea smiled in relief. "Yes. I think she is." Lea glanced toward the window. "And the darkness is gone."

Monty stood still, in a listening posture. "The whispers are gone."

Linda grabbed her son into her arms again. "Oh, baby. You did it. You helped her. And I'm going to help you too. We're going to talk to a therapist together."

Monty gave her another of his wise-beyond-his-years looks. "It's okay, Mom. I get it. I was doing what Bessie did, not forgiving myself. It's wrong. Joy wouldn't want me to blame myself for her death. She would want me to be happy."

Tears leaked down Linda's face. "That's right, baby. That's right."

⁂

An hour later, Lea and Montgomery finished using the infusing equipment to apply a static layer to the walls in Monty's room, covering over any traces of the depression, guilt, rage, and grief that were marking the place. They had given Monty's room an emotional atmosphere clean slate.

As Lea repacked the equipment, Montgomery talked to Linda, explaining what they had done and offering to do the whole house.

Linda declined the offer. "No, thank you. You've done enough already."

Kamika joined them. "I've finished typing out my recommendations for redesign for Monty's room, your living room, and the exterior of the house. You can implement them yourself, or I can come help you." Kamika glanced at Montgomery for confirmation.

He nodded at Kamika but said to Linda, "Kamika is an extremely talented interior designer. The changes she's recommending will help create a more cheerful sensory environment in each room. That will influence the moods of the people using the spaces. Influencing frame of mind via sensory input is a widely tested area of behavioral science with proven benefits in workplaces. The same sensory techniques can be used to great effect in your home."

Linda grinned up at Montgomery, who towered above her. "Ever the scientist, Montgomery." She turned to Kamika. "Thank you. I'll review what you've written and get back to you if I have any questions or need any help." She extended her hand and shook Kamika's hand.

Then Lea, Kamika, and Montgomery said their goodbyes and walked outside. Raquel stood on the porch behind her grandson with her hands on his shoulders as Linda walked toward the van with the others.

After they had loaded their equipment, Montgomery hugged Linda and said, "I promise I'll talk to you soon."

Then Lea, Kamika, and Montgomery climbed into the van, and Montgomery directed the vehicle back to the Bad Vibes Removal Services office.

THE END

Thank you for reading *Degrees of Deceit*. I hope you enjoyed reading the book as much as I enjoyed writing it. If you have a moment, please leave a review of the book on your preferred retailer's site. If you have any comments or questions, you can contact me through my website, nmcedeno.com.

ABOUT THE AUTHOR

N. M. CEDEÑO LIVES NEAR AUSTIN, Texas, and writes mystery short stories and novels that are typically set in Texas. These mysteries vary from traditional to romantic suspense and from science fiction to paranormal. Ms. Cedeño is a Plan II graduate of the University of Texas at Austin. She is an active member of Sisters in Crime, Heart of Texas Chapter, and has served as vice-president and president of the chapter. For more information, please visit nmcedeno.com.

ALSO BY N. M. CEDEÑO

The Bad Vibes Removal Services Series:
Bad Vibes Removal Services: Short Story Collection
The Walls Can Talk
Island Vibes and Other Stories: A Bad Vibes Removal Services Collection

Near Future Mystery Short Stories:
A Reasonable Expectation of Privacy
In the Interest of Public Safety
Pariah

Other Mystery Novels:
All in Her Head
For the Children's Sake

To connect with N. M. Cedeño please visit nmcedeno.com.